"Dr. Jalbert Isn't Going Anywhere," Said A Deep Voice From Behind Them.

Harriet started, dropping her purse. She looked over Aiden's shoulder as he clutched her tighter. A bright light was shining in her face. She could see several dark forms beyond the light but couldn't tell who or what they were.

"Ma'am, I need you to slowly move away from Dr. Jalbert. And both of you keep your hands where we can see them."

She did as she was told, and as she moved out of the glare, she could see the man was a uniformed police officer, and he was holding a large gun pointed in her direction.

"There must be some mistake," she protested, unable to stop herself from spouting the cliché that most people in this situation said.

"No mistake, ma'am. You aren't in any trouble. Move over to Officer Nguyen." He pointed with his free hand.

Why is it always Officer Nguyen? she wondered. There must be two dozen officers on the Foggy Point Police department, but any time she crossed paths with the police it was Officer Nguyen.

She looked at Aiden.

"Do what he says," he told her as he held his hands away from his sides and in the air where everyone could see them.

When Harriet reached Nguyen, the guy with the gun rushed up to Aiden and grabbed his right wrist, snapping a handcuff onto it in one smooth motion, quickly pulling his left hand down and back and cuffing it, too.

"What's going on?" Harriet asked Nguyen.

He didn't answer.

ALSO BY ARLENE SACHITANO

The Harriet Truman/Loose Threads Mysteries

Quilt As Desired

Quilter's Knot

Quilt As You Go

Quilt by Association

The Quilt Before the Storm

Make Quilts Not War

A Quilt in Time

Crazy as a Quilt

The Harley Spring Mysteries

Chip and Die

The Widowmaker

CRAZY AS A QUILT

A Harriet Truman/Loose Threads Mystery

ARLENE SACHITANO

ZUMAYA ENIGMA   AUSTIN TX

2015

A QUILT IN TIME

© 2015 by Arlene Sachitano

ISBN 978-1-61271-282-6

Cover art and design © April Martinez

"Zumaya Enigma" and the raven logo are trademarks of Zumaya Publications LLC, Austin TX. Look for us online at http://www.zumayapublications.com/enigma.php

Library of Congress Control Number: 2015939698

To My Favorite Knitter

Acknowledgments

Thank you to my friends and family for your unending support of my writing and promoting endeavors. You know who you are. Thanks also to my knitting students who always understand when I have to miss class for book related activities.

Special thanks to my sister-in-law, the real Beth for all the driving, cooking and the unfailing support of my writing activities. Also thanks to Beth and Sally for making blocks for the crazy quilt pictured around the edge of the cover.

I would also like to acknowledge Jack and Linne Lindquist of Craftsman's Touch Books for providing a venue for me to promote my books and for being so kind and supportive.

A huge shout out to my cover artist April Martinez—I love every one of the covers you've made for my stories.

Last and most important, thanks to Liz for making all this happen.

Chapter 1

Spring had arrived in Foggy Point, Washington, and nowhere was it more apparent than at Pins and Needles, the town's best and only quilt fabric store. Gone were the snowflake prints and snowman figurines. Easter bunnies, fuzzy chick candles, stuffed animals and ceramic figurines adorned the shelves. Pastel florals were on display in the front window in coordinated groupings with prints, stripes and solids.

The Loose Threads quilt group, in the larger of the two classrooms at the back of the store, sat around a table stacked with plastic-wrapped bolts of fabric.

"Does anyone need anything?" Harriet Truman called from the small kitchen next to the room. When no one answered, she joined her friends in their examination of the fabrics.

Lauren Sawyer stood and leaned to the center of the table, picking at the edge of the plastic on the nearest fabric bolt. The bundle appeared to be some sort of muslin backing fabric.

"This must be for the crazy quilt workshop."

"That's correct," Marjory Swain, the store's owner, said from the doorway. "They asked me to bring in backing fabric and some basic moiré colors."

Carla Salter, the group's youngest member, pulled the plastic off another bolt.

"What's mwa-ray?"

"That's the watery-looking pattern on the colored fabric," Harriet's aunt Beth explained. "When they were first invented, moirés were all silk, but now they're made from cotton and even synthetic blends."

"Thank heaven," Connie Escorcia added. "Cotton is a little more affordable and also much easier to work with."

"Did they give you a supply list?" Marjory asked. "The organizers asked me to bring in the moiré and backing, but they didn't tell me anything else about what you all might need. I assumed they're supplying some of the fabrics."

Harriet pulled a folded paper from her canvas project bag and handed it to Marjory.

"'Assorted pieces of ten different fabrics—velvet, satin, silk, rayon, etc.—in a variety of colors and prints. One or more ten-inch squares of each fiber,'" she read, scanning the list. "'Pieces of silk or satin ribbon and a variety of laces.' Wow, they expect a lot."

"I called the number at the bottom of the page to ask," Robin McLeod, the group's resident yoga teacher and a semi-retired lawyer told them. "The person who answered said some of the teachers will have kits available, and one of the ladies is bringing a lot of hand-dyed lace and ribbon for us to buy."

Harriet took a sip of her tea.

"That's good, but it sounds like a field trip to Seattle is in order."

Marjory handed the paper back to her.

"I don't know if it will help, but some of you may remember that this shop was geared toward dressmaking when I bought it. I sold off as much of the old inventory as possible, but I had a fair bit of bridal and prom dress fabric left. It's such nice material I couldn't bear to get rid of it, so I stuck it up in the attic. You all must have seen it when you were up there during the storm. In any case, I could give you a real good deal on that if you think it would work."

Harriet looked around the table at her fellow workshop-goers.

"That sounds good to me. Can we go up and look when we finish our meeting?"

"Sure. Carla, if you can watch the register a few minutes before everyone's finished, I can go up and pull the bolts out onto the table up there."

Lauren pulled a stack of fabric strips, a portable cutting mat, ruler and roller cutter from her bag and set them on the table.

"I'm a lot less worried about the crazy quilt supplies than I am about the out-of-town quilters we're supposed to be hosting. Whose idea was that, anyway?"

Mavis Willis, the Loose Threads' oldest member, got her hand-piecing project from her bag. She was stitching diamonds of Civil War fabric into Lemoyne Stars for an opportunity quilt at the Methodist church.

"I think the Small Stitches came up with that one."

"I told them we didn't have room," DeAnn Gault said. "I gave up my sewing room when we adopted Kissa. I can't imagine anyone would want to stay with a house full of kids, anyway."

Lauren sighed. "I didn't have a good excuse, so I'm going to have to put up with some stranger invading my space for a week."

"You could have said no," Aunt Beth pointed out.

"My landlord's mother-in-law is a Small Stitch, so, no, I couldn't. Edna is well aware that I have a three-bedroom apartment."

Harriet pulled her own project from her bag. She was embroidering a Christmas wreath on a square of off-white flannel.

"It could be worse. I *know* the person who's coming to stay with me."

"How did you pull that off?" Lauren asked.

Harriet put her hands to her face then swept her short dark hair back.

"This is not a good thing. I'm telling you. My past is coming back to haunt me. The wife of my husband Steve's best friend called and asked to stay with me."

Carla looked up from the binding she was sewing onto a baby quilt.

"Does it make you sad to see people from before he died?" Her face turned pink as she finished speaking.

"No, no, it's not that at all. It's complicated."

Carla looked down at her hands.

"I'm sorry, I shouldn't have asked."

"No, sweetie, it's okay. When my husband died, it turned out he'd been keeping a big secret about his health from me. The sad part is, he didn't have to die. His condition was treatable. Since he chose to never tell me about it, I have no idea why he didn't seek treatment or if I could have changed his mind about that decision.

"Since I'm not from California, and Steve was, most of our friends were his friends, and it turned out they all knew about his condition."

DeAnn stirred a packet of sweetener into her coffee.

"Wow, that must have made you mad."

"It did. Over time, I've accepted it was his decision, not his friends'. They were just respecting that decision."

"Yeah, but still..." Lauren said.

"Exactly. Which is why I'm not looking forward to having Sharon in my house for a whole week. For a few days, I can avoid having to talk about 'the subject,' but a week? I think not."

Lauren started measuring and cutting small squares.

"Hard to believe she'd want to stay with you. I mean, for that reason."

"Yeah, that's what I thought, but it is what it is."

Aunt Beth uncovered a plate she'd pulled from a paper bag sitting on the table.

"This coffee cake is an experiment, so don't be afraid to speak up if you don't like it." She pushed the plate to the middle of her end of the table. "All I know about my roommate is she'll be able to climb stairs."

"And mine won't," Mavis said. "I told them my place would be good for someone less mobile. My son even made a ramp I can put over the front porch step if I need to."

Carla glanced up again from her binding.

"Aiden said we could host someone, but I don't know who we're getting."

"Oh, honey, that's nice," Mavis said and patted Carla's knee.

Connie went to the kitchen and came back with the hot water carafe.

"Anyone need a warm-up?"

Robin raised her hand, and Connie went around the table to pour.

"Rod and I will have a pair of sisters—I told them we could take two people. They said they were coming in from Colorado and Texas and were hoping to be near each other."

"Well, you can't get much closer than that," Beth commented.

"On a slightly other subject," Lauren said with a smile. "I ran into Tom Bainbridge in Angel Harbor last week. Guess who's bringing a collection of crazy quilts to display at the workshop?"

Harriet lowered her forehead to the table.

"Oh, great," she said without looking up.

Lauren's smile broadened.

"Think of it this way. With all the romantic tension between your two men, you won't have time to worry about your house guest."

"You're not helping," Aunt Beth scolded.

Lauren shrugged.

Harriet sat up and sighed.

"Can this week get any worse?"

✂ - - - ✂ - - - ✂

Harriet straightened and rubbed her low back.

"This is a real treasure trove." She held up a strand of velvet ribbon from a bag on the attic floor. "This whole bag is velvet and satin ribbons, and the one beside it is cotton lace. Most of it is white or off-white, but we can dye it."

"You should look at these satins," Aunt Beth said from a table on the other side of the attic. "There are some pretty beiges and pinks."

Lauren looked up from the bolt of wine-colored velvet she was unfolding.

"You aren't going to go the traditional route?" she asked Harriet. "I figured your quilt would be all black and navy and wine."

"I'm going to wait to make a decision until I see all the materials we have available." Harriet rerolled the ribbon she was holding onto its spool. "I was telling Aunt Beth that if it's possible, I'd like to try making a lighter-colored quilt."

Carla unfolded a section of bright pink velour from a bolt she was holding in her arms.

"Are there any rules about color?"

Aunt Beth looked up from her satins.

"Honey, if you like that pink, I'm sure there will be a place for it in your quilt. I think the only rule is that there are no rules."

Lauren set her bolt on the pile the women had selected.

"Keep telling yourself that. If there weren't rules, we wouldn't need to take a week-long workshop on how to make these things."

Harriet picked up an armload of bolts and headed for the stairs. She paused and looked back at the group.

"I've got to go home and take Scooter out before Aiden brings his niece Lainie by." She and veterinarian Aiden Jalbert had been dating off and on since they'd both returned to Foggy Point the previous year.

"So, are you the new nanny or something?" Lauren asked.

"No, their mother is visiting. Again. I'm not sure what kind of custody arrangement Michelle has with her ex, but she and her kids are here along with a tutor and a real nanny. Lainie asked Carla to teach her to quilt, and Carla passed her off to me."

Carla pulled the bolt of pink fabric to her chest and cleared her throat.

"I could have showed her what I do, but I think she needs to get away from her mother sometimes. Did I do something wrong?" She dipped her chin to her chest so her hair fell across her eyes.

"No, honey," Aunt Beth said, "you did the right thing. Being the housekeeper, you see what goes on every day in that house. If you think the girl needs a breather, I'm sure you're right."

Carla set the fabric on the table and came over to Harriet.

"Michelle is saying all the right things, and she's being her version of nice to me, but she's not good with the kids."

Harriet shifted her armload of fabric and put her hand on the younger woman's arm.

5

"Aunt Beth's right—you did the right thing. I'm happy to help Lainie learn to quilt and to give her a break from her mother."

Carla's shoulders relaxed. Lauren stepped over and patted her on the back.

"You did good. We'll make a full-fledged Loose Thread out of you yet."

"She's kidding," Harriet said before Carla could react. "You *are* a full-fledged Thread. I better go. If you guys decide to go to Seattle to buy more supplies, let me know."

With that, she eased her way down the staircase with her fabric.

Chapter 2

Aiden's niece and nephew were playing with his dog Randy on the front lawn of the large Victorian home he'd inherited when his mother had passed away a year earlier.

"Harriet," they both called as she got out of her car. Randy beat them to the driveway and started bouncing on her back legs, her front feet grazing Harriet's thigh. She reached down to stroke the dog's head, but the kids took it as an invitation to a group hug and almost knocked her over in their enthusiasm.

"Slow down, everyone," she said as she regained her balance, hugging both kids as she did so.

"*Controlez-vous*," said a voice in French from the porch. A gray-haired woman stood ramrod straight, her arms folded across her navy blue-cardigan-clad chest. Her thin lips were pressed together, and she shook her head. "Mademoiselle Avalaine, go get your coat and bag, don't keep Ms. Truman waiting," she continued in accented English. She turned to Etienne. "Go inside and wash your hands."

She gave Randy a disgusted look, turned and went back into the house. Harriet looked down at the dog.

"What did you do to her?" she asked.

Carla came out the back door before the dog could answer. She stood at the top of the stairs.

"I guess you met the nanny."

"She's a real delight. Is she always that friendly, or is it me she doesn't like?"

7

Carla swept a strand of her long dark hair behind her ear and looked down at Harriet.

"She's like that all the time. Except when the kids step out of line, that is. Then she's worse."

"That's awful."

Carla came down the back porch steps and joined Harriet.

"Tell me about it. I feel sorry for the kids. At least Wendy and I can escape to our rooms. They're stuck with Madame all the time except for her half-day off on Sunday."

"Do you think they'd let Etienne come quilt?"

"Oh, no, it's not manly enough. She's real old school, and Michelle lets her do whatever she wants."

"I'll see if I can figure out something for him."

"Do you want to come inside and wait?" Carla asked.

"Not really, but I guess I should." Harriet locked her car and followed Carla into the house.

"Harriet, thank you so much for agreeing to teach Avalaine to quilt," Michelle said. She was sitting at the kitchen table, a cup of coffee in one hand and a pencil in the other. She set the pencil down on a folded segment of newspaper. "I was just trying to finish the Sunday *Times* crossword puzzle."

Who cares? Harriet thought, but she didn't say anything.

Michelle took a long sip from her cup.

"Did Carla tell you that one of my friends is going to be staying with us while she goes to the workshop you all are going to?"

"She mentioned that Aiden had agreed to host someone."

"It was amazing." Michelle set her cup down on her newspaper, leaving a wet ring on her crossword puzzle. "It could have been anyone, and it turns out it's an old friend of ours."

"That is amazing," Harriet said.

"Maybe you and your aunt can come over for dinner and meet her when she arrives. She's coming a few days early so we can visit before your program begins."

Harriet would rather have been trapped on an iceberg with a hungry polar bear.

"That sounds nice," she said.

She and Michelle were never going to be friends, but the woman was Aiden's sister; and now she was getting involved with Michelle's children. If Michelle was willing to try, so was she.

Avalaine came into the kitchen carrying her jacket and a small backpack.

"I brought a notebook and a pen. Do I need anything else?"

"That sounds perfect," Harriet told her and headed for the door. "Bye all."

✂- - - ✂- - - ✂

"When you're making a quilt, one of the most important skills you need to develop is accurate cutting. For example, if you have six squares in a row on your quilt top, and each one is one-quarter of an inch off in size, what will happen?"

Lainie's brows pulled together as she thought.

"Are they too big or too small or some of each?"

"Good question," Harriet replied. "For our first example, let's say they are all a quarter-inch larger."

Lainie's lips moved as she counted. Her eyes got big.

"That row would be an inch and a half longer than it was supposed to be."

"What happens if the blocks in the next row are all a quarter of an inch too small?"

"Whoa, that row would be an inch and a half smaller. When you tried to sew them together they would be three inches different from each other."

"Good," Harriet told her and smiled. "You'd notice if your blocks were a quarter of an inch too big or small. If you had twelve blocks and they were only an eighth of an inch off, you'd have the same problem, but it would be harder to spot until you finished."

"Or a sixteenth of an inch with twenty-four blocks."

"You get the idea. In real life, what you asked first is more typical. Some blocks are a bit too big and others a bit too small so they can cancel each other out. But the truth is, it's best to cut your fabric pieces as accurately as possible. We have plenty of tools to help us do that."

Harriet spent the next half-hour showing Lainie various rulers, cutting guides and roller cutters. She had just started to demonstrate the suction cup handle used to hold bigger rulers when they heard a knock on the studio door. Aunt Beth and Mavis entered. Lainie's look of relief was unmistakable.

"Have you been working this poor little thing to the bone?" Mavis asked. She set her bags down by the door and came over to Lainie, put her hands on the girl's shoulders, and began massaging.

"I might have gotten a little carried away."

"A little hard work never hurt anyone," Aunt Beth observed.

"It's really interesting," Lainie said. "I had no idea it was so complicated."

"I'm sure Harriet here is a wonderful teacher," Mavis agreed, "but how about a little break so you can digest what you've learned."

The smile on Lainie's face was all the answer they needed.

Mavis went back to the door for her things. She held up a white paper bag.

"We swung by Annie's on our way here, and she'd just put out a batch of cinnamon twists." Mavis looked at Lainie. "Annie makes the best cinnamon twists, bar none."

Beth looked at her friend.

"If you'll stop talking and bring them in here, the girls might get to taste them while they're still fresh."

"I'm coming," Mavis said and headed for the kitchen. "I just wanted to educate her on the finer points of pastry in Foggy Point."

Harriet fixed tea for herself, Mavis and her aunt and poured a glass of milk for Lainie. They ate in silence until each of them had consumed their first twist.

Lainie wiped her hands on her napkin and took a drink of her milk before speaking.

"Do you like my mom, Harriet?"

Harriet choked on her sip of tea. Aunt Beth reached over and put her hand on Lainie's arm.

"Honey, your mother has had a difficult year. Your grandmother died, and your mother has had trouble dealing with that."

Mavis picked up the story.

"Sometimes people do things we don't like, but that doesn't mean we don't like that person. We don't like what they did, but we can still like them. Does that make sense?"

"I guess so," Lainie said, all the while looking at Harriet.

"She's right. Your mom has had a tough year, but the important thing is that she's getting help." Harriet passed her the plate of cinnamon twists, ending the inquisition. She was glad the girl had waited to ask the question until a time when her aunt and Mavis were with them. "Let's have one more twist, and then we can get back to cutting out your first quilt."

Lainie smiled at her and bit into a pastry.

✂- - -✂- - -✂

"I think we have enough squares cut that you can start laying out your design next time."

Another hour had passed. Harriet was starting Lainie on a simple lap quilt made from six-inch squares cut from a combination of solid and print fabrics; she'd let her pupil choose the material from her stash.

Lainie tilted her head to the side and looked at Harriet.

"How will I know what squares to put where?"

Harriet went to her desk and pulled a pad of grid paper from a drawer then picked a plastic mechanical pencil from a ceramic cup on her desktop. She handed everything to Lainie.

"When you get home, you can draw your quilt on this paper and then color the squares with crayons or colored pencils. You can try out different arrangements to see which one you like best. If you want, you can take a scrap of each of the colors to remind you what we cut out."

"I can put the colors wherever I want?"

"Yes, you can. That's the great thing about quilting—you can make whatever design you want."

"Cool."

"Let me find you a bag to put your supplies in." Harriet went to a storage cupboard and rummaged around until she found a canvas bag with her company logo on it. "Here we go."

She handed the bag to Lainie.

"Why did you name your business Quilt as Desired?"

"I didn't," Harriet explained. "My aunt started this business, and she named it. She told me lots of people get frustrated by quilt patterns that tell them how to put the pieces together to make the quilt top but don't give any hints about how to quilt it. The patterns say to 'quilt as desired.' She thought that would be a good name for her business."

Lainie sat on one of the wheeled chairs and put her pad, pencil and fabric scraps into the canvas bag.

"Your aunt is cool. She said nice things about my mom even though I can tell no one thinks my mom is a good person."

"Has something happened? You seem pretty worried about what people think about your mother."

Lainie spun her chair around, avoiding eye contact.

"Carla picks up Wendy and takes her out of the room any time my mom comes in. And she won't speak to my mom except to say 'yes, ma'am' and 'no, ma'am'. And Uncle Aiden's jaw twitches when she talks to him. He says normal things to her, but his voice never sounds happy."

"Sweetie, everyone understands that your mother was sick. It's just that sometimes it's hard to pretend something never happened, especially if it was something that scared you. Your uncle Aiden loves your mother, and he'll keep talking to her until he can do it with a happy voice again."

Lainie jumped up and threw her arms around Harriet.

"You're the best." A smile lit up her face.

11

Harriet hugged her then rubbed the girl's back.

"I think things are going to get better from now on. You can stop worrying about your mom and start worrying about something important—like who is your favorite music group this week or what are you going to wear now that you don't have to wear a school uniform every day."

"Did you have to wear uniforms at your boarding school?" Lainie asked.

The ensuing discussion lasted until Harriet pulled to a stop at Aiden's back door. Carla leaned into the open window when Lainie was back in the house. She held the receiver to Wendy's baby monitor loosely in her left hand.

"So, you're telling me I have to be nice to Michelle?" she asked when Harriet had related her conversation with Aiden's niece.

"I didn't say that. But it was sad hearing Lainie ask if we all hated her mom. She's a sharp kid. I decided I'm going to make a better effort to accept Michelle."

"As long as Michelle keeps her hands off Wendy, I guess can try," Carla offered.

"Do the kids say anything about their father?"

"Not much, but..."

"What?"

"I shouldn't say anything if I don't know for sure."

"Come on. If I'm going to be spending time with Lainie, I need to know if you think something's going on."

Carla's expression became serious.

"Don't tell anyone I said anything."

"I can't promise that, but I won't tell anyone something they could use against you. How's that?"

"It's not that big a deal, I just don't need any more trouble than we've got here already. I'm pretty sure Michelle's husband has moved on."

"Wow, that was quick, if it's true. What makes you think so?"

"Well, first of all, when Michelle was going off the rails, the kids were with their dad full time—I heard Aiden say he didn't want Michelle to have any visitation. I guess the dad was quite vocal about it. He talked about having Michelle's parental rights terminated. Now, the kids are here with the nanny and the tutor, and he's the one arranging visitation."

"That might have been a court decision. They're both lawyers, after all."

"There's more. He bought a new car. He used to drive a big sedan the kids could fit in with all their stuff. Now he drives a Porsche Nine-eighteen Spyder. I didn't even know what it was; I had to look it up on the Internet. And the last time he came here, a pair of women's sunglasses was hooked on the passenger seat visor."

"I don't suppose they could have been Lainie's?" Harriet asked.

Carla stared at her.

"I guess not, huh? Well, that is an interesting twist on things. It's especially interesting since Michelle always complained about how poor they are. That's why she was trying to get Aiden to give her money all the time. Now, her husband can buy a car that, if I'm not mistaken, costs well into the six-figure range."

"I'm sure he has money she doesn't know about it. My mom always hid money from her boyfriends. We hid our escape money in my doll."

"If the car is his, I'm guessing Michelle's husband hid his escape money in the Cayman Islands."

"I feel sorry for the kids. Now nobody wants them."

"Their mom is getting better, and their uncle Aiden loves them. Plus, they have their uncle Marcel and his family."

Carla twirled a strand of her dark hair.

"I still feel sorry for them."

"Well, for as long as they're here, I plan to do my best to give Lainie some quality one-on-one time. I'll think about what we can do for Etienne, too."

"I guess that's all anyone can do. I better go check on Wendy. She fell asleep in the playroom, and if I don't wake her up pretty soon, she's going to want to party all night when she does get up."

Harriet smiled. "Good luck with that. Are you going to be able to come to lunch at Jorge's tomorrow? We're supposed to talk about our visitors and what, if anything, we'll do as a group apart from the workshop."

"Wendy has playgroup at the church, so that should work."

"See you then."

Harriet drove away, deep in thought about Lainie and her quilt project.

Chapter 3

Connie picked up a glass from the side table in the back room at Tico's Tacos and filled it with iced tea.

"I don't understand why that woman would want to stay with you after everything that happened." She came back to the table and sat opposite Harriet. "Didn't you say you weren't on friendly terms when you left California?"

Harriet stirred a packet of sugar into her own glass of tea.

"I wouldn't put it that way, exactly. We were never friends to begin with. Steve had a group he'd gone to high school with. When they all got back from college and were working, they took up where they left off, and all us partners were along for the ride. The men went to football and baseball games together, and we women joined them for group meals. We barbecued or went to the theater in smaller groups, but always still in a group.

"A couple of the wives had gone to the same high school, and I'm sure they did things together without the guys, but the rest of us didn't. We were all too different. Steve's friend Jason had four kids in three years, so his wife rarely got out of the house. Sharon was still modeling back then, so she was always off to LA for this, that, or the other photo shoot.

"Niko went back to Japan and married the girl his parents had picked out for him shortly after his birth. To their surprise, they fell in love after he moved her here. She was nice, but she spoke little English, which made it hard to exchange heartfelt secrets.

"Anyway, when Steve died, and I found out they'd all known about his condition, I pulled away from them. They didn't exactly fall all over themselves offering help or anything, but the few who did I ignored."

"I still don't see why you have to host one of them," Connie said.

"I can't believe she wants to stay with me. I'm assuming it's out of a misplaced sense of guilt. I could be wrong, though. And I'll admit I'm curious."

Lauren had arrived while they were talking. She plopped her bag on the bench beside Harriet and pulled out her tablet computer.

"Want me to see what she's been up to in the intervening years?"

"Yes," Connie said at the same time Harriet said, "No." Harriet looked at Connie.

"Okay, I guess I *am* a little curious."

Harriet spelled the full name for her friend.

Lauren's fingers tapped the face of her tablet.

"Oh, wow."

"What?" Harriet asked.

Lauren was silent while she continued reading and scrolling.

Connie put her hand over her heart. "The suspense is killing me. What have you found?"

Lauren clicked and scrolled for another moment.

"First of all, when she was modeling, she went by the name Charin, spelled C-H-A-R-I-N. And it looks like your friend suffered quite a career reversal. She was in a terrible car accident, and according to this, it may have been her fault. One of her legs was badly scarred. Not a good thing for a model."

"Were other people involved?" Connie asked.

Lauren turned back to her tablet and read some more.

"It says here that her passenger was another model, and she was also injured bad enough they airlifted her to the hospital. The other car held a mother and her two kids." She clicked to the next page. "One of the kids suffered a spinal cord injury; it doesn't mention the second child."

"Was she drunk?" Connie asked.

"No. It sounds like the other car came through an intersection at the end of a yellow light, and Harriet's friend was looking at her phone. The court decided they both were to blame. The press crucified Charin, though— I'm guessing because she was a celebrity as opposed to any determination of greater liability."

Harriet sipped her tea.

"Great, that's all I need. Someone else with issues."

Lauren put her tablet to sleep and put it back in her bag.

"Maybe she figured you two outcasts could bond over your ostracism."

"Let's hope not. Speaking of bonding with strangers, have you learned any more about *your* roommate?"

"Rumor has it she's a former nun."

"*Diós mio,*" Connie said.

"What have I missed?" Robin asked as she breezed into the room, picking up a glass for tea as she passed the side table. Aunt Beth and Mavis came in before anyone could respond.

Connie slid over to make room for the new arrivals on the bench.

"We should wait to talk about our guests until everyone is here."

"You're no fun," Lauren said, but her smile softened the complaint.

✂ - - - ✂ - - - ✂

"What do you all think about having a mixer Friday night when our guests have arrived?" Aunt Beth asked when everyone was present and Jorge's server was delivering their lunches.

Jorge entered with a basket of warm chips in one hand and a pitcher of lemonade in the other.

"Anyone need a refill?" He looked around the table. Harriet held her glass up, and he came to her spot. "This is a first."

She looked up at him. "What?"

"The entire group is eating the same meal."

"What's not to like about fish tacos made with halibut?" Deann asked him with a smile.

"Good point," he said and laughed. "I heard you mention a mixer. Would you like me to prepare some refreshments?"

"There's an idea," Lauren said. "If people have food in their mouth, they can't talk to us, and we don't have to talk to them."

Mavis set her glass down.

"Stop that right now," she scolded. "We want this event to be a success. If we all go into it with that kind of attitude, it's guaranteed it will be a flop."

Lauren broke the tortilla chip she was holding.

"Sorry, I was just kidding."

"I know you were, but I'm serious," Mavis said. "The success of this event not only reflects on the quilters in town, it reflects on our community as a whole. Just because it wasn't *our* idea doesn't mean it isn't a good idea."

"She's right," Aunt Beth added. "With the economy the way it's been, any opportunity to bring tourists into Foggy Point is important. Maybe they'll come back with their families in the summer."

16

Robin squeezed a wedge of lime over her tacos.

"I hadn't thought of that aspect. I'm just worried about gathering materials for the classes I'm taking. I'm also planning the stretching programs the organizing committee asked me to do."

"So, back to the mixer idea," Harriet said. "You said Friday? The official program starts on Sunday, doesn't it?"

Aunt Beth wiped her mouth on her napkin before answering.

"Yes, the quilting program starts on Sunday. We offered out-of-town visitors the option of arriving Friday so they would have a day to recover before we got serious about stitching. The Chamber of Commerce organized some tours of Foggy Point and the surrounding areas. One of the Small Stitches called me and asked if we could do something with them Friday."

"I heard they were offering a day trip by ferry to Victoria on Saturday," DeAnn offered. "They hired a bus to take people to Port Angeles for departure."

"That sounds fun," Harriet said. "Maybe Sharon will want to go."

Lauren sat back in her chair.

"What did you have in mind for the mixer?"

Connie went to the side table, picked up the iced tea pitcher, and carried it back, offering refills.

"I saw Glynnis at the store, and she told me that almost half of the people are taking them up on the Friday option. If even half of that half come, plus us and at least some of the Small Stitches, that will be too large a group for any of the restaurants in town."

"I can check and see if the basement room at the church is available," Mavis volunteered.

"We can ask Jorge to supply hors d'oeuvres," Beth suggested. "The Chamber said we could have a small budget to work with."

Lauren looked at Harriet and then back to Connie and Mavis.

"Harriet and I can come up with a get-to-know-each-other activity." She looked back at Harriet and smiled.

"Now, that's the spirit," Aunt Beth said.

✂- - -✂- - -✂

Lauren finished her tacos and laid her napkin on the table.

"I called an upholsterer in Angel Harbor," she said to Harriet, "and they have some of that heavy muslin that's on our class list. I know our teacher said she'll have some for us to buy. I don't know about you, but I'd like to practice on some of it before class starts so I can make sure I've got the best needle and thread combo. I'm going to get some this afternoon. Want to come with?"

"I guess I could spare a little time." Harriet mentally reviewed her schedule. "I'll have to stitch a couple of hours when we get back, but that should be no problem." She stood up. "Anyone want us to pick up some heavier muslin?"

Everyone wanted at least a half-yard. Lauren made a quick calculation and tapped the number into her smart phone.

✂- - - ✂- - - ✂

"You know, for a few brief moments, I thought this whole crazy quilt retreat week was going to be fun," Lauren said as she backed her car out of the parking lot of Tico's Tacos.

Harriet laughed. "Trade you my scarred model for your former nun."

"No way. My ex-nun has potential. She sounds like she knows what she wants from life. Your model sounds depressing."

Harriet looked out the car window. The sun was trying to push the clouds aside.

"I hope Carla isn't given anyone too difficult. She has her hands full with Michelle and the kids and their entourage."

"Connie told me she and Rod have been taking Wendy two afternoons a week. It's partly to give Wendy special time but also to give Carla a little break."

"That reminds me. I have Lainie coming to my house to quilt. I forgot to ask the Threads if anyone can come up with something her brother could do so he can get out of that house once in a while, too."

Lauren turned onto the highway that led out away from Foggy Point.

"He's a little young for me to teach him programming, but I ran into Tom Bainbridge in the coffee shop a couple of days ago. He's designing an addition to the house of those people he stayed with during last year's storm. I think he's going to do some work himself on the existing structure, too. He might be willing to take on an apprentice."

Tom's mother had run a fiber arts school and retreat center the Loose Threads had attended the previous year in the town of Angel Harbor.

"Great idea." Harriet closed her eyes. "My life isn't complicated enough with Aiden and his sister and my past coming to haunt me for a week. Let's stir the other man I've dated since I've lived here into the mix so Aiden can get all defensive and Sharon can go back to California and tell everyone how I've become a harlot."

"Hey, you're the one who needed ideas. You don't have to rescue every stray puppy that comes along, you know."

18

"Why does life have to be so complicated?"

"That's a small town for you. If you want to be anonymous, move back to a big city."

Harriet looked at her and shook her head.

"I'm assuming you have an idea for this mixer you volunteered us for."

"Not really, I was just sucking up to Mavis and your aunt. After her lecture about the economy and all that, I figured I needed to do a little damage control."

"What if we made color copies of crazy quilt blocks and cut them in half like puzzle pieces then gave every person who enters a half of the block? We could separate the halves into two groups; we locals would take from one pile and the visitors from the other. Everyone has to find the person with the matching half-block."

"That sounds easy enough. Where will we get the pictures?"

"The teachers all sent pictures of their work for promotional purposes. I'll email them and ask if we can use their quilt images for this," Harriet volunteered.

"Let me know when you have the okay. I have a good color copier that will take card stock without eating it. We can use that."

The women traveled in silence for a few minutes before Lauren spoke again.

"So, how *are* things going with Aiden? Is his sister really better?"

"Everything is improving. Michelle is never going to be my favorite person, but she seems to be trying. Her law license has been suspended, although if she can document that her actions were driven by a diagnosed mental illness that is now controlled by medication, she might have a chance of having the suspension lifted."

"Is she hanging out at Aiden's house while she waits for that to happen?"

Harriet smiled. "Believe it or not, she's doing volunteer law clerk work in the legal aid office."

Lauren glanced at Harriet then looked back to the road.

"Seriously? That really *is* a miracle."

"I told you, I think she's really trying."

"Want to stop for a drive-thru coffee?" Lauren asked. "There's a Dutch Bros coming up at the next exit."

"We haven't been driving for thirty minutes yet."

"And your point?"

Harriet laughed. "Sure, I'd love a coffee."

Chapter 4

The sky had turned the dark blue-gray that immediately follows sunset in the northwest.

"I'll call you when we have the go-ahead to use the crazy quilt pictures," Harriet said as she got out of Lauren's car in Jorge's parking lot.

"I'll wait with bated breath."

Alone by her car, she debated going into the restaurant; but dinner was in full swing, so Jorge would be busy, and she needed to get home and stitch on her customer's quilt.

She took the route past Mr. and Mrs. Renfro's tidy home. They had been friends of Tom's mother's, and he stayed with them whenever he was in Foggy Point for more than a day. It wouldn't hurt to see if his car was in their driveway, she reasoned.

It was, and before she could think about it, she was on their porch asking if Tom was there.

"Come in, dearie." Mrs. Renfro guided Harriet into a small entrance hall. "Tom will welcome the rescue. We don't get much company, so my husband has him trapped in the kitchen, talking his ear off."

The small woman took Harriet's coat, and before she knew it she was seated with Tom in a cozy kitchen eating nook, dining on homemade lasagna and green salad.

"I feel like I'm intruding," she told her host. "I really just wanted to talk to Tom briefly."

"It's no trouble at all," Mr. Renfro assured her. "We don't get much company since the grandkids are all off in college. Mamma still cooks like the whole tribe is coming over every night."

"I'll take the extra over to the homeless camp," his wife assured Harriet. "And I have a whole other pan for them cooling on the screened porch."

"Tom, here, made the camp folks an outdoor cook stove so they can reheat it," Mr. Renfro added proudly.

Harriet looked across the table at Tom. He smiled and raised his eyebrows.

"What did you want to talk to me about?"

"I'm looking for a project for a young man who needs to spend some time away from his iron-fisted nanny and annoying mother." She looked at each of the people seated at the table, waiting a beat for a reaction. When one wasn't forthcoming, she continued. "Aiden's niece and nephew are staying at his house with their mother, tutor and nanny. His niece is taking quilting lessons with me, and I'd like to find a man to spend some time with her brother. I was hoping you might be doing some sort of home-handy project Etienne could help with."

Tom put his hand to his chin and rubbed absently.

"I'm doing some design work for the Renfros, but I can't think of any hands-on activity I could include a child in. We won't start the construction phase for a few months. I take it he's young?"

Harriet's shoulders sagged slightly. "Yeah, he's nine or ten, I think."

Mr. Renfro cleared his throat.

"I could use a lad like that. I'm about to start working on the wooden toys I make for the church Christmas bazaar. It takes me most of the year to make enough to sell as well as some to donate to the hospital children's wing. He could help with sanding and painting...and cleaning up, of course."

"If you're sure, that would be great. I think Etienne will be thrilled. I was willing to teach him to quilt, but Carla didn't think the old-school nanny and tutor would go for it."

Mrs. Renfro passed her a basket of warm French bread.

"Here, dear, have some bread, and then you can tell us all about this quilt retreat we're hearing about all over town."

Harriet spent the rest of the dinner explaining what crazy quilting is and telling her hosts about the planned events.

"I'm going to be bringing a collection of quilts my mother had," Tom added when Harriet was through. "My whole life, my mother stopped at every garage sale, estate sale, yard sale or any other type of sale you can imagine searching for quilts. Most of the time, the stuff she found had been badly abused, but every once in a while she found real treasure. She has three crazy quilts she got at an estate sale that were made by the deceased's grandmother in the late eighteen-hundreds. They had been stored properly and are in mint condition."

"That's amazing. Considering how many women have quilted in the past, relatively few quilts have survived in perfect shape. And speaking of that, I need to go home and work on a quilt for one of my customers."

She thanked the Renfros, collected her purse and coat and headed for the door, followed by Tom. He stopped when they reached her car and put his hands on her shoulders.

"How are things with you and the good doctor?"

Harriet was silent for a moment.

"I guess you could say we're still in a holding pattern. His sister is back in town living at his house with her children. She's on medication and seems to be recovering from her problems. She and Aiden are working on building trust again."

He squeezed her shoulders gently.

"That's great, but, Harriet, I think you know what I'm asking. Are you and Aiden a couple or not?" He pulled her into his arms. "I know I keep telling you I won't pressure you, but I need to know if I'm fooling myself here."

She rested her head on his shoulder.

"Why do relationships have to be so complicated?"

He dropped his hands to her waist.

"They don't have to be."

"If you're tired of this dance we're doing, I'll understand if you want to opt out."

He held her out at arm's length so he could look into her eyes.

"Don't put words in my mouth. I just want to know if I'm still in the game. As long as you haven't made any commitments, I'm willing to wait and see how this all plays out. My money is on the good doctor self-destructing. He can't figure out how to put you first, and I'm thinking you're going to get tired of always taking a back seat to his family."

Harriet leaned back against his chest.

"Did I tell you the wife of my dead husband's best friend is coming to stay with me during quilt week? The friend that blames me for Steve not getting treatment."

"Oh, sweetheart, I'm sorry." He kissed the top of her head. "Can I do anything to help?" He laughed. "Besides stop asking you to make a decision?"

"Thanks for offering." She moved out of his arms but held on to both his hands. "I'm not sure why you're so good to me."

"Maybe it's because we're friends? No matter what happens in the future, we'll always be friends."

"I better get going—I really do have to work tonight. Can you tell Mr. Renfro I'll call him to set up a time for Etienne if everyone on that end of things agrees?"

He pulled her car door open for her.

"I will pass the message along, and if you think of anything I can do to help, let me know—and not just about the boy."

Harriet got in her car and opened the window, smiling up as he leaned in through the window and gave her a quick kiss.

"If anything comes to mind, you'll be the first person I call."

Tom straightened up, and she backed down the driveway, not closing her window until she reached the street.

Instead of heading up the hill to her house, she went downhill toward Foggy Point and the Steaming Cup coffee shop. Her head was swimming after talking to Tom. She knew if she tried to stitch right now she'd likely destroy her customer's quilt.

With Tom safely two hours away in Angel Harbor, she could pretend she didn't feel anything for him and concentrate on whatever her relationship was with Aiden. However, as much as she tried to deny it to herself, when she was around Tom, her body reacted to him. Maybe it wasn't the liquid fire that raced through her when Aiden kissed her, but her toes did tingle at Tom's touch. There was no denying it.

"I thought you were quilting this evening," Lauren said from behind her as she stood at the coffee bar waiting for her drink to be prepared.

Harriet's shoulders sagged. Lauren moved to her side.

"I know that look. Which of your men have you just seen?"

"Do you really want to hear about my sorry love life?" Harriet picked up her cup from the counter.

Lauren glanced at the face of her smartphone.

"I've got a few minutes. Lay it on me."

Harriet led the way to two overstuffed chairs near the fireplace. When they were seated, she gave her friend a short version of her visit to the Renfros' and the subsequent dinner.

"Do you think I'm hanging on to an impossible relationship with Aiden because he was my first relationship after my husband died?"

Lauren took a sip of her mocha.

"Does this mean Tom is a contender again?"

Harriet leaned her head in her hand, her elbow braced on the arm of the chair.

"I don't know *what* it means. All I know is I like Aiden, but everything is hard. I like Tom, maybe not in exactly the same way, but I like him— and he's so uncomplicated."

"Is uncomplicated another way of saying boring?" Lauren asked her.

"No, it's not, and that's what's so confusing. I really do like Tom, and he's an interesting guy. He's definitely there for me when I need him to be. I can't say the same about Aiden. He's there as long as his family doesn't need anything at the same time."

"But if Tom was all that, we wouldn't be having this conversation."

Harriet sighed. "That's why I'm sitting here instead of at home doing my work. I can't figure out if I'm not allowing myself to fully engage with Tom because I'm not willing to commit to someone who's really available. Maybe I'm sticking with Aiden no matter how unavailable he is for that very reason. If he's never available I don't have to risk losing someone again."

"Whoa, back up. I thought your husband was a liar and your marriage a sham."

"I'm not sure where you got that. Steve did keep his health problem a secret, along with his misguided decision to not seek treatment for it. But why do you think it hurt so much? I loved him, and I know he loved me. I may not understand why he did what he did, but I know he loved me. We were happy."

Lauren set her cup on a table beside her chair and leaned toward Harriet, staring her in the face.

"Do you feel guilty about his failure to get treatment? Like it was somehow your fault? You have to know that's not true."

"I do know that. I also know his friends think it *was* my fault. After Steve died, I went to a therapist for a while. A lot of what we talked about was personal responsibility and our inability to ever truly know why other people do what they do."

"But?"

"In my dark moments, I wonder if, deep down inside, part of me still believes I could have done something different that would have resulted in a different outcome."

"And that makes you think you don't deserve to be happy?"

Harriet attempted a weak smile.

"Something like that."

Lauren straightened in her chair and picked her drink back up.

"Well, guilty or not, I don't think you're sticking by Aiden to punish yourself. Anyone can see the way you light up when he's around. That's not guilt-driven." She rubbed her chin with her free hand. "I have to admit, though, you and Tom looked pretty happy when you were driving around in the storm delivering food last winter."

"So you could see me with either one of them?"

"Unfortunately, I can't be of any help on this one. I can tell you one thing, though. Aiden may be endlessly unavailable while he deals with his family issues, but I wouldn't bet on a guy like Tom waiting around forever to find out. He's no one's second fiddle."

"You're no help at all."

Lauren shrugged. "I never said I was Dear Abby."

They finished their drinks in silence, each lost in her own thoughts.

Harriet stood up.

"Now I really do need to go stitch on that customer quilt."

Lauren pulled her tablet computer from her bag.

"I'm going to do some work before I go home. I was stuck and thought a change of venue might help."

"Shall we meet tomorrow to work on the mixer?"

Lauren agreed, and Harriet left, her stomach still tied in knots.

Chapter 5

*H*arriet held out a small red fleece jacket for Etienne.

"Mr. Renfro is a very friendly fellow, and I think you're going to have a lot of fun helping him build toys."

The boy slipped his arms into his jacket and turned to face her.

"Do I need to pack a lunch?"

Harriet smiled at him.

"Every time I've been to the Renfro house, Mrs. R has made enough food to feed a small army. She bakes a lot of cookies, too."

Etienne's eyes opened wider, and he started to smile.

"Only one cookie for you," Madame deCloutier, the nanny, said in a stern voice. "We can't be spoiling our dinner."

The smile left his face, and Harriet bit her tongue to avoid telling Madame what she thought about taking the joy out of everything the kids did. She settled for squeezing Etienne's hand in a way she hoped conveyed her intention to give him as many cookies as he wanted.

Lainie skipped down the servant's stairs and into the kitchen.

"I found my bag," she told Harriet.

"Mademoiselle, you must use the front stairs," the nanny scolded.

"But your stairs are closer."

Harriet handed the girl her coat before Madame could launch into a lecture on stairway etiquette.

"Let's get your brother to the Renfros' so we can quilt. I'll bring them back in about..." She looked at her phone screen. "Two and a half..."

She trailed off when Aiden strode into the kitchen from the dining room. He clearly understood which stairs the lord of the manor was to use, she noticed; he would have used the sweeping front staircase to reach the dining room. A blue backpack was slung over one shoulder, and he held the handles of a large duffel bag in his opposite hand.

"Are you going on a trip?" she asked.

Michelle came in from behind him.

"He's escaping the estrogen. My friend arrives tonight, and he's feeling badly outnumbered."

Aiden looked at Etienne and shrugged.

"Sorry, buddy. I'd take you with me, if I could, but I'll be working." He turned and looked at Harriet. "I'm not going far. I'll be staying in my old apartment over the clinic. They never re-rented it, and it'll actually be convenient this week. We ran a coupon special for discounts on spaying or neutering feral cats, and we have a full schedule."

The children moved to Harriet, standing one on each side, and she put her hands on their shoulders.

"That sounds like a worthy cause."

Aiden's jaw tensed. "It is. We're making headway with the feral cats, but people have this romantic idea that when they're tired of their animals or when they have kittens they can't give away, they can turn them loose in the park and it will be like they're in a fairy tale forest. Unfortunately, the result is more Grimm than Disney." He smiled. "Like my sister said, I'm badly outnumbered here, so I'm getting out of Dodge."

"Aiden doesn't want to be here when Marine arrives," Michelle said. "They used to be an item."

"That is completely untrue," Aiden protested. "I had a crush on her when I was twelve and she came home from school with Michelle for spring break. It lasted all of a week, and she didn't even know I was alive."

"Oh, she knew you were alive, all right. All my friends did. Besides, we couldn't miss you sneaking around and snooping on us. And then Mom told them to stop drooling over you or she was going to send them away."

"No, she didn't," he countered.

"You can ask Marine. She'll tell you. Your hair was long that summer, and they took one look at your black hair and crazy white-blue eyes and were goners. It was actually a little creepy."

Harriet grinned. "He still has that effect on older women."

Aiden turned to her.

"That's a total lie. They didn't know I was alive. They all were hot for some guy named Colt Parker. He was the quarterback of their football team."

Michelle stepped in front of him and glared at him.

"You little sneak. You were listening in when we were talking in my bedroom."

27

Aiden laughed. "You gotta love the vent system in these old houses. The closet in mom's office was right over your room, and all I had to do was make sure the vents were open in both places and I could hear it all."

Michelle swung at her brother, but he danced out of her reach.

"I think it's time for me to leave," he said. "You kids have fun." With that, he opened the back door and left.

"We better go, too," Harriet told Michelle.

"Thanks a lot for taking the kids. Lainie is enjoying her quilting, and Etienne has been talking nonstop about going to make toys. I really do appreciate you arranging that for him."

"You're welcome," Harriet mumbled as she guided the kids to the door. This was possibly the first sincere thing Michelle had said to her, and it was a bit disconcerting.

Aiden was waiting outside by her car when she came out.

"Hey, can you two go get Randy from the kennel? Bring the black leash and collar, too, will you?" The children dropped their bags and ran off in the direction of the kennel, jostling each other in an effort to reach the dog first.

As soon as they turned their backs, Aiden pulled Harriet into his arms and kissed her soundly.

"What was that for?" she asked when the kiss ended and she could catch her breath.

"I wasn't sure when the next opportunity would present itself, given the hordes of women descending on our town. I figured I'd better take my chance while I had it. I would like to point out that I'll be alone all week in my lonely apartment should you find yourself available and willing to help save me from dying of boredom."

"What about all that surgery? It sounded like a noble sacrifice you were making."

"It is, but I can't do surgery day and night. Our days are scheduled, but not much more than usual. Mostly, I didn't want to be around with Marine coming. I didn't want to say anything in front of the kids, but she was all too willing to initiate a young lad in the ways of women. And I was all too willing to let her."

Harriet broke free and pushed him away.

"You didn't!"

"No. No, I wasn't that willing. She didn't do anything she could get arrested for, but, boy, could she kiss. We took every opportunity."

"Was she your first?"

He laughed. "No, that would have been Pammy-Lynn Bates in the third grade."

"Third grade? Really? You little Lothario."

"It wasn't like that. Her girlfriend dared her to kiss me. I was unsuspecting, and after she kissed me, she punched me just to make sure I didn't get any ideas."

"I was in love with my horse in the third grade. I cried myself to sleep when I had to come to Foggy Point and stay with Aunt Beth for spring break and Henry had to stay in France."

Aiden pulled her back into his arms.

"I'd have come and dried your tears, if I'd known."

"You mean if you'd been born yet?" Harriet grimaced. "Now *I* sound like the creepy lecher."

He kissed the top of her head.

"You aren't a creepy lecher, and you know it. At our ages now, the difference is inconsequential and you know that, too." He let her go as niece, nephew and dog came running toward them. "I thought I was going to have to send a search party to find you, you were gone so long," he scolded them in a teasing tone.

"It's Etienne's fault. We tried to do rock-paper-scissors to decide who got to open the kennel and who got to put the leash on, and he kept messing up so then we had to do eenie-meenie-miney-moe, and we had to start over three times."

Aiden put his hands into his pockets.

"Sounds like you need a better method for making decisions." He pulled out two quarters and gave one to each child. "Carry these with you everywhere, and when you need to decide something, you can each choose a side and then flip the coin." He demonstrated. "See? You'll never have trouble with decisions again."

Harriet looked at him as the kids tucked their quarters away and then climbed into the back seat of her car.

If only decisions really were that easy, she thought as she got in and drove away.

Chapter 6

*H*arriet unlocked the door to her studio and propped the kitchen door open before going upstairs to check the guest room Sharon would be using one more time. The day had finally arrived, and in a few short hours, quilters would begin descending on Foggy Point.

"Anybody home?" Lauren called a few minutes later.

"Be right there," Harriet answered and, with one last survey, shut the bedroom door and returned to the kitchen.

Lauren pulled a stack of laminated crazy quilt pictures from a paper bag and set them on the counter. She scooped her long blonde hair in her two hands and into a ponytail in one practiced move, securing it with a scrunchie she pulled from her jeans pocket.

"I brought these over whole so we could make sure we were on the same page about how we're cutting them."

Harriet picked up the stack and leafed through the images.

"How were you thinking of cutting them?"

"I was thinking of doing the standard jigsaw puzzle innie and outie, but then I worried it might be too hard. Maybe we should just cut them in half and keep it simple."

"Where's your sense of adventure? Let's go with your original plan. These people are quilters—they're used to matching shapes."

"If you say so." Lauren pulled three white pages with black outlines on them from the paper bag. "I made templates in case you chose the puzzle piece option." She handed one of the templates to Harriet and kept the other two for herself. "Got any coffee?"

Harriet finished cutting her final puzzle piece, placing the two halves in their respective stacks.

"Do you think it's weird that I don't have any pictures of Steve on display?"

"I think it would be weird if you had pictures of the rest of your family and excluded your dead husband, but, Harriet, you don't have any family pictures anywhere in the house that I've ever seen."

"If you had my family, would you? The only pictures I have of my parents are either publicity photos or formal portraits done by some important artist."

Lauren set her last laminated piece on the table.

"If you're asking me if I think your houseguest is going to think it's weird, that's a whole other thing."

Harriet played with the edge of her template, curling and uncurling the corner.

"Will she?"

"You're the one who knows her, but if she and her husband were good friends of your husband, she probably *will* expect to see his picture." Lauren gathered all the quilt pieces and put them back in the paper bag. "Don't you have a simple wedding picture? Maybe a four-by-six, or a five-by-seven—nothing too flashy. You and him and a bunch of flowers. You could put it on the mantle in the living room with some of your aunt's ceramic knickknacks. It wouldn't stand out, but it would be there if she's looking for it."

"I think I have something like that. Thanks, I've been driving myself crazy preparing for this visit. I just don't get why this woman wants to stay with me. It's not like we were good friends or anything. And she and her cronies certainly didn't have the time of day for me when Steve died. I really don't need any more drama in my life." She rubbed her hands through her hair. "I hope she doesn't have an agenda apart from wanting to learn to crazy quilt."

"It's entirely possible—" Lauren started, but she was interrupted by Aunt Beth and Mavis coming through the door.

Beth set a drink holder with four paper coffee cups on the table and shrugged out of her tan hip-length coat.

"Mavis and I thought we'd come wait with you. Isn't your guest supposed to be arriving this morning?"

Harriet shook her head and looked at the drink carrier.

"How did you know there'd be four of us?"

Mavis set a plate of brownies beside the coffee.

"That would be me," she said as she took her coat off and set it and her purse on the wingback chair in Harriet's customer reception area. "I ran into Lauren when I was at the store getting chocolate chips to add to the brownies. She was on her way here, and I figured it would take you guys a while to cut all those pieces."

"If you don't want company, we can leave," Beth added.

Lauren grabbed the plate of brownies and clutched them to her chest.

"We'd love to have you stay."

Mavis looked at Harriet.

Harriet laughed. "I wouldn't want to see a grown woman cry."

She looked at Lauren, who set the brownies back on the table.

"Don't you all have people to wait for?" Harriet asked when they were all settled around the kitchen table, each with what turned out to be a vanilla latte in front of them.

Lauren took a sip of her drink, then set it down.

"My lady comes at three-thirty this afternoon."

Mavis reached for a brownie.

"Mine is going straight to the reception and then following me home."

Beth set her cell phone on the table beside her cup.

"My visitor is coming from Portland. She's going to call me when she reaches Seattle."

Harriet twirled the plastic travel plug she'd pulled from her drink.

"Sharon should be arriving in the next hour or so. But I guess you knew that, since you're here waiting with me."

"You said she was taking an eight o'clock flight to Seattle from Oakland," Beth reminded her. "If you add a two-and-a-half-hour drive to that plus time to get her car and luggage when she arrived in Seattle…" She glanced at her wristwatch. "…she should get here in about a half-hour or so."

"And you're expecting her arrival to be a train wreck? You and Mavis are here for what? To pick up the pieces when I fall apart?"

Aunt Beth reached across the table and patted her hand.

"Now, honey, it's nothing like that. I just never heard you talk about this woman. You mentioned Lindsay and Kelly, but I've never heard you talk about Sharon."

"There's a reason for that. Lindsay and Kelly are quilters who had nothing to do with Steve or his friends. I didn't really know Sharon, so there couldn't be much of a problem. She probably thought it would be weird if she came to a quilt retreat in my small town and didn't stay with me."

"Good point," Lauren said.

Mavis chewed thoughtfully on her brownie.

"That may be," she said when she'd swallowed her bite. "But she hasn't called you since she signed up, has she? Other than to arrange an arrival time? She's married to your husband's best friend, and they haven't so much as mailed you a postcard, and now she's coming to stay here?" She set the brownie down on her plate. "Something feels off about that."

"And if everything is fine, it won't matter that your aunt is here with her friend," Aunt Beth added.

The two women looked at each other and nodded then turned in unison to look at Harriet.

Lauren smirked. "Do you two practice that?"

✂- - - ✂- - - ✂

Lauren crumpled her napkin and stood up.

"I think I hear a car coming up the driveway." She looked at Beth and Mavis. "Since you two have the arrival covered, I'm going to drop our puzzle pieces by the church and go home and get some work done before my ex-nun arrives."

Mavis pulled a second package of brownies from the bag she'd brought.

"What are those?" Harriet asked.

"I brought some store-bought brownies for your guest."

Harriet raised her left eyebrow in question.

"Never you mind," Mavis told her.

"I'm out of here," Lauren announced and exited the kitchen. After a moment, Harriet heard her open the studio door.

"Incoming," Lauren called out. "Nice car, too," she said before the door closed.

Harriet got up and went out to greet her guest.

Sharon parked her rented BMW Sports Wagon and got out, stretching as she did so. She left her car in the middle of the circular drive, blocking Aunt Beth's Beetle.

"You *are* out here in the middle of nowhere, aren't you," she said.

"I hope the drive wasn't too taxing," Harriet shot back, but if her words hit their mark, Sharon didn't show it. "Can I help you with your bags?"

"Sure, they're in the back. It's open." She went up the steps past Harriet and into the house.

"No problem," Harriet said to her back then located the two large suitcases. She struggled first one and then the other into the studio. Sharon came out of the half-bath off the kitchen as she entered.

33

"Sorry," she said when she saw Harriet. "I didn't mean for you to unload my luggage by yourself. My bladder was just bursting after that long drive."

Harriet was fairly sure the words were an attempt to soften the stern glares her visitor was receiving from Aunt Beth and Mavis.

"Would you like some tea or coffee and brownies?" Mavis asked.

"No, thanks, I don't eat sugar."

"These are sugar-free and gluten-free," Mavis said with a smile.

"I said no."

Harriet brought one of the suitcases into the kitchen.

"Let me show you to your room so you can rest and freshen up a little before this evening's mixer." She didn't wait for a response, just headed up the stairs.

$$\sim\!\!-\,-\,-\sim\!\!-\,-\,-\sim$$

Harriet let Scooter out of her bedroom, where she'd shut him in before her guest's arrival, and headed back downstairs.

"What was that all about?" she demanded in a firm whisper.

Mavis gave her a sheepish look.

"I was testing the waters. I figured we might as well find out what we would be dealing with."

"I'm glad she did," Aunt Beth said, defending her friend. "Now we know we've got a prima donna on our hands."

Harriet sat down at the table.

"All you've done is stirred the hornet's nest."

"We're just trying to help," Aunt Beth said. "And we'll help you with her."

"If this is your idea of help, I'll take a pass."

"You say that now, but you'll appreciate our help. A week is a long time."

"Thanks for the reminder," Harriet said and grabbed a brownie.

Aunt Beth looked at Mavis as she stood up.

"Our work here is done."

Mavis laughed.

"We'll see you at the mixer."

Chapter 7

The aroma of Jorge's hors d'oeuvres wafted over the meeting room at the Methodist church. He had prepared spicy shrimp cocktails, guacamole, and smoky queso with blue corn chips, but he'd outdone himself with the quesadillas. To mirror the quilt theme, he'd used red pepper-and-spinach tortillas cut into small rectangles and squares and arranged them to look like quilt blocks. Waiting in the kitchen was his famous flan.

Harriet joined Lauren and her new roommate at the check in table. Her own guest was in the restroom adjusting her makeup, even though they'd just arrived and she looked perfect.

"Wow, Jorge's outdone himself."

"No kidding," Lauren said. "Harriet, meet Jessica."

Jessica took Harriet's proffered hand in both of hers.

"Lauren's told me so much about you. Do you really speak seven languages?"

Harriet looked at Lauren, who shrugged.

"Yes, I do. My parents worked internationally when I was young, and they wanted me to be prepared when I joined them."

Jessica's red hair was cut short and gelled into a faux-hawk. Her ears sported half a dozen metal rings.

"You must have a real ear for it. I struggled with Latin and barely got by in Spanish when I lived in Mexico."

If Lauren's roommate was truly an ex-nun, Harriet was beginning to suspect why the convent hadn't suited her.

35

"I think it helps that I started young."

Jessica looped her arm through Harriet's and turned toward the growing crowd.

"Okay, so, tell me who some of these people are." She pointed with her free hand. "I'm guessing, by the matching name tag, the little lady over there is part of your group."

Harriet looked where she was pointing.

"That's Connie Escorcia. She's not only in our group, she's also a retired kindergarten and first-grade teacher. It seems like half the town has been in her class. Those two ladies beside her must be the sisters she's hosting."

"What kind of quilting does she do?"

"She machine pieces and appliqués and dabbles in art quilting."

"What about the white-haired lady in purple standing beside the woman with rust-colored hair?"

"My aunt Beth Carlson and her friend Mavis Willis. Along with Connie, you've picked out the power players in the Loose Threads quilting group." Harriet turned them slightly. "See the woman over there with the blond pixie cut, wearing yoga pants?"

"With the younger woman?"

"Yes. The blonde is our resident quilting lawyer, Robin, and beside her is our youngest member, Carla."

"I'm guessing that cluster of women across the way are *not* Loose Threads."

"Give the girl a prize," Harriet said with a laugh. "I recognize a few of them. They belong to the other quilt group in town, the Small Stitches."

Jessica pulled back and looked at her.

"That's really their name?"

"What can I say? I guess they're proud of their work."

"Oh, that's too funny."

"So, what's your quilt group's name?" Harriet asked her.

Jessica slipped her arm free.

"Promise you won't laugh."

"No guarantees,"

She looked at Lauren.

"It can't be worse than what we've just told you."

"It can be. Okay, here goes. We call ourselves 'Out of the Habit.'"

Harriet and Lauren laughed, and several other groups of women stopped talking to stare at them.

"That's priceless," Harriet said when she could speak.

"I love it," Lauren said at the same time.

A tall skinny woman with bleached blond hair streaked with purple approached the table. Heavy makeup covered the pockmarked surface of her skin. Harriet and her two companions fell silent as the woman completed the check-in process and headed for the food table.

"Who's the tweaker?" Jessica whispered.

Before Harriet or Lauren could answer, Michelle approached the table. She noticed Harriet and joined the group.

"Did you see Marine come in?"

"Is that her at the food table?" Lauren asked.

"Oh, there she is. I was parking the car, but she was afraid we were late. I told her I'd come in and introduce her to a few people. Let me go get her."

Harriet turned to face Jessica.

"Why did you call her the tweaker?"

"I'm sorry, I shouldn't have said that. Sometimes my mouth operates before my brain. I work for a Catholic charity that helps people get off the streets and reengage with society. I see a lot of people who look like her. Maybe not the makeup and designer jeans, but you get to know the look. I shouldn't judge. She's probably in the early stages of her recovery and more power to her for coming to the quilt retreat."

Michelle returned with the woman.

"Everyone, meet Marine. Marine, this is Harriet and her friend Lauren and...I'm sorry." She turned to Jessica. "I don't know your name."

Jessica held her hand out, and Marine had to juggle her plate to free her own.

"I'm Jessica."

"Marine and I were in high school together," Michelle explained. "She left Foggy Point and became an actress in Hollywood."

Everyone looked at Marine.

"Michelle exaggerates. I went to acting school in Los Angeles after high school. I got a few parts in the soap operas, but then the networks started canceling soaps and replacing them with cooking shows and talk shows," She shrugged. "I did a play, but mostly I was waiting tables—and there's a lot of competition for those jobs. I decided to come home and do some regional theater."

"And...you're a quilter?" Lauren asked.

"Not yet, but I've always been fascinated by the costumes in theater work and the crazy quilts look like they use the same kind of material. Besides, I don't have a lot else to do until the casting call for the next play at the Foggy Point Theater. I thought I'd give it a try." She popped the last square of quesadilla into her mouth. "These are really good." She turned and looked at Michelle. "I'm going to go get more. Do you want anything?"

Michelle shook her head, and Marine headed back to the food. Michelle looked to be sure she was out of earshot.

"Her mother remarried while she was in LA, and new hubby isn't interested in having an adult child return to the nest. I ran into Marine while I was in Seattle, and when I told her I was coming back to Foggy Point to do some work, she asked if she could visit.

"I gather she came back here once when my mom was still alive, and when her own mother wouldn't let her stay at home, Mom ended up taking her in. I don't know how that all happened, but what could I do? The old me would have told her to get lost, but my therapist says I have to be more empathetic. Besides, Carla had already signed us up to be a host house."

Lauren picked up a stack of puzzle pieces and handed it to Harriet. She picked up a group of opposite pieces for herself.

"Let's get this show on the road. I'll do the out-of-towners while you do locals." She handed Jessica the first piece.

Harriet shuffled her pieces.

"Give us a few minutes to distribute these, and then you can begin the hunt to find your match."

Jessica looked at her piece.

"This should be fun. Too bad there aren't any men." She laughed. "Don't look so shocked, and don't tell me you didn't think it."

Harriet smiled and shook her head.

"Not me. I've got my hands full."

"Speak for yourself," Lauren said and walked away.

✂- - -✂- - -✂

The noise level in the room increased as quilters queried each other, trying to find their match.

"This worked better than I'd hoped," Harriet told Lauren as they stood by the food table.

Lauren fanned herself with her remaining piece of puzzle.

"I've still got to find my match."

Harriet held her piece up.

"Me, too," She scanned the room. "Okay, what are the chances of this?" She pointed across the room at Connie's two sisters. Each woman clutched a laminated crazy quilt piece in her hand. She wove her way through the crowd, followed by Lauren.

"Are you my partner?" Harriet asked and held her puzzle piece up.

The younger-looking sister smiled with relief.

"I am," she said and matched her piece to Harriet's.

Lauren held her piece out to the other woman.

"That must mean we're a pair."

An exchange of information ensued. Lauren was delighted to learn the Texas sister was a recently retired computer programmer.

"I have no idea what my sister is talking about with your friend," the Colorado sister, Pam, told Harriet.

"I'm glad they found each other. Lauren doesn't have many women to talk tech with."

As they spoke, Harriet scanned the room to locate her roommate, finally spotting her in a cluster of women.

"Do you know that woman? The tall skinny one?" Pam asked. "I tried talking to her, but she didn't seem very interested in meeting people. At least, she didn't want to meet me. She heard that redhead say she was from the Bay area, and I no longer existed."

"I'm sorry. That wasn't very nice."

"She looks vaguely familiar."

"She used to be a fashion model. She did a lot of print work in magazines. I think she did a few TV commercials, too."

Pam put her hand over her mouth.

"I'm sorry if she's a friend of yours. I didn't mean to speak out of turn."

"No problem. She's the wife of my deceased husband's best friend."

"Oh, now I've really made a mess of things."

"Don't worry, I find her rather pretentious myself, and my husband's death isn't recent."

Pam gave Sharon a last glance and turned back to Harriet.

"I suppose I've spent too much time in the People's Republic of Boulder. We're all a bunch of aging hippies—no makeup, no designer clothes, and no posturing."

"Sounds like Foggy Point," Harriet said and held her hand out. "Can I take your plate?"

Glynnis Miller of the Small Stitches quilt group picked up a black handheld microphone from atop a podium that had been brought in during the quilt-piece matching exercise. She tapped and blew on it before calling the group to attention. Teachers were introduced, quilt samples were shown, and schedules were explained before the group was dismissed for the evening.

Lauren came to stand beside Harriet.

"Jessica wants to go get lattes on the way home. Do you want to come with?"

Harriet's roommate was still talking to her new friend from the Bay area.

"I'd like to, but I need to take Sharon home. If she came here to talk to me about Steve and his death, I'd like to give her the opportunity to get that over with so we can get on with our week without that hanging over us."

"You don't owe that woman anything."

"I know, but she seems to have an agenda, so I'd rather get it out on the table and move on."

Chapter 8

Harriet took Scooter's leash from the kitchen coat closet and attached it to his collar. She turned toward Sharon, who was looking a little lost in the middle of the kitchen.

"I'm going to take my dog out for a minute. There's cut-up fruit in the fridge and chocolate chip cookies in the jar on the counter, if you're hungry."

She paused a moment, but when Sharon didn't say anything, she picked her dog up and headed for the door.

"Well, she's not very friendly," she said to Scooter as she set him down.

"Who isn't?"

"Aiden? What are you doing hiding in my bushes?"

Aiden's dog Randy rustled out of the hedge that bordered one side of Harriet's drive.

"I thought I'd hike over here through the woods and see how your opening soiree went. Bringing this little rascal along was a big mistake." He bent down and rubbed his dog's ear, removing a dried twig that had attached itself to her. "She thinks she saw a rabbit or a rat or something and took off. I'm lucky she stopped in your hedge."

"Yeah, how would that look if she'd ended up chomping on someone's cat? Dr. Jalbert flaunting the leash law."

Aiden barely contained his smile as he grabbed Harriet's arm and pulled her to his chest. His voice dropped to the husky whisper that made her heart race.

"So, are you going to turn me in to the police?"

She bit her bottom lip and looked up at him.

"I'm thinking."

"Let me help you." Aiden tilted his head down and lightly brushed his lips across hers, teasing her mouth. "Are you convinced of my innocence yet?"

"Hmmm, I may need more data."

He wrapped his arms around her, sliding his hands to her lower back, and kissed her thoroughly.

"Okay, so maybe we can let it go this one time," Harriet said when they finally separated. "I'm always happy to see you, but what are you really doing here?"

"My sister invited me over for dinner with the kids since you-all were having your quilt party. Randy and I decided to go for a run before we go back to the apartment, and I wanted to see how it's going with your house-guest."

Harriet slid her hands slowly up his arms.

"It's going great, since I'm out here with you and she's in the house." She put her hands behind his neck and pulled him to her for another kiss.

He groaned. "I'm trying to be the interested, supportive boyfriend here, but you're making it difficult to listen attentively."

She stepped back.

"I appreciate that you were willing to listen, but I'm all talked out."

Aiden sighed. "I tried."

"And you did very well." Harriet smiled up at him.

"Someone is looking for you." He turned her slightly so she could see the dining room window and the silhouette of Sharon.

Harriet took another step back.

"Don't worry, we're in the shadow of the hedge. I should let you get back in before she comes out, though." He leaned in for one more quick kiss.

"Thanks for stopping by."

She watched while he and Randy, now on her leash, jogged down the drive and out of sight.

✂- - - ✂- - - ✂

"Is that your boyfriend?" Sharon asked when Harriet had returned to the kitchen. So, they hadn't been as concealed in the shadows as Aiden had thought.

Harriet rubbed the back of her neck.

"It's complicated, but the simple answer is yes."

42

Sharon looked at her but didn't say anything. Harriet ran her hand through her hair then dropped it to her side.

"Look, this is going to be a long week if we keep walking on eggs around each other. If you have something to say about Steve or anything else, just say it. If it's that you're uncomfortable around me and maybe you didn't expect to be, we can find you a room somewhere else. Foggy Point has a motel not far from downtown. I'll pay for a room for you. It's not the Hilton, but it's clean and we could move you there tonight. The workshop organizers reserved several rooms just in case there were problems, so I know we can get you in there."

Sharon twisted a hank of her fine blond hair in her fingers.

"Harriet, no. You've got it all wrong. I *am* uncomfortable, but not for the reasons you think. I feel terrible about how everyone treated you when Steve died. We weren't there for you."

"Would you like some tea?" Harriet asked as she put the kettle on the stove.

"That would be nice."

It was the first genuine thing Harriet had heard come out of the woman's mouth since she'd arrived.

"I didn't expect anything from any of Steve's friends when he passed. We'd never really been friends. You all were a close group who had known each other since you were children. I get that I was never going to fit, even if Steve had lived."

"You make us sound like monsters."

"Not at all." Harriet handed her a box of mixed flavored tea bags to choose from. "I had a very nontraditional childhood. I don't fit in many people's groups of friends. Thankfully, Steve understood that and didn't expect me to be anything but what I was."

"That's what I'm talking about. We didn't even bother to know that. Steve brought you to a dinner one day, and all we knew is you weren't from Oakland. I'm not making excuses, but where we went to school, we were the minorities.

"Except for Niko—about a third of our school was Asian—but less than ten percent of our school was Caucasian. Most of the white parents had the money to send their kids to private schools. Ours didn't. We had to stick together. Jason was bullied by some of the other kids, and that brought us closer than we already were. After that, it was us against the world."

"Steve told me about your group. Frankly, he was getting tired of it." Sharon started to say something, but Harriet held her hand up. "He was clear that he still liked his friends. He was just tired of doing everything

43

as a group. He felt like a traitor if he went to a baseball game with his co-workers instead of the gang."

The kettle whistled, and Harriet poured water into their mugs and carried them to the kitchen table.

"I know Steve used me as an excuse to do things apart from the group, and I didn't mind because, like I said, I was never going to fit in the group. I mostly grew up in Europe. My schools didn't have a baseball team or a football team, because football is really soccer there, and most of the schools I went to didn't have boys. Every now and then, I'd be sent to stay here with my aunt. She taught me to quilt, but I didn't make any friends here. Just about the time I'd meet someone my age, my parents would ship me off somewhere else."

"It sounds glamorous." Sharon attempted a smile.

"It wasn't. I had some amazing experiences, to be sure. I met the Queen of England and the Emperor of Japan, Queen Margrethe of Denmark and a bunch of lesser dignitaries. My parents are internationally renowned scientists. My job was always to be seen but not heard, while maintaining a suitable list of accomplishments for them to recite when the subject came up. Their great disappointment was that, after graduating college with the required degree in physics, I switched to studying textiles."

"Pretty impressive, if you ask me."

Harriet dunked her teabag up and down in her mug then plopped it on an empty saucer she'd put on the table for that purpose.

"Not really. I wasn't always able to come back to Foggy Point, so I spent a lot of holidays with paid employees while everyone else in my school went home to their families." She sipped her tea. "Enough about my pathetic past. I'm grown up now and have a great life. If you aren't here to punish me about Steve, why *are* you here?"

"I'm here because of you, but not because of Steve's death. I'll admit it was easy to blame you at first. Eventually, we—or I should say some of us—realized that if we'd been the friends we always pretended to be maybe Steve would have felt comfortable getting treatment. We knew he had a health condition, but no one realized how serious it was.

"After my accident, I realized just how much we'd picked at other peoples flaws growing up. Hours of therapy later, I know it was a defense mechanism on our part. If we pretended we were cooler than everybody else, the bullies left us alone. We had safety in numbers. But, Steve must have thought we'd turn on him if he had a weakness."

"That all sounds rather dramatic. I can believe that was the case in high school, but you all went off to different colleges, didn't you?" Harriet spooned a glob of honey into her cup and stirred. "I think it's much simpler than all that. Steve was in denial. He didn't want the condition, and if he didn't acknowledge it, it didn't exist."

"Maybe I'm giving us too much credit."

Harriet tasted her tea. She'd added too much honey, but she took another long sip, hoping Sharon would reveal why she was really sitting opposite her at the kitchen table.

"Since my accident, not very many modeling jobs are coming my way. I can do hand modeling, but those calls are few and far between. I majored in partying in school and then quit after two years to model in Europe."

Harriet waited in silence for her to complete a sip-tea stalling maneuver.

"You probably don't remember, but Rick and I came over for dinner one night, and your quilting friends were just leaving. One of them had a beautiful quilt draped over her arm, and you were putting away some pretty quilt pieces. I didn't think too much of it then, but while I was in the hospital I had a lot of time to think. It really hit me—I don't create anything.

"I was always totally dependent on my looks, which I know now are only too fleeting. I thought about those quilts. Your family will have them forever, no matter what happens to you. I know that sounds morbid, but I was in the hospital on drugs.

"I realized I want that. I want to make something...anything. I may turn out to be a wretched quilter, but I at least want to try. Besides, you and your friends seemed so happy. I'm not sure I know what that word means anymore."

Harriet folded her hands in her lap.

"Okay," she finally said. "Have you ever quilted before?"

The other woman's shoulders sagged.

"Have you sewn anything?"

Sharon brightened. "I can hem pants with a stapler."

"It's a start," Harriet said with a laugh.

They sipped their tea.

"Let's go into my studio. I have a couple of books on beginning quilting. Maybe you can page through them tonight before you go to bed. That will at least help you get familiar with the terminology."

"That sounds great. I'm actually a pretty quick learner."

Harriet took their cups to the sink then led the way to her studio. Maybe this wasn't going to be so bad after all.

Chapter 9

A fine sheen of sweat frosted Marine's brow as she and Harriet left their classroom in the basement of the Methodist church. Jessica came up behind them and put her hand on Marine's arm.

"Are you okay? You don't look well."

Marine glared at her.

"Do you have something that will cure what ails me?"

"No, and if I did, I wouldn't give it to you. You know that wouldn't help you. Are you in a program?"

Marine jerked her arm free.

"I'm sure I don't know what you're talking about. My breakfast didn't agree with me, that's all." She stormed off down the hallway and up the stairs.

Jessica laughed. "Was it something I said?"

Harriet shifted her tote bag up onto her shoulder.

"Do you really think she's using drugs?"

"I don't have a single doubt. She's a user, and it looks like her supply ran out. She'll have to make an excuse and go find something on the street."

"In Foggy Point?"

"Come on, you're not that naive. Drugs are everywhere. She might be trying to clean up, but she's not succeeding. Not today, anyway."

"It must have been hard for her, sitting through this morning's lecture on the history of crazy quilts."

Jessica laughed again.

"It was hard for me, and I wasn't coming off of anything. That lady was a really dry speaker."

"I thought the first part was interesting," Harriet said. "I'd heard people say that crazy quilts were the first patterns made in America. She makes a good argument for why that isn't true."

"You're right. I hadn't realized they were constructed on a larger piece of backing, making them not a good choice for the early settlers who didn't have big pieces of fabric to work with."

"There's also the age-old problem of no surviving samples from before the late eighteen-hundreds, at which point suddenly there are a lot of them." Harriet pulled her smartphone from her pocket. "Lauren just sent me a text. She and my aunt and our friends Connie and Mavis are waiting for us by the front door. My roommate needs to buy a little more fabric for her afternoon session, so we thought we'd go to lunch at the sandwich place just down the block from Pins and Needles. We have two hours for lunch. Does that work for you?"

"Sounds great if you have room for me."

"My car can take seven if the three in back are agile enough to get in," Harriet told her as they reached the stairs and went up to join the others.

Harriet put her phone to her ear but couldn't hear her caller.

"Wait a minute, I need to walk outside so I can hear."

Pins and Needles was full of crazy quilt students, and it sounded like they were all talking at once. Harriet stepped outside to the sidewalk.

"Hello? Michelle, is that you?" She listened for a minute. "Yes, I still plan to have my weekly session with Lainie...Sure, I can pick her up on my way home from my afternoon class. Tell her I can be there around four-thirty...No problem. Bye."

"Everything okay?" Aunt Beth asked. She'd followed her niece outside.

Harriet slid her phone back into her pocket.

"Yeah, that was Michelle. She wanted to be sure I was still going to give Lainie her weekly quilting lesson. Since we're on our own for dinner tonight, I said yes. I'd told her that before, but she asked if I can pick her up at Aiden's."

Beth shook her head.

"Why can't she drive the girl herself? It is her daughter, after all."

"I didn't ask, and she didn't offer a reason. If it's easier on Lainie for me to pick her up, I'm happy to do it."

"What about your roommate?"

Harriet smiled.

"Funny thing, that. It turns out she really does want to learn to quilt. I told her about Lainie, and she asked if she could join the lesson, too."

"So, all that worry about her coming here to torture you about Steve was for nothing?"

"That may still be in play, but we've talked, and it would seem that things are a lot more complicated than what I was thinking."

Aunt Beth picked a stray thread from her jacket sleeve.

"You just be careful. I still don't like the way she was talking to you when she first arrived."

"I will, but I think she was as nervous about coming to my house as I was to have her come."

"It was her idea, though."

"Aren't you the one who always says 'Don't borrow trouble'?"

"Don't you throw my words back at me, Missy," Aunt Beth said and then laughed. "I hope you're right is all I'm going to say about it."

Music came from Harriet's pocket, and she pulled her phone out and tapped the face.

"We better round up our crews. That was our twenty-minute warning." She slid the phone into her pocket and followed her aunt back into the store.

><---><---><

Aiden got out of his vintage Bronco and walked over to Harriet's SUV.

"What are you doing here?"

She turned her engine off and opened her door.

"I came to pick up Lainie for our quilting lesson."

"That's why I'm here." Aiden pushed Harriet's door closed behind her. "Lainie called me and asked if I could take her to your place. Michelle's car is in the shop."

"Michelle had already asked me to come pick her up."

Aiden's jaw tightened. "My sister must have forgotten to tell her daughter what the plan was. I'm not surprised. She's not the most organized person. We're really slammed at the clinic. I only came because it was Lainie asking."

"You can go back. I've got it covered."

He looked at his car and then toward the house.

"I better go in and at least say hello and tell Lainie it isn't her fault. She's a sensitive kid and will be upset if she thinks she took me away from something important."

"Uh, she *did* take you away from something important."

"I know, but she doesn't need to know that." He took a deep breath and looked at her. "Okay, I'm calm, cool and collected. No stress here at all."

Harriet shook her head.

"I don't think there's anything wrong with her learning to be considerate of other people, but what do I know."

He put his arm around her shoulders.

"Come on, back me up here."

"Lead the way."

They found Lainie with her mother, brother and Marine. Their houseguest had either gotten over her illness or found something to cure what ailed her. The group was clustered around a book that lay open on the dining room table.

"Look, Uncle Aiden," Lainie called out. "Here's your picture with Marine at the prom." She spun the book around so he could see the picture.

Aiden smiled, but it looked more than a little forced to Harriet.

"That was a long time ago."

Lainie grinned. "You looked really handsome, Uncle Aiden."

"I looked handsome?" he said with mock horror. "You mean I'm not the most handsome guy you know now?"

Lainie's face turned crimson, and she looked to her mother for help.

Marine seemed to be somewhere else.

"We did look good didn't we?" she said to no one in particular.

"Don't worry, Lainie," Harriet said. "Uncle Aiden in teasing you. Do you have your quilting bag ready?"

Lainie glanced at her with obvious relief.

"My bag is by the front door, I'll go get it."

She hurried out of the dining room, followed by her brother. Harriet watched until the dining room door closed then looked at Aiden.

"I didn't realize you two were an item."

"They were more than an item," Michelle said before Aiden could answer. "She was the love of his life. They went steady for most of high school."

Aiden turned abruptly. "I've got patients to see."

Harriet watched as he strode across the dining room and into the kitchen. The nerves of her spine bristled. She took a deep breath and reminded herself most people had dramatic teen romances that didn't stand the test of time.

"I'm going to go lay down," Marine said. She left through the door Lainie had used.

Michelle closed the yearbook.

"Marine and I were having a little trip down memory lane. If I'd known he was coming, I would never have gotten the book out. She broke his heart when she went to LA after high school. Everyone, including Aiden thought she was going to go to the community college near here until he graduated and then they were going to go off to university together. I know my mom thought they would eventually get married. We all did.

"I think Mom thought there was still hope when Marine came back from LA and stayed with her, but Aiden had just left for his research trip to Africa for three years. But you know all that." She picked the book up. "Why was he here, anyway?"

"Lainie called him to take her to my house."

"I'll have to talk to her. I told her you were coming to get her."

Harriet was ready for this conversation to be over before Michelle dropped any more revelations about Aiden that he'd not chosen to share with her.

"Speaking of Lainie and her lesson, we better get going. My house-guest is waiting for us."

"Lainie," Michelle screeched. "Come on, you're making Harriet wait after she's been so nice, coming and getting you."

As if on cue, Lainie returned, her bag clutched to her chest.

"I'll feed her dinner," Harriet told Michelle as she followed Lainie out to the car before Michelle could reply.

Lainie shivered.

"I don't like Marine. Madame du Cloutier says we're not supposed to talk about people unless it's something nice, but she's really weird."

Harriet backed up and then turned down the driveway.

"Weird how?"

"Well, she gets sweaty when it's cold in the house. And she smells a lot of the time. She wears a lot of perfume to cover it up, but that makes it worse. She talks to herself."

"What does she say?"

Lainie puffed her chest out and deepened her voice.

"You can do this, Marine, it's just dinner. You just have to make it through dinner." Lainie's voice returned to normal, and she relaxed her shoulders. "Stuff like that. It seems like she's always giving herself a pep talk. She doesn't really seem to like quilting, either."

"Well, now, that's downright sacrilegious."

Lainie's brows pulled toward each other and furrows formed between them.

"Is it really?"

"Honey, no. That's just a figure of speech." What sort of education were these poor children getting with their French tutor and nanny? Harriet wondered. Her own education was largely European, but she'd still learned English, including slang and idioms.

50

Lainie's cheeks turned pink.

"Sweetie, it's okay. Every language has figures of speech that don't make sense. Let's get back to Marine. Is there anything else that makes you uneasy? She hasn't said anything inappropriate to you or your brother, has she?"

Lainie shook her head. "She ignores us, just like everyone else in that house, except our nanny and tutor. Our nanny says we are to be seen but not heard."

"That doesn't sound like much fun."

The girl chewed on her lower lip.

Harriet thought for a moment. Her desire for information was at war with her desire to protect Aiden's niece.

"Tell you what. You listen to what Marine says—to herself or to others. If she says anything you think is weird, or even just a little off, you can tell me at our next lesson. If it's something big, you can call me on my cell phone. I'll give you the number when we get to my house. I think you're very smart, and I'd like to hear what you have to say."

Lainie smiled.

A few minutes later, they pulled into Harriet's driveway.

"Can I take Scooter out when we get there?" Lainie asked.

"I think he'd like that."

✂ - - ✂ - - - ✂

Sharon lay her four-patch block beside Lainie's on Harriet's cutting table. Carla had picked Lainie up after Harriet had fed everyone a simple stir-fry with rice. She shook her head.

"Hers looks so much better than mine."

"Don't be so hard on yourself. This isn't her first lesson, and I've been giving her homework. She's had practice cutting precisely and sewing a straight line." Harriet picked up Sharon's lopsided block. The two women looked at each other and laughed.

"It'll get easier with practice," Harriet told her when they could speak again. "No one who hasn't sewn before just sits down and starts making perfect quilt blocks. Don't pressure yourself. You can practice while you're here. We spent most of this lesson on cutting. It will be better when you can just sew for an hour or two at a time."

Sharon raised her eyebrows. "If you say so." She looked at Harriet and blew air out of pursed lips. "Since my modeling career ended, I've been mostly a bust at everything I've tried. I designed our kitchen and the refrigerator spot was too small for a normal-sized unit. I got that corrected and took up gourmet cooking. That lasted until I blew up the pressure cooker in the kitchen.

"Rick banned me from the golf course when I over-swung and hit him in the eye with my club." She smiled. "I was hoping this would be a success. Your quilts were always so beautiful. I knew I couldn't do anything like that, but I'd hoped I could create something."

"I don't know about all that other stuff, but I do know you can do this. You told me before you learn quickly, and I believe it. Your work shows promise. You've a good eye for color, and crazy quilting allows for a lot of irregularity. Lainie is learning the basics, but much of that doesn't apply to crazy quilts."

"Are you going to be working with Lainie again tomorrow?"

"I'll have to check with Michelle. We're only scheduled to meet weekly, but I was hoping to have her over after class tomorrow before our group dinner."

"I'd like to try my corner technique again tomorrow, if that's okay." Sharon tilted her head and looked past Harriet's shoulder. "I think your friend is waiting outside for you."

Harriet turned around and looked out the front window of her studio. Aiden was leaning against his Bronco in her driveway.

"I better go out."

Sharon smiled. "Don't worry about me. I'll see you in the morning."

Harriet waited until Sharon was out of the studio and the connecting door was shut. She opened the outside door.

"Are you coming in, or do I have to come outside and freeze with you?" It was springtime in Foggy Point, but evenings were still cold.

"I didn't want to interrupt you and your roommate. I figured you'd take Scooter out eventually."

She stepped aside and held the door open.

"Sharon is upstairs for the night. How long have you been waiting out here?"

"I just got here. I had nothing better to do, since I can't go to my real home, so I volunteered to do the evening hours at the clinic tonight."

"I'm guessing you didn't have to ask twice."

"Yeah, Ron was glad to go see his kid's soccer game."

She looked at his face. He wasn't smiling.

"What's wrong?"

He was silent for a moment.

"I didn't want you to get the wrong impression about me and Marine."

Harriet shut the door behind him and sat in one of the two wingback chairs in her client reception area. She pointed to the other one, and he sat down.

"I didn't have any impression, right, wrong or indifferent."

"Even when Michelle said Marine was the 'love of my life'?"

"I would have been more surprised if a guy as good-looking as you still are didn't break a few hearts in his youth. Besides, I've learned not to believe most of what your sister says, even this reborn version. Having said that, she does seem to be trying. I get the impression she didn't really want to invite Marine to stay at your house."

Aiden leaned his head back against his chair.

"So, I've been worrying for nothing?"

"I wouldn't go that far, but you don't have to worry what I think. Even the kids can see Marine's a troubled soul."

He let out a big breath.

"She always has been. Contrary to my sister's romantic notions, Marine wasn't the love of my life. I'd always brought home stray kittens and puppies. She was my first stray human. I realized later what was wrong with her would take more than a few normal dates and some of my mom's home cooking. She wasn't that easy to get rid of once I'd figured things out."

Harriet stood up and went over to his chair. He opened his arms, and she sat down in his lap. She stroked a lock of silky black hair back off his face.

"How so?"

"You name it, she tried it. She threatened suicide. She scratched my car door with a key. She left long rambling messages on our phone machine. One time, she called all my friends and said she and her fictitious baby couldn't live without me and then hid and wouldn't answer her phone. The whole town was searching for her. I looked like a schmuck for ditching her in her hour of need."

"But you did take her to the prom?"

"Only after she bought a dress and told everyone she was going with me. Half the town still believed I'd made her get rid of the pretend baby at that point. I hadn't asked anyone else—I'd been planning on going to a program at the University of Washington with Julio that weekend. Jorge was taking us. It was a pre-college thing. Julio and I were big science nerds back then."

"What did Jorge say about it?"

"To no surprise, he thought I was making a big mistake giving in to her demands. Peer pressure was intense, and I caved in. He was right. It only got worse."

"How did things end?"

"I went off to college. After she'd spent some time trying to get acting jobs in California with no training, she came back to Foggy Point and tried to trap me into marrying her. Remember, she's a couple of years older than me—I was in high school when she went to LA.

"Eventually, she got a scholarship to a drama program at a junior college. I guess she got involved in that and forgot me. There were rumors she got into drugs at that school, but I don't really know. I didn't want to know anything about what she was doing or where she was doing it." He wrapped his arms around her and pulled her against his chest. She leaned her head on his shoulder.

"I should go," he said. "I just wanted to be sure my sister hadn't caused us any more trouble."

"We're fine. I really do think the time your sister spent in the mental hospital has done her some good. She's still no fun to be around, but it seems like she's beginning to understand that and is trying to change her behavior."

"I'm tired of talking about my sister." He kissed her forehead then worked his way down to her mouth, ending all possibility of further discussion.

Chapter 10

A light rain was falling the next morning as Harriet guided her car into a visitor parking spot near the covered entrance to the Methodist church.

"You can get out here, and I'll park down below in the workshop parking area. There's no sense in both of us getting wet," she told Sharon.

Sharon gathered her quilting bag and purse.

"Thanks. It's silly of me not to have brought an umbrella."

"It makes you look like a local. Only visitors carry umbrellas. Besides, I can use the exercise."

Sharon opened the door and got out.

"Thanks again," she said before turning and heading for the entrance.

"Aren't we the good hostess," Lauren said as Harriet got out of her car and locked the door.

Lauren was locking her own car door, but her roommate, Jessica, was with her. Jessica waved a hand at Harriet and joined her.

"Don't let her fool you—she tried to drop me by the covered entrance, but I refused to get out. I need every bit of activity I can get. I'm not used to sitting all day."

Lauren walked over to them.

"I hope your guest isn't as surly as this one."

Jessica poked her arm.

"You love it, and you know it. I bet you don't get sparring partners as skilled with zingers as I am every day."

Harriet laughed. "You're right. I'm more of the straight-man type."

Lauren slid her messenger bag crosswise over her chest after positioning her quilting bag on her left shoulder.

"I hope we get to sew something today. History is all good, but a full day of it was a little much."

"Weren't you listening? The morning was quilt history, and the afternoon was design."

"That's what I'm trying to tell you. My design lady spent half the time reviewing the history again."

Harriet looked at Jessica with raised eyebrows. Jessica shrugged.

"I have to agree with the blonde. Our teacher seemed to have one lecture, and it included history, whether you needed it or not."

"That's too bad," Harriet said. "My teacher taught us a lot about color values and appropriate fabric choices."

Jessica led the way through the rows of cars.

"Let's hope for a day of sewing," she said over her shoulder.

✂ - - - ✂ - - - ✂

"Get away from me!" they heard Sharon yell before they reached the top of the stairs that led up from the lower parking lot. Harriet took the remaining steps two at a time, followed by Lauren and Jessica.

"What's going on?"

Sharon turned to her.

"This woman is harassing me."

Marine stood close to Sharon, staggering slightly as she twisted her body in Harriet's direction.

"She won't help me. They told me she could help me, and now she's being all high and mighty and pretending like she doesn't know me."

Sharon threw her hands in the air and backed up.

"That's because I don't know her. I have no idea who 'they' are, and I never saw her before the meet-and-greet the other night."

Marine swayed as she attempted to close the distance between herself and Sharon. Jessica stepped in and grabbed her by both arms. She looked back at Harriet.

"I got this. You guys go ahead in, I'll catch up."

She led Marine into the building before anyone could protest.

Sharon dropped her hands to her sides and then settled her quilt bag on her shoulder.

"That was weird."

"And you've never met her before?" Lauren asked.

Sharon rearranged the front of her hair.

"Not that I know of. I mean, that would be awfully random. Isn't she from around here?"

"She is, but Michelle said she was an actress in a soap opera in LA for a while," Harriet explained.

Sharon was thoughtful for a moment.

"I modeled in a couple of commercials in LA. I sure don't remember her, though—and I'm usually good with faces."

"Jessica thinks she's a drug user who's had her supply dry up," Lauren said.

Harriet started toward the door.

"Let's go have some quilting fun and try to forget this little episode. Jessica says she has experience with this sort of thing."

Sharon straightened her blouse.

"I guess we're lucky she was here, then."

Aunt Beth opened the church door.

"There's coffee, tea and breakfast pastries set up in the cafeteria. You all look like you could use a little caffeine."

✂- - -✂- - -✂

Harriet hung back with her aunt when everyone had finished their coffee and left to find the restroom before going to their individual classes.

"We had a bit of a scene in the parking lot."

Beth set her empty cup on the table.

"I figured something had happened. Your roommate seemed rattled, and Lauren's gal seemed unusually subdued when she finally joined us."

"Marine accosted Sharon when we arrived. She claimed she knew Sharon and wanted something from her we're all assuming is drugs."

Beth's brows drew together.

"That doesn't sound good. Are you sure Sharon doesn't know her?"

"She says she doesn't. She says it's possible they were at the same party sometime when they were both in LA. Jessica has experience with troubled people, so she took Marine into the church office. I assume she called Michelle to come get her."

"I'm not sure what Marine is doing here anyway. Your cat is more interested in crazy quilts than that girl is."

"The week is young, so we have plenty of time to find out."

Beth put her arm around Harriet's shoulder.

"Let's not borrow trouble. I'm looking forward to starting my first quilt block today."

Sharon was waiting in the hallway when they came out.

"If you don't mind, I think I'd like to go home. I've got a migraine coming on. If I take my medicine and lie down, I can nip it in the bud."

"Okay, I'll go get the car."

Sharon put her hand on Harriet's arm.

"You don't need to do that. I went to the office to find out about getting a cab, and your pastor said he was going near your place to visit an elderly woman. He volunteered to drop me on his way."

"Let me know if I can do anything. If you feel better by lunchtime, I can bring you back."

"Thanks. I better go back to the office so I don't hold Pastor Hafer up."

Chapter 11

The private dining room at Tico's Tacos was full of quilters. Each of the Loose Threads had brought her roommate with her for the buffet lunch Jorge had prepared.

He entered the room, raising a pitcher of tea in one hand and lemonade in the other.

"Welcome to the Loose Threads clubhouse. I hope you are enjoying your visit to our town." He began filling glasses and passing them to Aunt Beth, who distributed them around the table.

Jessica raised hers to Jorge.

"We thank you for all the wonderful food you've prepared for us. I, for one, will come back to Foggy Point again just to have your guacamole."

Jorge smiled.

"I've trained her well," Lauren told the group. "I had Jorge's guacamole and chips waiting for her when she arrived."

Connie's Colorado roommate Pam took a glass of tea from Aunt Beth.

"Bobbi and I already decided we're bringing our husband here at the end of summer to salmon fish. Rod said he'd take them."

"You have a wonderful town here," Bobbi agreed.

Lauren dipped a chip into the bowl of guacamole in front of her.

"Bring your quilts with you, and we can do a show-and-tell."

Pam looked at Bobbi.

"Oh, dear. They think we're going to finish these things this year."

Bobbi laughed. "I hope we don't have to wait until they're done to come back."

"Of course not," Mavis assured them. "At least half of us won't have ours done, either."

Two servers brought in large bowls of warm queso dip to go with the chips, and conversation stopped while people sampled the warm spicy cheese.

Jorge delivered another meal the group wouldn't soon forget. Camarones al mojo de ajo—white prawns in garlic—and chiles with plantains and re-fried black beans were served with a grilled cactus salad. When the quilters were convinced they couldn't eat another bite, he proved them wrong by serving his signature flan.

Bobbi leaned back in her chair.

"I am in love," she declared.

Lauren set her napkin beside her plate.

"It's going to be hard to sew this afternoon after all this. I need a nap."

Sharon appeared in the doorway.

"Am I too late?"

Connie stood and pulled a chair to the end of her table.

"Sit down. We're just getting finished. Jorge!" she called out, mindful of the intercom system in the big room. "We have a late arrival."

Sharon set her purse beside the chair and sat down.

"I took my medication and then slept for a hour. When I woke, my migraine was gone, so I thought I'd come here and see how things went in this morning's class."

"Well, honey, we're glad you came back," Aunt Beth said with a warm smile.

Harriet was impressed. Her aunt had told her she thought Sharon was faking a headache to get out of quilting. The Threads had all agreed to be good ambassadors of Foggy Point, though, and she knew her aunt wasn't going to be the one to let the group down.

Lauren leaned toward her.

"Anyone else notice that Marine never came back?"

Carla leaned in from Harriet's opposite side.

"I hope she went back to wherever she came from." Her cheeks turned pink, and she cast her gaze down.

"I doubt you'll be that lucky," Harriet said in a quiet tone. "If we're lucky, Jessica handed her off to professionals. Hopefully, she's in a detox somewhere."

Mavis stood up. "Would anyone like to go for a walk in the park along the Muckleshoot River?"

Jorge handed Sharon a paper bag as the group stood and gathered their coats and purses.

"I packed you some taquitos and a little container of the nopales salad. I'm thinking after a migraine you don't want a lot of food. I can give you more if I'm wrong."

"No, thank you. You're right. This is perfect."

Harriet pulled her car keys from her pocket.

"I'll bring my car up to the door for anyone who doesn't want to walk to the start of the river trail."

Several of the less mobile visitors indicated they'd appreciate the ride.

She was a few feet from her car when Michelle pulled into the parking lot. She stopped and rolled her window down.

"Have you seen Marine?"

"Last I saw of her, she was with Jessica at the church. Jessica was going to try to find her some help. Marine had a little confrontation with my friend Sharon."

"I know, Jessica called me. The detox center couldn't take her for a few hours. They had to discharge some people or something. I had her in the car, and we were going through town. I stopped at a red light, and she jumped out. I've been looking for her ever since."

"How long ago was that?"

"I don't know. An hour? Two hours? I've looked everywhere I could think of."

"I doubt she'll show up at quilting, but if she does, I'll let you know."

"Can't you help me search for her?"

Harriet looked her in the face.

"You're joking, right? I've got a carload of quilters I have to take to the river walk and then back to the church. Besides, you said you've looked everywhere. I don't know what else I could do. Why don't you go talk to the police and see if they can help you?"

Michelle hit the button to raise her window.

"Thanks for nothing," she said as it closed. She backed up and then shot forward and out of the parking lot, spraying Harriet with gravel.

Harriet laughed to herself.

"Bye, Michelle."

Sharon and Bobbi were standing in the hall laughing when Harriet and Lauren came out of their classroom.

"I take it things went better this afternoon," Harriet said.

The two women laughed harder. Lauren and Harriet exchanged a look.

61

"Maybe their teacher put drugs in the water pitcher."

Sharon finally dug in her bag and handed Harriet a square of muslin that was covered in a mountain of fabric scraps.

"My fabric glue bottle malfunctioned. My teacher said to cover the excess glue with fabric." She giggled.

Bobbi took up the story.

"She never came back to see how much glue had blobbed out. It soaked right through the first piece of fabric, so Sharon kept adding fabric pieces until the glue was soaked up."

"I'm guessing your teacher wasn't thrilled when she saw it," Lauren said.

"She was very cool about it," Sharon told her. "She kept trying to figure out how to make it work. She was trying hard not to hurt my feelings. She told me how original my work was."

"It was sweet, really," Bobbi added.

Sharon put the fabric mess back into her bag.

"I assured her I'd get another glue bottle and would remake my square tonight so I'd be ready to start embellishing tomorrow."

"I wish you could have seen the teacher's face," Bobbi said. "It was priceless."

Jessica came up from the direction of the office.

"Have any of you heard from Michelle or Marine? I just called the detox center, and they said Marine never arrived."

"I saw Michelle on the way back from lunch. She was looking for Marine," Harriet said. "She said they were on the way back to Aiden's to wait for an hour or two until the center had discharged people and had a space for her. Marine jumped out of the car at a stop sign and took off. As of when I talked to her, Marine was still MIA."

Jessica pulled at her lower lip.

"This is not good," she said. "That girl needs help in a big way." She looked at Harriet and Lauren. "Does either of you know where people can access drugs in this town?"

Harriet frowned. "Not from firsthand experience, of course, but I've heard there's a problem with people dealing drugs down by the industrial docks."

"I think I'd better go look for her."

"You shouldn't go alone," Harriet cautioned.

"The youth pastor was in the office when I went to get the detox number from them. Maybe he can go with me."

"Be careful," Lauren warned.

"We better get going," Harriet said. "We've got some stitching to do before dinner."

Chapter 12

$\mathcal{H}$arriet pressed the two four-patch squares Sharon and Lainie had just stitched.

"These are both great. See, what did I tell you? Practice makes perfect."

The corners of the two blue and two white squares met exactly in the middle of Sharon's block. Lainie's pink and green squares were equally precise.

Lauren held up a large square of muslin.

"I cut a new base square for Sharon to remake her class project."

"Can I make another four-patch?" Lainie asked.

"I think that's a good idea," Harriet told her. She made sure the girl had her next fabric strips laid out and then turned to her roommate. "I have some crazy quilt fabric on the left side of the third shelf over there." She pointed to a bookcase with six shelves of neatly folded fabrics. "Choose a couple of pieces that resemble the ones that got ruined today, and we'll see if we can recreate your block, minus the glue."

A knock sounded on the studio door, and Jessica came in before anyone could answer it. Her hair was standing on end, and a sheen of sweat covered her forehead.

"I don't suppose Marine showed up here, did she?"

Harriet slid a wheeled chair toward her.

"Here sit. Can I get you some water or tea?"

"Water would be good," Jessica replied. "I had Pastor Andy drop me at the bottom of your hill. It's steeper than it looks."

Harriet went to the under-counter refrigerator next to her desk as Lauren slid her chair closer to Jessica.

64

"To answer your question, no. But then, we came straight here and haven't left. I take it you didn't find her at the docks."

Jessica took the bottle of water Harriet handed her, opened it and took a drink.

"No, I didn't. There are some really creepy people down there, but none of them seemed to know Marine. Or if they did, they didn't admit it."

"Michelle will be here soon to pick Lainie up. Maybe she'll know something. Hopefully, Marine went back to Aiden's."

Jessica set her water on the cutting table.

"Aiden's the vet, right?"

Harriet slid her chair away from Lainie and toward Lauren and Jessica.

"Why do you ask?"

"I went by an animal clinic between the docks and here and its parking lot was full of police cars and an ambulance and fire truck."

Lauren and Harriet looked at each other.

"Maybe it was one of their elderly clients," Harriet said. "Aiden told me Mrs. Novack had a seizure in the waiting room last week. It turned out she ran out of money so she was buying prescribed medicine for her dog, instead of buying her own."

"That must be it," Jessica said. "If this is like most small towns, I'm sure you'll know the whole story by class time tomorrow."

Sharon brought her fabric selections to the cutting table. She looked at Jessica.

"I had a little mishap with a glue bottle so I have to restart my class project."

Jessica brightened. "Do you have enough spare fabric that I could make one, too? I can use the practice. I'll pay you for it."

Harriet laughed. "I bought enough fabric to make ten crazy quilts. We got a great deal from our local fabric shop. Help yourself."

✂- - - ✂- - - ✂

"You better pack your bag," Harriet told Lainie an hour later. "I hear someone coming up the drive."

Lauren pushed the curtain aside and looked out the window.

"Uh, that's not Michelle."

Harriet looked over her friend's shoulder and saw a dark-haired man getting out of a gray Volvo sedan. He had the same silky black hair as his brother Aiden, but he wasn't as tall or fine-boned as his younger sibling. He, too, had blue eyes but his were more robin's-egg, not the ice blue that made Aiden's so distinctive.

65

"Lainie, is your uncle Marcel picking you up?"

Lainie looked confused.

"When I got out of the car, my mom said she'd see me in two hours."

"She must have gotten called in to work or something," Harriet assured her.

Lauren looked at Harriet and rolled her eyes. They both knew court-appointed community service work would be the last reason Michelle wasn't there. She could be getting a mani-pedi or taking a nap or any of a dozen other egocentric activities. The surprising thing was that *Marcel* was picking Lainie up. He usually kept his sister at arm's length and, unlike Aiden, did not enable her inconsiderate behaviors.

Marcel tapped on the door and entered. He held out his arms to Lainie. *"Avez-vous une étreinte pour votre oncle?"*

Lainie smiled and rushed into his arms for the requested hug.

"Are you picking me up?" she asked with a smile when he released her.

"Indeed, I am. We're going to go to Santa's workshop and get your brother, and then the both of you are coming to spend the night with your aunt Cookie and me. And don't worry, I have the bag your nanny packed in the car."

Harriet looked at him with a raised eyebrow. He patted Lainie on the back.

"Can you go get in the car? I need to talk to Harriet for a moment, and I don't want to leave our new puppy Adele alone that long."

A smile lit Lainie's face.

"You have a new dog? Can I go see now?"

Marcel laughed. "Yes and yes. And she has a leash on the front seat. You can take her out on the grass, if you want."

He watched until Lainie had safely gotten the puppy under control and out in Harriet's yard. When he turned back, his face had lost all humor.

"Can we talk privately?"

Lauren, Sharon and Jessica stood up.

"We'll go get some tea or something." They went into the kitchen and pulled the connecting door shut.

The smile left Marcel's face. Harriet felt the blood drain from hers.

"What's wrong?"

"Aiden's fine. A little shaken, but physically, he's fine. Marine Moreau was not so lucky."

"What do you mean?"

"I can only tell you what Michelle told me. Marine was found dead in Aiden's apartment over the vet clinic. Michelle stopped by the clinic to

66

pick up some flea medicine for the kids' cat. She said the parking lot was full of police cars when she got there.

"Aiden was sitting in the back of one of them. He told her he'd been out running, and he went to the apartment to clean up before going back to work and found Marine sprawled on his sofa—dead. He called the police, and they took him down to the station to make a statement. The apartment is a crime scene, so they couldn't do it there.

"Michelle is guessing he'll go back to the house. She figured he might not want to deal with her and her kids, so she asked if Cookie and I could take the kids for a few days. She's sending the tutor and nanny off, too. I don't know where she's going, and I didn't ask. I also didn't invite her to come to our house."

"What a shock. I just saw Marine this morning."

"I hadn't seen her lately. I didn't even know she was back in town. I do know she gave Aiden a lot of grief when he was in school. Her whole family is a train wreck."

"Is there anything I can do?"

"I'm sure Aiden would take comfort from seeing you when the police are through with him. I'm not sure when that will be. I suspect he has to wait for the detectives to finish at the crime scene before they come talk to him."

"They can't possibly think he had anything to do with it, can they?"

"No, I'm sure it's just routine stuff, since he's been staying in the apartment. They probably want to know how she could have gotten in. Stuff like that."

Harriet sank into a wingback chair.

"I'm shocked."

"Sorry to dump it on you, but Michelle called us a few minutes before I came to get Lainie. Speaking of which, I better scoop her up and go find her brother."

"Could you let me know if you hear anything else?"

"Of course. I'm guessing you'll see Aiden this evening some time, though?"

✂- - -✂- - -✂

The kitchen door flew open before the outside door had closed.

"Did he say Marine was *dead*?" Lauren asked as she burst into the room, closely followed by Jessica and Sharon. "We couldn't hear very well."

Harriet brushed past them and headed for the kitchen.

"I need a cup of tea."

Once everyone was there, Lauren took the teakettle from her at the sink when water began spilling out the spout.

"Give me that. You go sit down. Jessica, can you get the mugs from that cupboard." She pointed as she set the kettle on the stove. "Where do you hide the ginger snaps?" she asked Harriet.

Fifteen minutes later, all four were seated at the kitchen table, tea and cookies in front of them.

"Marine *is* dead," Harriet said without preamble. "Michelle stopped at the clinic to get flea medicine, and I guess Aiden was in the back of a squad car being questioned after he found Marine's body in his apartment."

Lauren sucked in a breath.

"Did she commit suicide because he's with you?"

"Oh, please," Jessica protested. "She must have found drugs and OD'd."

"Why would she do that at Aiden's apartment?" Lauren asked.

Sharon reached across the table and patted Harriet's arm.

"Can I do anything? Do you need me to drive you to wherever Aiden is?"

Harriet picked up a cookie.

"Thank you, but, no. I'm not sure he's going to want to see me tonight. I don't even know where he is right now. All Marcel knows is that Marine is dead, and the last he knew Aiden was at the police station having his statement taken."

Jessica stirred honey into her tea.

"I can't say I'm surprised. Don't know what to say about her choice of location, unless she knew he kept animal meds there, and she broke in to find them. Addicts do crazy things when they need a fix."

Lauren bit into her gingersnap.

"Remind me to bring you a fresh box of these. You could break a tooth." She chewed thoughtfully and swallowed. "I'm thinking we should call your aunt and Mavis. Maybe Connie."

"I was about to dial up Robin."

"Good idea," Lauren agreed. "I'll call your aunt and see if she thinks they need to come over."

"Didn't you tell me Robin is an attorney?" Jessica said.

Harriet paused before touching the face of her phone.

"She *is* an attorney. She keeps her license current, but she doesn't work many hours. She's taking time off while her kids are young. She works a little for her old firm and helps out the Loose Threads when we get in trouble."

"We don't know anyone's in trouble yet." Jessica pointed out.

68

Harriet started tapping numbers.

"Better safe than sorry."

Lauren and Harriet had just completed their calls when they heard a soft tap on the studio door.

"That was quick," Harriet said and went to see who had arrived. "Carla?"

The Loose Threads' youngest member followed her into the kitchen, her toddler Wendy balanced on her hip.

"I hope it's okay we came by. We're on our way to Connie's. Michelle cleared everyone else out of Aiden's, and I didn't want to be home alone with just her."

"Of course it's okay." Harriet looked over at Jessica and Sharon, who were both smiling at Wendy.

"Can she have a cookie?" Jessica asked Carla.

Carla pulled a sippy cup from the bag slung over her shoulder.

"Sure, she'd like that. Here's her juice." She set the cup on the table and put Wendy on the chair next to Jessica. When the child was situated, she got out a portable DVD player and pink earphones and set up her daughter with an educational cartoon. "All I heard from Michelle is Marine was found dead in Aiden's apartment at the clinic. Do you know anything?"

Harriet got a mug from the kitchen cupboard.

"Tea?" She filled it with hot water when Carla nodded. "That's all we heard, too. Marcel came to get Lainie and told us what you just said. If Aiden hasn't come home, he's probably still waiting at the police station to give his statement."

Jessica looked up from feeding Wendy bits of cookie.

"I hate to say it, but this should be routine. Drug overdoses are the leading cause of accidental death in this country—more than traffic accidents and guns. That woman was definitely an addict, too."

Sharon sipped her tea.

"I saw a bit on our local news in Oakland that several of the social service agencies are providing training and kits for the local opiate addicts. They give them naloxone to inject in case of an overdose. I guess it's an antidote."

"Kind of sad that it's come to that," Harriet mused.

The group pondered this latest fact until the studio door opened and Jorge came in, followed by Aunt Beth and Mavis. He carried a bulging white bag in each hand.

"Can you give me a plate?" he asked Harriet. She handed him one and he opened a bag and began placing cinnamon-sugar-covered churros on the provided dish. "I thought you ladies might need a snack for this discussion."

Harriet didn't ask him how he knew about "this discussion." She'd noticed that every time she called her aunt or Jorge lately, the other one was nearby. She wasn't sure how she felt about that. She knew she should be happy for her aunt, but the child in her wasn't sure she wanted to share.

Aunt Beth shrugged out of her jacket and hung it on a hook in the kitchen closet.

"I wonder if anyone has informed any of the Small Stitches."

Harriet got more mugs out while Lauren refilled the water kettle.

"I hadn't even thought about that," she said. "They'll need to make some sort of announcement to the group."

Mavis picked up Harriet's telephone.

"I'll tell Glynnis," she said as she dialed a number from memory. After a short conversation, she returned to the kitchen table and picked up a churro. "They hadn't heard, so it's good we decided to call. She said she'll make an announcement during the Continental breakfast, and in addition, she'll call all the teachers and have them each tell their morning class, just in case anyone skips breakfast."

Jorge shook his head.

"I don't mean to speak ill of the dead, but that girl has been trouble for Aiden for years. Why would she go to his apartment? And how could she get in?"

Lauren grabbed a second churro.

"I'm sure that's what the police are asking Aiden."

"My bet is, he has no idea what she was doing there," Harriet said. "He told me when he was in high school she scratched his car and told everyone she was pregnant with his child—which she was not—all to try to pressure him into staying with her. She was pretty resourceful."

Jessica took a churro when the plate was passed to her.

"I'm telling you, she was an addict and probably went to his place 'cause she thought he'd have animal drugs she could take. They'll use anyone and everyone to get their next fix."

Robin came in from the studio.

"I let myself in. I hope you don't mind." She hung her coat on the closet doorknob and helped herself to a mug, filling it with hot water from the kettle before coming to the table.

"Let's move to the dining room," Harriet suggested. "We can spread out and be comfortable."

70

The group relocated, and when they were settled, they all looked expectantly at Robin.

"I spoke to Aiden. The detectives finally came back to the station, and someone took his statement. As expected, they didn't really tell him anything. He told his story several times, and they typed it up, had him sign it, and sent him on his way. The apartment is still off-limits for now, so he's returning to his house. I told him to call me if he has any more contact with the police. I don't expect that to happen, but you never know."

"Could he get in trouble if she got into animal drugs that weren't safely secured?" Carla asked.

"Good question," Lauren said to her. The girl's face turned red.

"There are rules about securing controlled substances," Robin told them. "But I think those are mainly around settings where the public could gain access. If he had something in his medical bag, I think the lock on his front door would be considered adequate control. I don't know that for a fact, though." She pulled a yellow pad from her bag and made a note. "I'll check on it."

"Hard to imagine they could hold him liable for something someone does when they're in the process of committing a crime," Aunt Beth said.

They reviewed what was known for another fifteen minutes but weren't able to tease anything new out of the few facts they had.

"The law can be very crazy," Jorge finally stated. His phone rang, and he got up and went into the kitchen to answer it.

Connie arrived a few minutes later.

"Sorry I'm late. I was putting fresh linens on the beds." She smiled at Carla.

"You didn't have to do that," the young woman said.

"Of course we did. We want you to be as comfortable as possible while you're staying with us. Heaven knows you'll have to go back to work at Aiden's soon enough."

Carla twirled a strand of hair around her finger.

"It's not that bad. Michelle is better than she's ever been, and I'm getting used to the nanny and tutor. They spend a lot of time together in their rooms, speaking French." She got up. "I'll get your tea."

Connie smiled at her and turned to the group seated around the table.

"*Diós mio!* Marine is dead? And she died in the apartment at the vet clinic?"

Harriet slid the plate of churros to her.

"That's what everyone is telling us. We don't really know more than that."

"Will the workshop continue?" Connie wondered.

71

Aunt Beth set her cup back on the table.

"I can't imagine anyone would suggest canceling it. They're going to tell everyone, of course, but Marine killing herself has nothing to do with our quilting workshop."

Jorge returned to the dining room.

"That was Aiden on the phone. He was looking for Julio. I told him we were all here and invited him to come over."

Carla picked Wendy up.

"Is it okay if Wendy and I go on over to your house?" she asked Connie. "I don't want her to hear anything Aiden might have to say. I mean, details or something. And she can only watch videos for so long."

"We knew what you meant, honey. And Grandpa Rod is waiting for Wendy so he can read her some stories." Connie smiled.

Robin stood up. "I better get going, too. I need to do a little research. Someone call me if Aiden tells you anything new."

Lauren put two fingers to her forehead in a mock salute.

"Will do, Chief."

Sharon took her empty mug to the kitchen and came back to the doorway.

"If you don't mind, I'm going to take a couple of Harriet's quilting books upstairs and do a little reading."

She was right, Harriet thought. Aiden wouldn't feel comfortable with strangers hearing about his trouble.

"I think I'll help her," Jessica said. "Holler when it's time to go back to your place," she added to Lauren as she followed Sharon out of the room.

Chapter 13

*H*ere, come sit down by Harriet," Jorge told Aiden setting a cup of Mexican hot chocolate he'd whipped up in Harriet's kitchen in front him. Lauren slid the plate of churros to him. He picked one up and dunked it into his chocolate before taking a bite then looked at the people seated around him.

"I guess you all want to know what happened today."

Harriet put a hand on his arm.

"Only if you want to talk about it. If you don't, we're okay with that."

Lauren glared at her but didn't say anything.

"I'm sure you all heard I found Marine dead in the apartment over the clinic."

"We did," Harriet affirmed. "What I don't understand is why they had to take you to the police station to make a statement. I mean, if you were with patients and then went in for lunch and found her, what else is there to say?"

Aiden looked down at his hands. His pale blue eyes looked white in the soft light of the dining room.

"It isn't quite that simple. I wasn't in the clinic before I found her. I wish I had been. I worked evening hours last night, so I didn't have to take appointments this morning. I went out for a run, and while I was out I got a call from someone at the homeless camp. I'd posted my cell phone number there, offering emergency animal care.

"I came back, got my car, drove over to Fogg Park and started looking for the caller. No one in the camp knew anything, so I drove around to the back side of the park. I've seen a few people camping in those woods before.

"I found a big area of blood on the side of the road. It looked like a fairly large animal had been hit by a car, but other than the blood and a little hair, I couldn't find anything. I saw a trail and followed it into the woods, but still no dog. I worked my way over to the strait and got a bite to eat.

"I needed to get to work so I drove back to the homeless camp to see if anyone had appeared while I was gone. They hadn't. I told the people there to let me know if the dog or his owner showed up and went back to the apartment to change clothes for work...and you know the rest."

Lauren toyed with her teaspoon.

"So, you were wandering the wilderness while Marine broke into your apartment and killed herself with an overdose."

Aiden gave her an icy stare and turned to Harriet.

"That's why they had me at the police station for hours. I have no alibi. I have no idea how she got into my apartment. I had the key with me, but they told me there's no sign of forced entry."

"That may or may not be true," Harriet said. "They aren't obligated to tell you the truth when they're questioning you."

"They asked me all sorts of questions about Marine and our relationship. I tried to tell them I hadn't seen her in years before she showed up for this quilt deal. I could tell they didn't believe me. They pointed out that she didn't seem like a very likely quilter. I couldn't argue with that."

Harriet took her hand off his arm.

"Did you tell them that your mom had taken her in while you were in Uganda?"

"I told them I had *heard* my mom had taken her in for a few weeks during that time. I have no direct knowledge about that, though, since I wasn't here. They twisted that around. They made out that she had a closer relationship with me than I was letting on if she stayed with my own mother." He propped his elbows on the table and lowered his head into his hands. "This is a nightmare."

"*Diós mio,*" Connie said. "They can't accuse you of wrongdoing because you dated in high school. And that apartment isn't really yours. You were there temporarily. The other vets must have keys. Maybe one of *them* had a relationship with Marine."

Aiden raised his head and smiled weakly.

"Thanks for that. None of the other vets grew up around here, so it isn't likely. I guess anything's possible, though."

Harriet sat back in her chair and thought for a moment.

"If Marine died from an overdose, why does it matter where you were when it happened?"

"I suppose they think I supplied her with the drugs. They don't know yet what she OD'd on. If it turns out to be something we don't stock, it will help, but that's not proof I didn't give her whatever it was."

Mavis reached across Harriet and patted his hand.

"Oh, honey, is there anything we can do for you?"

Aiden attempted a laugh.

"Yeah. Find out how Marine got into my apartment and what she died from. Oh, and if you can, find the person who called and asked me to come take care of their dog."

Mavis pulled her hand back.

"I'm sure this will all be cleared up by tomorrow. Speaking of which, I better go home so I can get ready for class. I've got to sort out my ribbons and threads now that I know what my block looks like."

Connie stood up.

"I better go make sure Carla and Wendy get settled in. Aiden, you let Rod and me know if there's anything we can do for you."

"Thanks, I'll do that."

"Come on, mi'jo," Jorge said. "Let's get you to my place." He looked at Beth. "Can you take my truck home? I'll get it from you tomorrow. I'd like to ride with Aiden." He dug keys from his pocket and handed them to her.

Harriet looked at her aunt with eyebrow raised once no one but the three of them was left at the big table. Beth blushed.

"Jorge and I were cooking at his house."

"I didn't say anything," Harriet said with a wicked smile.

Lauren drained the dregs of her tea and set her mug on the table.

"What Harriet is trying to say is 'good for you.' Now, what are we going to do for Aiden?"

"We need to wait and see what the police have to say tomorrow," Beth said.

Harriet shook her head.

"I'm with Lauren. I don't trust the Foggy Point police. If they questioned Aiden for as long as they did, they aren't thinking he's an innocent bystander. We need to go to the homeless camp and talk to Joyce Elias. Nothing goes on at that camp she doesn't know about. If someone had a dog, and it got hurt, she'll be able to tell us."

Lauren smiled. "Now you're talking. When do you want to go?"

Aunt Beth stood and collected her empty mug and the half-empty plate of churros.

"We have enough time during lunch to drive over there. We could call in an order of sandwiches from the Sandwich Board during our morning break and pick them up on the way to the park."

Harriet picked up several empty mugs.

"Works for me." She turned and headed for the kitchen.

"I'm going up to collect my roommate," Lauren told them and headed for the staircase.

"Your roommate is here," Jessica said from the kitchen. "And count me in on the lunch adventure." She looked from Lauren to Harriet. "I was already in the kitchen, and I heard you make the plan. I might be able to help—you never know. Homeless, drunks, addicts…those are my peeps."

"I really appreciate your help," Harriet said. She did appreciate all her friends' help, but right now all she wanted to do was crawl into her bed and pull the covers over her head. "I'll see you all tomorrow at class."

Chapter 14

arriet took the white shopping bag from the counter at the Sandwich Board and handed it to Lauren. She took the second bag herself, supporting the bottom with her free hand.

Lauren hefted her bag up and down.

"I guess your aunt thought we were going to be real hungry today."

"She asked if the Sandwich Board would go halfsies with her on lunch for the homeless people. They agreed, so we're delivering lunch to the whole camp."

"That was generous."

"Aunt Beth is like that. Besides, Mavis and Connie probably split the cost with her. I'll ask. Am I hearing you offering to donate?"

Lauren rolled her eyes.

"I will if you will."

Harriet led the way to the door.

"Aunt Beth will be happy we're both giving to her favorite cause. She and Jorge have been regular volunteers at the camp since the big storm last winter. She keeps trying to talk Joyce into moving indoors. Joyce keeps politely telling her she's happy outside."

The rear passenger door to Harriet's car swung open as they approached it.

"Here, let me take that," Aunt Beth said from the middle row of seats. She leaned out and took the bag of food from Harriet. Lauren opened the opposite side door and climbed in with her sack.

"I hope Joyce can tell us who the dog owner is," Harriet said as she guided her car back onto the road.

Lauren buckled her seat belt.

"I think we're borrowing trouble. Marine obviously overdosed. That had nothing to do with Aiden, so what does it matter where he was yesterday morning?"

"I wish I had your confidence," Harriet told her.

Jessica leaned forward from her perch in the third row of seats.

"I hate to be a pessimist, but I've been thinking about it, and if Marine was such an obvious OD, it doesn't seem like they would have been so interested in whether Aiden had an alibi or not."

Harriet tapped her fingers on the steering wheel.

"I don't know why, but I've got a bad feeling about this."

It took a few minutes to get everyone out after they arrived in the parking lot at Fogg Park.

"The camp is down the trail behind the restrooms," Harriet told Jessica. "I'll go make sure they're home."

She returned a few minutes later followed by a petite white-haired woman wearing tidy blue jeans and a plaid flannel shirt topped by a dark-green fleece jacket who smiled when she saw Mavis and Beth.

"How nice to see you again," she said, clasping Aunt Beth's hand in greeting. She looked at Jessica and extended a hand to her. "I don't believe we've met. I'm Joyce Elias."

There was a hint of the British Isles in her voice. The smile that creased her face was echoed in the lines around her bright blue eyes.

Lauren raised her white paper bag.

"We brought you lunch."

"That's so good of you, dear. Shall I go get the others?"

"We brought enough to feed a small army," Lauren answered.

"You know where our dining room is," Joyce said with a chuckle.

Indeed, they did. Most of the Loose Threads had spent time volunteering in one capacity or the other at the camp, helping clear away dropped branches after storms or spreading fresh bark mulch or gravel on the trails that would otherwise be slick with mud. The Threads also provided flannel rag quilts for the residents so they could stay warm in the winter.

Harriet led the way down the trail, stopping in a large clearing.

"Wow, did Tom Bainbridge make you a new table?"

The previous table had been a piece of plywood balanced on mismatched legs. The new one was large and sturdy, with shelves and two deep drawers with locks. It was painted a green that blended with the colors of the forest and looked to be waterproof, if the beaded liquid on the surface was any indication. Three matching benches were arrayed around the clearing.

"Tom has been a good friend to our camp," Joyce told them. "Thanks to him, we have secure lockable boxes to keep our personal possessions in. He chained them to trees, so no one can haul them off without cutting the trees down. But enough about us. What is it that brings you to the camp today? Don't get me wrong, we appreciate the food, but I can see you aren't dressed for a work day."

Several more camp residents edged into the clearing as Harriet and her aunt looked at each other. Finally Harriet spoke.

"I think you know. Aiden took a call from someone who said he lived at the camp here. The guy said his dog had been hit by a car and was gravely injured. Aiden came to help and couldn't find them."

Joyce looked thoughtful, staring at her feet for a moment.

"I did talk to Aiden. I told him no one has been here lately with a dog."

"Jimmy," one of the other camp residents grunted.

"It's true enough that Jimmy has a dog, but Jimmy's daughter took him away two weeks ago." She turned to Harriet. "His girl takes him for a month once or twice a year; takes him to the doctor and dentist and such. He and his dog stay for a while, and then one day she'll leave him alone and next thing you know, he and his dog are back here. It would be unlikely it was him, but I suppose it's possible."

Harriet was silent while Aunt Beth and Mavis unpacked the lunch bags. Joyce took her foil-wrapped sandwich and set it in her lap.

"What is it you aren't telling me? Kind as you are, I know you didn't come because you're worried about a dog."

"You're right," Harriet said. "Aiden came home from looking for the man and his dog and found a woman who seems to have committed suicide in the living room of the apartment over the vet clinic where he was staying while the quilters are in town."

"And you're thinking it would be good if he had an alibi," Joyce concluded.

Harriet's shoulders sagged.

"Something like that."

Lauren swallowed the bite of sandwich she'd been chewing.

"They took him to the police station to make a statement, but they kept him there for hours. We're thinking that can't be good, and if we could rustle up some proof he wasn't around the apartment, it would help."

"We did see him yesterday when he asked us about the dog, but then he was gone for more than an hour before he came back by."

Joyce let the implications settle before she continued.

"I'll ask the rest when they get back from doing their laundry," she promised and then visibly brightened. "Do you have time to tell me about this quilt event you're all going to?"

Jessica stood up once the Loose Threads had, each in turn, given their rendition of their crazy quilt classes.

"This camp is amazing. When I was still a nun, I worked with a number of homeless people, but none of them lived in such a nice community."

"We've gotten a lot of help from the people of Foggy Point," Joyce said and smiled. "Your friends here have done a lot for us, making quilts and tarps and bringing us nutritious food. Their friend Tom is quite a handyman, as you can see from all our outdoor furniture."

Harriet crumpled her empty sandwich wrapper.

"What you're seeing is the difference between big city and small town homelessness." She smiled at Joyce. "We consider Joyce and the other people here an integral part of our community."

"Joyce does volunteer work at the grade school with the reading program," Connie added.

"I'm able to do that because here I don't have to worry about the security of my belongings, and Robin convinced the city to add a bus stop near us and give us free passes so we don't have to spend so much time walking in the weather."

"That's amazing," Jessica told her.

Mavis checked her watch and looked around; everyone had finished their sandwich.

"We should probably head back," she announced.

Harriet stood up.

"I'll swing back by tomorrow and see if you learned anything."

"I'll look forward to your visit," Joyce said. "We'll go to the other side of the park and talk to the people camping there, too. Since we don't condone drug and alcohol use in our community, those people tend to stay on the other side of the forest from us. Rest assured, we'll find out who called your young man if he's anywhere around here."

"That's all I can ask," Harriet told her. "Thanks."

"And thank you all for the wonderful lunch."

With that, the quilters went back up the trail to Harriet's car for the drive back to their classes.

✂- - -✂- - -✂

Harriet carefully arranged her three class blocks in a flat plastic box then began gathering piles of ribbon and thread and sorting them into small plastic bags. Connie was doing the same at the table to her left.

"I feel like there's hope after today's class," Harriet said.

"Me, too." Connie finished packing her bags and began helping Harriet. "Have you heard from Aiden?"

"He texted me this afternoon and wants to meet for coffee or dinner. I told him I'd have to check our schedule here first. I know there isn't a planned event tonight, but at afternoon break, Aunt Beth was organizing something with some of the out-of-town people."

Connie put her arm around Harriet's shoulders.

"Querida, I think everyone will understand if you need to be with that boy. He must be a wreck. He's such a tender soul. He was all teared up the other day when Rod and I saw him after an animal had died at the clinic. I know that girl gave him a lot of grief in the past, but it must have been just awful for him, finding her like that."

"You're right. Originally, I was planning to quilt with Lainie this afternoon, but Michelle had Marcel pick up her kids and sent the nanny and tutor away so Aiden didn't have to deal with a house full of people. I'll have to check with Cookie to see what they think is happening."

"Don't worry about that. I'll call Marcel, and if they were planning on Lainie being with you, I'll go get her and take her home with me. Carla and I can work with her."

"Won't she be going to whatever event Aunt Beth is cooking up?"

"She's planning on staying home with Wendy tonight."

Harriet felt some of the tension leave her shoulders.

"Thank you so much. I'll feel better when I can talk to Aiden without everyone around and see how he's really doing. Even though he didn't have anything to do with that woman, I know him—I'd guarantee he's blaming himself."

"You go take care of him, and I'll talk to Beth and Mavis and call Marcel and deal with the kids, if need be."

Harriet slung her tote over her shoulder and picked up her purse.

"Thanks again for doing this. I'll talk to you tomorrow."

"It's the least I can do."

Chapter 15

Harriet scooped food from two different cans into her pets' dishes. Her cat Fred wove between her legs meowing while Scooter danced on his back legs, falling forward onto Fred when he overbalanced and earning himself a well-placed swat on the rear from the cat.

"How about the Alder Wood Bistro in Sequim?" she asked Aiden.

"You need to teach your pets some manners," he told her. He was perched on one of the wooden bar stools pulled up to the kitchen island. "Fred's probably a lost cause, but Scooter could learn to sit and wait while you prepare his food."

"Thanks for the assessment of my animal wrangling skills, O great one. Don't forget I've seen *your* dog in action."

His mouth turned up in a brief smile.

"Randy's a special case. She's still learning English."

Aiden's dog was a stray he'd rescued and brought home with him when he'd returned from Uganda the year before.

"So, what do you think? Alder Wood?"

He was silent, his perfect face a mixture of anger and hurt.

"Or we could get takeout and stay home," she offered.

"I'd like to take you to Sequim or Port Angeles or anywhere but here. The only problem is, I've been told not to leave town."

"You can't be serious. They didn't say that, did they?"

The set of his jaw told her he was. He stood and started pacing, his back to her.

"They did say it, and they were dead serious. I answered every question they had. I mean, what else could I say? I came home, and Marine was

82

lying dead on my couch with a needle sticking out of her arm. They didn't believe me."

"Was Detective Morse there?"

"I didn't see her. It was two guys I've never seen before."

"That's weird. Have you got an attorney?"

"I talked to a friend of Julio's on the phone, and the guy's coming here first thing in the morning. And why is Jane not being there weird?"

"Foggy Point isn't that big. I think Jane said there are five other detectives besides her. Two are detective sergeants, one is a detective corporal, and then Jane and the two others. They have to cover robbery, drugs, sex crimes and everything. I figured with her success rate on the recent homicides she'd be assigned."

"Apparently not. Can we not talk about this? I'd like to try to have a normal dinner with my sweetie."

Harriet smiled. She turned and pulled him into her arms as he paced back in her direction.

"Come here." She tilted her face up to his, and he didn't disappoint. He wrapped his arms around her and met her lips with his.

"I wish we could shut the rest of the world out and stay like this, just you and me."

Fred meowed, holding the last unpleasant note.

Aiden laughed.

"Okay, you, me and our pets." He reached down and scratched Fred's ear. Fred head-butted his leg.

Harriet smiled. "See, he has sympathy for you even after you made disparaging remarks about his dinner manners."

"Speaking of dinner, let's go see what we can find within the boundaries of Foggy Point."

✂ - - - ✂ - - - ✂

Harriet wiped her mouth on her napkin.

"So, how did you find this place?"

"When I couldn't find the dog or the person who called about it, I did a grid search, spiraling out until I reached water. I didn't find them, so I decided to drive home along the strait. And..." He spread his arms. "Here we are. With a name like Hot Diggity Dog, how could I not stop and try the fare."

"I'm surprised I've never heard of it."

"I was here on their first day open. They gave me a free milkshake with my dog."

"Mine was delicious. I didn't know sauerkraut could be fermented instead of pickled."

Aiden smiled at her.

"It's the little things in life." He reached across the table and took her hands in his. "Thank you for coming to dinner with me tonight. I know you're in the middle of your quilt thing."

She squeezed his hands. "You're doing me a favor. The quilters are pleasant, and my roommate has turned out better than I feared, but still, it's good to have a break. Besides, there's no place I'd rather be than having dinner with you."

He slid out of his seat and pulled her to her feet.

"Come on, let's go across the street. There's a path along the water."

There weren't many cars out at this time of night to disrupt their peace. The sound of water washing over the rocky beach helped Harriet relax for the first time in more than a week. Aiden had his arm around her shoulders and walked along lost in his own thoughts.

Down the beach, they came to a large flat rock, and Aiden led Harriet to it, easing her onto his lap when he was seated.

"It's easy to forget everything that's happened when we're out here."

She turned her face to his. "I was thinking that very thought a minute ago. Do we have to go back?"

Aiden smiled briefly. "Not right away, but eventually, yeah, we do."

"We can't run away?"

He laughed. "I love that you would even consider it, especially given our last year, but we both know it wouldn't fix anything."

"Does Marine have any friends or family in the area anymore?"

"I don't know. Her mother was in town when she lived with my mom a few years ago, but who knows now. She was always chasing after some man." He sighed. "Marine never really had a chance. She had big dreams, but her family was awful. Her mom had a bunch of kids she didn't want. Their only value was to earn her child support or welfare payments. I think her mom dabbled in prostitution and tried to get Marine to join her."

"Did she?"

"There were rumors, but I didn't ask her and she didn't volunteer the information. At that point in time, I was avoiding her. She'd spread her stories about me being her baby daddy, and I was pretty mad at her. And before you ask, no, I was never mad enough back then to wish her harm. Even when I was angry about what she was doing to me, I still felt more sorry for her than anything."

Flashing blue lights on the road above the beach caught Harriet's eye.

"I wonder what's going on up there?" she said, and pointed.

"They were probably called as backup for something happening at the docks. This road would be faster than going through the neighborhoods." He turned his attention back to her. "Now, where were we?" he asked and kissed her, wrapping his arms around her in the process.

"Are you sure we can't run away?" she asked when they came up for air.

"Dr. Jalbert isn't going anywhere," said a deep voice from behind them.

Harriet started, dropping her purse. She looked over Aiden's shoulder as he clutched her tighter. A bright light was shining in her face. She could see several dark forms beyond the light but couldn't tell who or what they were.

"Ma'am, I need you to slowly move away from Dr. Jalbert. And both of you keep your hands where we can see them."

She did as she was told, and as she moved out of the glare, she could see the man was a uniformed police officer, and he was holding a large gun pointed in her direction.

"There must be some mistake," she protested, unable to stop herself from spouting the cliché that most people in this situation said.

"No mistake, ma'am. You aren't in any trouble. Move over to Officer Nguyen." He pointed with his free hand.

Why is it always Officer Nguyen? she wondered. There must be two dozen officers on the Foggy Point Police department, but any time she crossed paths with the police it was Officer Nguyen.

She looked at Aiden.

"Do what he says," he told her as he held his hands away from his sides and in the air where everyone could see them.

When Harriet reached Nguyen, the guy with the gun rushed up to Aiden and grabbed his right wrist, snapping a handcuff onto it in one smooth motion, quickly pulling his left hand down and back and cuffing it, too.

"What's going on?" Harriet asked Nguyen.

He didn't answer.

"You have the right to remain silent," the cop holding Aiden recited. "Anything you say can and will be used against you in a court of law. You have the right to an attorney. If you cannot afford an attorney, one will be provided for you. Do you understand the rights I have just read to you? With these rights in mind, do you wish to speak to me?"

Aiden looked at the man.

"What are you arresting me for?"

"You are under arrest for the murder of Marine Moreau." The cop's shoulders sagged a little. "Before we go, I'd just like to say I really appreciate how you saved Peppi last winter when she was hit by a car. I'm sure this is some sort of mix-up, but when we get an order to arrest someone, we have to do it and do it by the book. I'm really sorry about this."

"Jerry. It is Jerry, right?"

The cop nodded.

"I was doing my job when I saved your dog, and I understand you're doing yours now. You're right, this is some sort of mistake, and when I call my lawyer, I'm sure he'll get it straightened out. Can you give Harriet my keys so she can drive herself home? They're in my right front pocket."

Harriet could feel tears filling her eyes as she watched Jerry dig in Aiden's pocket and toss the keys to Officer Nguyen. She reached for them, but Nguyen held them out of her reach.

"We should be arresting you and squeezing you until you tell us what you know about this. If the past is any indication, your presence here means you know something you haven't shared with the police.

"You've turned up at every major crime we've had in the last year, and in every case, you've ended up knowing something that solves the crime and makes us cops look incompetent in the process. Not this time. I'm letting my commander know you were here when we arrested the good doctor. You can expect to be hearing from him."

"I came here with Aiden for dinner. I don't—"

"Save it," he interrupted. "And by the way—don't leave town."

He turned and walked away, following the cluster of policemen who had been providing backup.

Harriet stood for a minute, digging through her purse for a tissue to wipe her eyes with before she returned to the restaurant parking lot. Her fingers found her smartphone.

Meet me at my house, she texted to Lauren. *Aiden's been arrested. Gather the Threads.*

She pressed send and headed for Aiden's car.

Chapter 16

*M*ost of the Loose Threads were assembled in Harriet's dining room when she finally got back to her house. Connie met her at the studio door and pulled her into a hug. Harriet inhaled the flowery scent of her friend's familiar perfume.

"*Pobrecita*," Connie soothed. "Come on, take your coat off and get something to drink. Then you can tell us what's going on."

Aunt Beth put her arm around Harriet and guided her into the kitchen, where Mavis handed her a cup of tea.

"DeAnn couldn't come; but she said she'll be thinking of you, and if you can think of anything she can do, let her know." She lowered her voice. "Lauren brought her roommate, and yours is in there, too." Beth nodded toward the dining room.

"Thanks for coming and getting everyone settled."

"I wouldn't be anywhere else," Beth told her. "Now, let's go in and sit down, and you can tell us all what happened."

Harriet took a seat between Lauren and Beth. She picked up her tea and sipped, then sat back in her chair. The women around the table were all focused on her.

"Aiden and I went to dinner tonight, and afterward, we went for a walk on the beach by the strait. While we were sitting on a rock watching the water, the police appeared, guns drawn, and arrested Aiden for killing Marine."

Lauren gave a low whistle.

"Whoa. They really drew their guns?"

"Hush," Connie scolded.

Robin pulled a legal pad from her bag.

"Did they say anything to explain why they were arresting him?" Harriet stirred her tea.

"No. The arresting officer apologized to Aiden and thanked him for saving his dog. Officer Nguyen was there as backup, and he threatened *me*. He told me not to leave town, and said he was going to tell his commander I might be involved."

Carla looked at Robin.

"Can he do that?"

"Not if Harriet isn't a legitimate suspect. I can't imagine she could be. Of course, it's hard to imagine what evidence they have that caused them to arrest *Aiden*. I guess we'll have to wait and see."

"We didn't talk about it a lot, but he was confused by why they were questioning him so long. He said what Robin just said. He already has a criminal lawyer coming to meet with him in the morning." She raised her mug to her lips and set it down again without taking a sip. "Would someone call Detective Morse and see if she can come over?"

"Oh, honey, don't you think she's a little busy right now?" Mavis asked her.

Lauren pulled her phone out and began tapping in a number.

"On it."

"Aiden told me she's not assigned to his case," Harriet told them. "He said two men were the ones questioning him."

Robin took a pen from her bag and set it on the yellow tablet in front of her.

"I asked when I was at the police station yesterday. Morse has been assigned to the cold case squad."

"Foggy Point PD has a cold case squad?" Lauren asked.

"They didn't until Morse was assigned to start one," Robin explained. "She hasn't been feeling the love from her fellow detectives since she's solved the recent murders in town. Add that to her being female and not from here, and you get a bunch of jealous hometown boys who manipulated the situation to their advantage."

Lauren dropped her phone into her bag.

"She's on her way and is willing to trade info for whatever tasty treat she's sure you have waiting for her."

Mavis looked at Beth.

"What do we have in Harriet's freezer?"

"We better go look." Beth headed for the garage; Mavis followed.

Lauren laughed at the confused look that passed between Jessica and Sharon.

"This used to be Beth's house. Since we meet here so much, she and Mavis and Connie keep a supply of cookies and other treats in the freezer."

By the time Detective Jane Morse arrived, Connie was spreading cream cheese frosting on a pan of freshly thawed and warmed double chocolate brownies. Morse shrugged out of her coat and let it fall over the back of a chair.

"Before you ask me anything, let me make something clear. No matter how I feel about the other detectives in my department right now, I cannot and will not tell you anything that will compromise their investigation."

Lauren started to speak, but Morse held her hand up to stop her.

"Let me finish. Anything that is in a public record or anything that I've observed that isn't part of their investigation is fair game. I can also tell you how things will likely play out."

Beth set a cup of tea at Morse's place while Connie carried in the pan of brownies and Mavis brought a stack of saucers and fistful of napkins. Detective Morse waited until everyone had a brownie in front of them and she'd taken a bite from her own.

"I'm guessing the first thing you want to know is why Aiden was arrested." She looked around the table as people nodded. "The medical examiner is classifying the cause of death as undetermined at the moment. He just got here from Seattle this morning.

"You all probably know this, but for those who don't, our county has a coroner who is also the prosecuting attorney. She called her buddy the medical examiner from King County—he steps in when we have a situation that requires an autopsy. He's taught our coroner to do a few basic tests. Based on those tests, she concluded Marine's death was suspicious enough to call for an official autopsy."

"Can you say what those tests were?" Harriet asked.

"I can't tell you the specifics, but I do know that, when she's attended deaths where I've been the primary, she tested algor mortis and checked for rigor mortis and livor mortis. Basically, body temperature, stiffness and blood pooling. These all are helpful in determining time of death and also whether the person died where they are found. I think we can assume one or more of those were not consistent with an overdose death in the time frame we're talking about."

She took another bite of her brownie while the group digested what she'd just told them. She followed it with a sip of tea.

"I also happened to see Darcy Lewis logging in evidence she'd collected at the scene. She had a packet of black hairs and what looked like a saliva sample. I can't ask her, and she didn't say anything, but she made sure I was able to see what she was checking in. And I heard one of the other crime scene techs say that the detectives asked them to lift fingerprints from every possible surface in that apartment."

Harriet twisted her napkin into a rope and threaded it through her fingers. Her knuckles turned white, and Aunt Beth reached over and put one hand over hers.

"They can't have DNA results from the saliva this quick, can they?"

"No. It's theoretically possible to get it in twenty-four hours, but not in Foggy Point," Morse agreed. "They probably did a new test they have that can tell them the blood type of the sample if it's from a secretor. And eighty percent of us are secretors. That means our blood antigens are in all our body fluids.

"If their saliva sample was from a secretor, and the blood type matched Aiden, that may be one of the pieces of evidence they used to get their arrest warrant. Also, where and how much saliva they found would factor into the situation, and that I can't tell you."

Lauren sat back in her chair.

"So, if they found his hair and saliva on Marine's body, it suggests he didn't just see her sprawled in his living room and call the paramedics."

"Of course he would have gone to see if she was alive and needed CPR," Connie told Lauren and glared at her. "He would, wouldn't he?"

"I didn't say he did anything wrong," Lauren shot back. "I'm just saying, if he didn't tell them he did that, it could make them suspicious."

Mavis passed the pan of brownies around the table again.

"Let's not borrow trouble," she said. "We can imagine all we want, but until we know something for sure, we'll just make ourselves crazy."

Harriet sighed and asked Detective Morse, "Can you tell us anything else?"

Morse drank tea and set her mug down.

"I don't know anything else, but I can tell you he's unlikely to be allowed bail."

"But he has ties to our community," Connie protested.

"And he lived and worked in Africa until last year," Morse pointed out. "He has contacts in Uganda and who knows where else who might be willing to help him hide. He also has the financial resources to plan and execute an escape plan."

Harriet swirled the tea remaining in her cup, studying the liquid before downing it.

"If he's stuck inside, what can we do for him?"

Morse sighed thoughtfully.

"First of all, you need to see what his attorney is doing. If the attorney hires a private investigator, you need to let that person do their job. If Aiden's defense team doesn't object to your help, let them know if you do discover anything useful, and keep them informed of what you're doing. If they don't want your help, stay out of their way. I know you all get tired of hearing this, but you need to let the professionals do their jobs.

"Now, having said all that, I understand Aiden said he was trying to find a homeless person with an injured dog during the time period in question. Finding them would go a long way toward establishing his alibi."

Jessica brought the teakettle of hot water from the kitchen and went around the table, refilling teacups.

"We went to the homeless camp for lunch, but they don't know anyone who has a dog," she told Morse.

"Not all of our homeless people live in the main camp, as I'm sure Joyce told you. If you want to help, canvass the neighborhoods near the park. See if anyone saw a man with a dog. You can also ask if they noticed Aiden's car in the area," Detective Morse suggested.

"Does anyone know who delivers mail in that area?" Aunt Beth asked.

Mavis pressed her lips together thoughtfully.

"I think Jim Park does. When my mail carrier takes a day off, Jim delivers my neighborhood. I think he said his normal area is toward the park. We were on the auction committee together. I can call him in the morning."

Morse picked up her plate and mug and stood up.

"I better get going. Let me know if you learn anything, and if I hear anything I can share, I'll let you know."

Aunt Beth stood up and reached for the detective's dishes.

"Here, I'll take those. Thank you for coming and talking to us. We appreciate your support, and we do understand you're in a delicate position."

Morse put her coat on.

"The internal politics of the Foggy Point Police Department are what they are, and they will be difficult no matter what you ladies do or don't do."

Beth and Mavis walked her to the studio door.

"Okay," Harriet said when she heard Morse's car leaving, "we need to find out if Marine's mother or other family still live in Foggy Point. Maybe they would know who her drug contact is."

Aunt Beth came back and sat down at the table again.

"I hope you're not suggesting we talk to a drug dealer."

Harriet twirled a shred of her napkin.

"If she died of an overdose, don't you think her dealer is the most likely to have provided the drugs?"

"Only if she died from street drugs," Lauren answered. "I think we have to consider the possibility that the reason the cops arrested Aiden is because she died from an overdose of some sort of animal medicine. And before you get wound up, I don't think Aiden killed Marine. I'm just thinking—if someone was trying to set Aiden up, they could have used something a vet would have."

Robin wrote on her legal pad.

"So, you don't think Marine broke into Aiden's."

"Do we need our flip chart?" Aunt Beth asked. "Never mind, we do need it. Is it still in the studio?"

Harriet nodded, and her aunt retrieved the flip chart and a handful of markers.

"What I'm hearing you say," Beth said when she had the chart set up on one end of the table, a clean page facing the group, "is there are two possibilities to consider." She drew a vertical line down the middle of the page. "First, Marine broke in and invited her drug dealer or other unknown person to meet her there." She wrote "Marine invited someone" over one column. "Second, someone else broke in and lured Marine there for the purpose of killing her." She wrote "Someone lured Marine" over the other column.

"I don't think we can assume they planned on killing her in the second scenario," Harriet said. "Maybe they wanted to blackmail Aiden and were going to 'discover' him there with her passed out on the sofa, but they overdid the drugs and killed her instead. From what I've heard about her family, it wouldn't be impossible to think they might do something like that."

Beth added a note in the second column.

Harriet put a hand over her mouth and stared at the chart.

"A lot of the medicines Aiden uses on dogs are the exact same as people use, just different doses."

"What's your point?" Lauren asked.

"My point is, they must have some other evidence against Aiden. We need to figure out what else they have."

"Didn't Morse say hair and saliva?" Robin pointed out.

Beth set her marking pen on the table and sat down.

"I would think finding Aiden's hair on someone found on his sofa in his apartment wouldn't be very strong as evidence goes."

Mavis picked up her teaspoon and twirled it between her fingers.

"If he did do mouth-to-mouth, that would explain the saliva. They have to know that. There must have something else."

Lauren sat up straight.

"Let's cut to the chase. What are our assignments?"

Robin put the cap back on her pen and tucked it into her bag.

"We need to be careful. We don't want to make things any worse for Aiden, and it sounds like Officer Nguyen has already warned Harriet to keep away from the investigation."

Aunt Beth flipped to a new page of the chart and wrote "assignments" across the top.

"Since Marine was attending our quilt retreat when she died, I don't think it would be out of order for the Loose Threads to reach out to her family."

"Maybe we could take up a collection for her funeral expenses," Carla suggested, speaking for the first time since the meeting started. "If her mom is like my mom, all you have to do is offer money, and you'll have her attention."

Beth wrote "collect money for funeral expenses" on the flip chart.

"Mavis and I can do that one," she said as she wrote.

"I can go canvass the neighborhood for Aiden sightings," Jessica volunteered. "I don't mind going during our lunch break. I've got a protein bar I can eat for lunch."

"If you want company, I'll join you," Connie told her.

"I'll research Marine's family on the Internet and see what I can find out," Lauren said.

Beth wrote everyone's tasks on the chart page.

Harriet pulled the pan of brownies toward her and cut one in half before removing it from the pan and taking a bite.

"I'm going to see if I can get in to visit Aiden, assuming he doesn't get out on bail. I'd like to ask him directly if he did CPR on Marine, and if not, how he thinks his saliva ended up on her body."

"I've got to go make sure my kids are getting to bed," Robin told them. "I'll call DeAnn in the morning and see if she can help find Marine's family." She looked at Lauren's roommate. "DeAnn's family owns a video store in town. A lot of people are still old school in Foggy Point," she explained. "She can check their customer database and see if any of them rent movies."

"If anyone comes up with anything, let Harriet know," Mavis said.

Connie picked up two empty mugs.

"You go on ahead home," she told Carla. "If I know Grandpa Rod, he'll still be reading 'one more story' to Wendy when you get there. Tell him I'm going to help Harriet clean up."

She and Aunt Beth went into the kitchen while the rest of the Threads gathered purses and coats and headed for the door.

Chapter 17

Mavis wiped the kitchen counter with a hand-knit dishcloth. "Did you make this?" she asked Harriet and held the cotton square up.

"I did. I added strips of netting to the cotton yarn in the middle of it to give it scrubbing power." She knew Mavis was well aware of the details of her knitting projects, but she appreciated the attempt to talk about anything else but Aiden.

Beth pushed the start button on the dishwasher and wiped her hands on a dishtowel.

"If you need anything or hear anything, you call. I don't care what time of day or night it is."

Harriet attempted a smile.

"Thanks, I will. I wonder—" She was interrupted by loud knocking on her studio door.

Connie looked at her.

"You want me to answer it?"

Harriet nodded, and Connie left, returning a moment later with Michelle Jalbert in tow.

"I need to talk to Harriet," Michelle was saying as she followed Connie through the door.

"My day is complete," Harriet said and slumped into one of her kitchen chairs. "What do you want, Michelle?"

"I'm going to ignore that, since I know you're upset about my brother. Actually, that's why I'm here. Two detectives just left Aiden's house. They wanted me to give them permission to search the place. I told them it wasn't my house, so I was unable to help them. They assured me they'd return in the morning with a warrant. I may be inactive right now due to my recent troubles, but I'm still an officer of the court, which limits what I'm able to do."

She sat down opposite Harriet. Beth remained standing.

"What are you suggesting?" she asked.

"I'm going to take my laptop to the coffee shop where I know the cops take their breaks and be very visible. I left the kitchen door unlocked when I left. Since they have Aiden locked up, no one has a reason to stake out his house. I can't say any more." She stood up and looked at her watch. "I expect to be gone two or three hours."

"Okay," Harriet said.

Michelle turned and went back through the kitchen door. A moment later, they heard the outside door open and shut.

Aunt Beth looked at Mavis and Connie and then turned to Harriet.

"We'll go with you."

Harriet stood up.

"Are you sure you want to do that? What if we find incriminating evidence? Would you remove it? Would you stop me if I wanted to remove it?"

Beth put her hand on Harriet's arm. "I've known that boy since he was he was in knee pants," she said. "There is no way he killed Marine or gave her drugs or anything else. There will be no evidence."

"You're right. We should go look, just to be sure there isn't anything innocent that could be twisted into something else." Harriet grabbed her purse and jacket from the closet. "I'll drive."

Aiden's long driveway was dark and quiet as Harriet guided her car up the hill and around to the back of the large Victorian home that had belonged to his parents. True to her word, Michelle had left the door unlocked.

Harriet headed for the servants' stairs that led from the kitchen to the second and third floors.

"Aiden's bedroom and sitting room are on the second floor. I think we should start there."

"Don't touch anything," Aunt Beth instructed the other three when they'd entered the first room. She held out a handful of one-size-fits-all plastic food handling gloves.

"These are from when I was helping Jorge package his homemade tortillas. I only have one for each of us. If you have to touch anything, do it with your glove hand."

Connie took her glove and put it on.

"Good thinking."

What had once been an upstairs parlor in the Victorian house had been modernized with a flat-screen TV, a gas fireplace inset, and black leather furniture. African masks and weavings adorned the walls.

Harriet sat on the sofa and picked a book up off the coffee table.

"This is the yearbook Michelle was looking at the other day. It has a picture of Marine and Aiden at the prom. Do you suppose this is what she wanted us to take away?"

"All the detectives have to do is go to the high school, and they can get a copy of the yearbook." Connie told her.

"We need to keep looking, then. Michelle must have seen something she thinks we need to remove." Harriet got up and went into the bedroom.

Dark wood bookshelves filled one long wall. She recognized the family albums from when his parents lived in France. He'd helped Lainie and Etienne with a family history project a few weeks before and had showed them the books.

A carved cherry bed was centered on the short wall, with matching nightstands on either side. A lamp and a clock were on the near stand; this was clearly the side of the bed Aiden slept on. A stack of leather-bound journals sat in front of the clock. Harriet picked up the top book from the stack with her gloved hand and flipped it open. She recognized the handwriting. It was less mature but definitely Aiden's.

She took the first two books and sat down on the edge of the bed to read. He had chronicled his troubles with Marine. When she'd skimmed the first two, she reached for the rest of the stack and paged through them, slowing down when she reached the section where he talked about Marine's scheme to convince the whole town he was her baby-daddy.

Aunt Beth came into the bedroom.

"We've been through everything, but other than the yearbook, there isn't anything here. Have you found something?"

Harriet looked up from the journal.

"Oh, yeah." She ran her gloved finger down the page in front of her, stopping when she found the place. "'She's ruining my life,'" she read. "'I wish she was dead'." She shut the book. "I think we've found what Michelle was talking about." She looked at the wall of books.

"What are you looking for?" her aunt asked when Harriet stood up to get a closer look.

"Aiden numbered his journals. The ones by the bed are from the middle of a series. I'm just wondering where the rest of them are. I don't see any similar volumes in here."

"Maybe he brought them down from the attic," Mavis said from the doorway. "His mother always kept her old pictures up there. Maybe his journals were up there, too."

Connie joined them.

"I'm not comfortable removing anything the police might be looking for from the house, but I don't have a problem with returning these journals to the box they came from in the attic, if we find that box."

Harriet went back toward the hallway.

"Let's go find that box."

It took a half-hour and several sneezing fits before they found two boxes marked "Aiden's Journals."

"Hallelujah," Harriet exclaimed. She folded the flaps back on the first box and could see the space the journals in Aiden's bedroom had occupied. "I'm a little surprised he put these back under so many others."

Connie looked up from a box she was returning to the industrial storage shelves that had been erected in one of the gable niches.

"Maybe he got them out when he heard who was coming to stay with Michelle. He could have planned on destroying them, but he hasn't been home to do it."

"I suppose," Harriet mused. "If we all agree, I'm going to go down and get them. I think we should put them back in with the other journals and then bury them deep."

"Would it be too obvious if we moved them over to this section where all the old clothes are?" Mavis asked.

Harriet paused at the top of the stairs.

"It can't hurt. Just remember to keep your hands covered when you move the boxes."

✂- - -✂- - -✂

Beth pulled her sleeve back and looked at her watch.

"We better wrap it up here. We've been here almost an hour and a half. How long did Michelle say she'd be gone?"

"She said two or three hours," Connie answered.

"I'd like to check out the room Marine was staying in," Harriet told them.

"Do you know which one it is?" Connie asked.

"I know Michelle and the kids stay at the other end of this floor," Harriet said. "Let's see if her room is down there."

They made their way down the hallway, across the landing that looked down on the entry hall, and into the opposite wing.

"Let's each try a door," Harriet suggested.

Mavis opened the third door down on the left.

"Jackpot. There's no mistaking this ratty fur-collared coat." She entered the room, followed by Harriet.

Harriet turned slowly in a circle then stepped over to a fake leather hobo bag sitting on a wooden chair by the door. She reached into the bag and stirred the clothing around, verifying there was nothing else inside.

"This is really sad. She was supposed to be staying for a week or more, and there are only two changes of clothes here—no undies and no night clothes." She went to the closet and opened the door. "Nothing in here, either."

Mavis crossed the room to the desk.

"She actually did a little work on her quilt block." She held the piece up and showed it to Harriet.

"Are you ladies finding anything?" Beth asked from the doorway.

"Not really," Harriet said. "I want to check one more thing, though."

She went to the bed and shoved her gloved hand and forearm between the mattress and box spring, sweeping it along the length of the bed, stopping when her hand encountered something. She slowly pulled her arm back out, clutching a worn black leather zip case in her hand.

"What have we there?" Aunt Beth asked.

Harriet unzipped the case and separated the two halves.

"This is interesting. I'm not well versed on my illegal drugs, but there are two syringes, a small spoon and two cellophane packages with crumbly whitish stuff inside."

Mavis stepped over to take a closer look.

"Looks like heroin to me."

Beth laughed. "Based on your vast knowledge of illicit drugs?"

"Hey, I watch the crime channel. They always pull these little bags from the suspect's pocket."

Harriet zipped the case back up and returned it to its hiding place.

"Does anyone else find it weird that Marine seemed desperate for drugs when she came to class and ended up at Aiden's with what we guess is animal medicine in her arm, but she had a supply of some drug she could have been using the whole time?"

"That *is* a little strange," Beth said.

"Maybe Michelle didn't leave her alone long enough for her to use her own supply," Connie suggested.

"I'm guessing addicts are pretty adept at getting away to use their drugs," Harriet said.

Aunt Beth glanced at her watch again.

"We better get going."

✂- - - ✂- - - ✂

Harriet guided her car into the parking lot of the Steaming Cup coffee shop. She had called Lauren from Aiden's driveway to give her the update, and Lauren confessed she and Jessica were having a hot cocoa nightcap and invited Harriet and her coconspirators to join them.

"That makes no sense," Jessica said when Harriet and the other Threads had their hot drinks and were seated in upholstered chairs and a sofa in front of the coffee shop's gas fireplace. "Marine was definitely hurting when we saw her at the church. She needed her drugs. Why would she leave home without them?"

Harriet stirred the whipped cream into her hot chocolate.

"Could she have been so impaired she didn't remember she'd stashed drugs under her mattress?"

"Anything's possible," Jessica told her. "I've been around addicts, but I'm certainly no expert. My training was aimed more at their soul than their body."

Lauren slid her tablet from her bag and woke it up.

"I think we need to change our focus. We're concentrating too much on Aiden."

Harriet felt her cheeks flush.

"He *is* the one sitting in jail."

"Calm down, I get it. I'm just saying, since we already know he didn't do it, maybe we should be concentrating more on who else wanted Marine dead. As near as I can tell, her mom is still somewhere in the area. From all her address changes, I'm pretty sure she does a lot of couch surfing. Or maybe she's just had a lot of live-in boyfriends with the men having the living quarters. Michelle mentioned a new husband, but all the marriage records I've found have a matching divorce or annulment."

"Does Marine have any other family?" Jessica asked.

"Funny you should ask." Lauren tapped the screen. "She has no full siblings, but she has at least four halves."

"Have you found where they live?" Connie asked.

"Her elder brother is currently incarcerated on federal drug charges. Her next brother has an arrest record but is not jailed at this time. I don't know where he is, but his arrests were all in this area, so chances are he's around. The third is a half-sister. She is currently a student on scholarship at University of Washington." Lauren chuckled. "You guys are going to love this. Marine's youngest sibling is *really* a young sibling." She looked briefly at the ceiling, her lips moving silently. "She is currently eight years old."

"Do they share the same father?" Aunt Beth asked.

"No. Marine doesn't have a father listed on her birth certificate. Her mom was fifteen when she had Marine, so she was probably thirty-six when she had this last one."

"So, we can eliminate the one in jail," Harriet said.

"Unless he has friends on the outside," Mavis said.

"Okay," Harriet continued, "the older of the two brothers would have to have help from someone on the outside. And we can eliminate the eight-year-old. The sister in college is probably less likely, so that leaves us Mom and the second half-sib."

Lauren drained the last chocolate from her mug.

"I have some other resources I can tap tomorrow. Unless they're in witness protection, I should be able to locate both of them."

"Do we know if Marine had a boyfriend or even a john?" Aunt Beth asked.

"Good point," Harriet said. She looked at Lauren. "Did you check to see if Marine has a record?"

"No, but I can do that." She tapped in a note.

Jessica swirled the chocolate sludge in the bottom of her cup.

"I should have thought of that. Female addicts often turn to prostitution to pay for their drugs."

Aunt Beth crumpled her napkin and picked up her mug.

"We probably aren't going to be able to come up with answers tonight, and we have class early in the morning."

"Beth's right," Connie agreed and stood up, followed by the rest of the group.

"We'll see you at the church in the morning," Harriet said to Lauren and Jessica. "Thanks for all the information."

"No problem," Lauren said, and they went to their respective cars and headed for home.

Chapter 18

Blue skies greeted the quilters as they made their way up to the church entrance from the lower parking lot. Sharon had refused Harriet's offer to drop her by the door, since it wasn't raining. Lauren and Jessica were approaching from the left as Mavis climbed out of Aunt Beth's silver Beetle, parked in the row ahead of them.

Harriet had to look twice before she could be sure the woman with Lauren was, in fact, her roommate.

"Jessica? Is that you?"

She wore a dark-blue A-line skirt that stopped several inches south of her knees. A white blouse with a Peter Pan collar was topped by a cardigan sweater in the same shade of blue as her skirt. Her hair was now a mousy brown.

Jessica twirled around.

"You like? This is my 'I'm going to church' outfit—or really, going to the church charity office outfit. Of course, we all know God doesn't care what we wear, but I've found that most people are more willing to open their purse strings for a good cause if the ex-nun asking for donations looks more *nun* than *ex*. It seemed appropriate for knocking on doors in Foggy Point."

"What happened to your hair?" Aunt Beth asked when they had joined her and Mavis.

Jessica twirled a lock of her now longer hair.

"It's a wig."

Mavis circled her.

102

"It really looks natural."

"It's the color mine used to be. The trick with wigs is to stick to hair colors that match your skin tone. That, and be willing to spend a little money. Not millions, but you can't buy it from a discount store."

"Good to know," Lauren said as she turned and led the way to the church.

The Loose Threads gathered around the breakfast buffet in the basement reception room a few minutes later. Chocolate croissants were stacked next to cinnamon rolls and blueberry mini-muffins. Slices of coffee cake were arranged next to a bowl of cut melon and berries. A large pitcher of orange juice sat next to carafes of coffee and tea.

Lauren bit into a croissant, and warm chocolate oozed out onto her fingers. She groaned as she licked the escaped filling.

"Boy, they're upping the ante foodwise."

Glynnis Miller joined them.

"We thought we should provide a little extra comfort food, given the announcement we're going to be making."

Aunt Beth showed her a flowered metal can with a hinged lid.

"We're going to take up a collection for her family to pay for funeral expenses."

"Oh, good. The Small Stitches were talking about doing something similar. I'll include that in the announcement each teacher will read to their morning class. Can we put the can in the program office? We have someone in there all the time in case students have problems with anything."

"Sounds good," Mavis said.

Sharon poured herself a cup of coffee and stirred a package of artificial sweetener into it.

"I'm going to go to my classroom so I can work a little more on my practice embroidery piece."

"See you in a few minutes," Harriet said.

Mavis and Aunt Beth went with Glynnis to the office, and Robin went with Carla to the restroom, leaving Lauren and Harriet standing by the food with Jessica.

"It's a good thing we've only got two days left," Harriet said. "I'm going to have to go on a celery-and-water diet to make up for all the calories we've been consuming."

Lauren picked up a mini-muffin.

"You and me both."

"Speaking of the event ending," Jessica said, "this may not be the best time to mention it, but I may not get another opportunity to see you without your roommate."

"That sounds ominous," Harriet said.

"It may be nothing. In case it *is* something, you should know."

Harriet looked at Lauren, who shrugged. So, she didn't know whatever it was, either.

"When you were all having your meeting, I went upstairs for a while to check on Sharon. I didn't find her in the TV room because, as it turned out, she was in the bathroom. I didn't know that at first, so I started opening doors, and the first one I tried was obviously her bedroom. I know I shouldn't have snooped, but I admit I'm nosey."

Harriet realized she was hunching her shoulders up around her ears and forced herself to relax.

"What did you find?"

"There was this photo album lying on her open suitcase. Of course I had to look. I thought maybe it was pictures of her past glory as a model."

"Spit it out, girl," Lauren prompted.

"It was pictures of her with Harriet's husband."

Harriet relaxed. "That's because Sharon and her husband Rick and a couple of other friends grew up with Steve in Oakland. They went to the same schools and remained friends till Steve died."

"Uh, okay. I'm sure they were all friends, but these looked like they were friends with benefits." Jessica reached over and put her hand on Harriet's arm. "I'm not trying to be mean, but did you know that Sharon and your husband had been that close in the past?"

Harriet shook her head.

"I think it's a little strange this woman brings a book with dozens of pictures of her younger self in compromising positions with your husband. Clearly, it was before your marriage. I'm not saying there was an affair or anything. I'm just wondering why she has a book like that in your house all these years later."

"That is pretty weird," Lauren said.

Harriet shook her head slowly.

"I don't know what to say. I have no idea what to think."

"I thought you should know," Jessica said. "I mean, think about it. Someone framed your boyfriend. Maybe someone who thinks you took their boyfriend could be a candidate."

"Steve wasn't seeing anyone when we started dating. He made a point of telling me that. I'm going to have think about whether that's even possible." Harriet ran her hand through her hair. "It's all crazy."

"I'm not trying to trash your husband, but you know how people are in relationships. It might have been over for him, but not for her. As long as he wasn't with someone, she might have had illusions they weren't really broken up. That ended when you came on the scene."

"That was years ago, though," Harriet protested. "Why wait until now?"

"Who knows? I'm not saying she did anything for sure. I'm just saying it's weird, and you guys can't seem to think of anyone else who'd want to set your boyfriend up."

"She's got a point," Lauren said. "We can at least tell the Threads about it next time we meet."

"I still want to see where Marine's mom and half-brother were during the critical time period. I think they're a better bet than my roommate," Harriet said.

"Just watch yourself around Sharon," Jessica told her. "We better get to class."

"Want me to drive you to the jail during lunch?" Lauren asked Harriet.

Harriet headed for the stairs up to the classrooms.

"Sure. I'll meet you out front as soon as they let us out."

✂- - -✂- - -✂

Harriet and Lauren weren't the only people meeting in the church foyer when the morning session was over. Connie was waiting by the door for Jesssica; Beth and Mavis had set up a table and put their money box, along with a sign saying the donations were for the funeral expenses of their recently deceased classmate. Several quilters dropped bills into the box on their way through.

"Have you checked with the jail to see what their visiting hours are?" Lauren asked Harriet.

"No."

"I think they can receive visitors on Saturday. Not that we care, but the rest of the alphabet gets their visits on Sunday."

Harriet felt frustration wash over her. She knew seeing Aiden in person wouldn't change anything, but somehow it would make her feel better.

"Great. There goes that plan."

"The jail site says they encourage phone calls between inmates and their family, friends and attorneys. And according to this, all cell blocks have phones."

"Give me the number."

"Let's go to that alcove over there. No sense broadcasting we're calling the jail."

Harriet dialed, left a message; and a few minutes later, her phone rang and Aiden was on the line.

"Are you okay," she asked. "I mean, of course you're not *okay* okay. But can I do anything for you? Do you need anything?"

"Slow down. I'm fine. I mean, considering everything. My lawyer is working on getting me out of here, and I did emergency surgery on a dog for one of the guards, and he's grateful and seems to have influence with the rest of them. As long as they've got room, I have private accommodations."

"Has your lawyer been able to find out what they have that caused them to arrest you?"

"It doesn't make sense. They said they searched her cell phone records, and my number shows up a bunch of times. *Her* calling *me*. I swear I haven't talked to her, by phone or otherwise, since she's been here. They found hair and saliva on her body. They are consistent with mine, but even if they get priority testing, it will still take days to get DNA results. I don't get it."

"I do. Someone is setting you up. And I hope your jailers are listening to this call. You did not kill Marine, and the sooner they realize that, the sooner they can get on with finding whoever is setting you up."

"I know I have to trust the police to find out who's behind this, but it's really hard to keep thinking positive sitting in here."

"Who would want to frame you for this? Assuming someone is trying, that is. Lauren is tracking down Marine's less savory family members to see if one of them had a reason to want her dead. Connie and Lauren's roommate are trying to find your homeless guy, or failing that, someone who saw you looking for him."

"So, the Loose Threads are on the case? I feel better already." He tried to laugh, but it came out more like a gasp. "I gotta go."

"Call me when you can," Harriet said and tapped her phone off.

Lauren had discreetly stepped away while Harriet was talking but returned when she dropped her phone into her purse.

"I called in an order for us at the Sandwich Board while you were talking to Aiden. I'd like to stop in the quilt store while we're near by and see if Marjorie has any of those pre-embroidered motifs we're supposed to use in our embellishments."

"They have some for sale at the supply table here."

"Have you looked at them? We're supposed to use at least one owl image, and the ones they have look like cartoons. After I've spent all this time doing perfect little herringbone stitches, I'm at least going to try to get a more realistic-looking owl."

"I have to admit, I'm not thrilled with my lime-green option. Do you want to drive, or shall I?"

"I'll drive, and you can tell me what the jailbird had to say."

✂ - - - ✂ - - - ✂

Lauren slowly turned the wire display rack full of embellishments.

"Incoming," she said in a quiet voice.

Harriet looked up in time to see Michelle come down the aisle.

"I'm so glad I found you here. The kids are still staying with my brother, and I guess Cookie has a sewing machine she's willing to let Lainie use. She's not a quilter, so Lainie gave me a list of things she needs. I have no idea what this stuff is." She shoved the list at Harriet.

"Cutting mat and cutter, big ruler, square ruler, ruler handle," Harriet read out loud. "I can see how this might be a little confusing. Lauren, you want to do cutter and mat or rulers?"

"I'll get the rulers." Lauren turned and headed toward the back of the store where notions were kept.

"Do you know how much space she'll have to work in?" Harriet looked at Michelle.

"Not a clue."

"Hmmm. I hesitate to get her one of the smaller ones while she's still learning."

"Don't look at me," Michelle said.

Harriet ignored her and walked over to a rack of cutting mats of various sizes and colors. She leafed through them, finally selecting a green twenty-four by thirty-six inch model.

"I think this will work. Tell Cookie if it's too big to fit her space, she can cut it down, but not to make it too small." She held it out, and when Michelle didn't immediately take it, Harriet shoved it into her hand.

Lauren set the rulers up front by the cash register before returning with Harriet to the embellishment rack. Michelle followed them and stood watching.

"Was there something else?" Harriet asked her without turning around.

"Lainie has been whining about wanting to come over to your house to have another lesson."

Harriet turned around.

"Of course—"

Jesssica burst through the front door.

"I found him," she said, pausing to catch her breath. "I mean, I saw him. I'm so glad I saw Lauren's car out front."

"Slow down," Harriet said. "You saw or found who? The homeless guy?" Jessica nodded.

"So, was that a yes to Lainie coming over?" Michelle looked at Jessica. "Sorry to interrupt, but I have to get back to legal aid."

"Yes, I need to figure out what we're doing, and then I'll call and make the arrangements. It might be tomorrow, but I'll call today."

Michelle carried her cutting mat to the register, paid for her purchases and left.

"Does that woman ever say thank you?" Lauren asked.

Harriet ignored her and nodded to Jessica.

"Continue."

"When the guy saw me coming toward him, he took off into the woods," Jessica explained. "I followed him a little way, but..." She gestured at her outfit. "...in this getup I couldn't catch him. He went off the trail into the brush, and it was hopeless. I thought we could change clothes and go back."

"Slow down, Nancy Drew," Lauren cautioned her.

"Lauren's right. We have to be careful where the police are concerned. I'll call Detective Morse, and she can tell whoever the right person is. My first inclination is to go look, too, but we can't do anything that will jeopardize Aiden's defense," Harriet told her. "I'll call Robin and see if she knows Aiden's attorney. Maybe she can call him, and if they have a private investigator maybe *they* can go look."

Lauren picked a couple of owls from the embellishments rack.

"Do you want a couple of these?" She held up a package. The owls were stitched from brown and gold thread.

Harriet took the package and looked.

"These do look a lot more natural."

In the end, all three women bought several of the owls and a couple of spiders.

"Thanks for spending your lunch looking," Harriet said to Jessica. "I'll call everyone while we're driving back to the church."

"No problem. It was nice getting some exercise. I didn't find anyone who had seen Aiden's car, but I did collect a few donations for the local women's shelter." She smiled. "When you look like a nun and knock on their door, people tend to think you're asking for a donation. Who am I to deny them the opportunity to salve their guilt by giving me their dollars?"

She went out the door and to her rental car.

Harriet paid for their purchases then followed Lauren to her car.

"I'm beginning to see why being a full-fledged nun wasn't working out for Jessica."

Lauren laughed.

'You think? She does seem to like to color outside the lines a little more than the church probably likes." She reached for her wallet.

"The embellishments are on me. You did drive, after all."

"Speaking of which, we're going to be late if we don't hurry."

It was Harriet's turn to laugh.

"What are they going to do, send us to the principal's office?"

Chapter 19

*H*arriet hung up her last call but kept her phone in her hand.

"I left messages with Robin and Detective Morse. Hopefully, someone will respond before the homeless guy is in the next county."

"I can't call the nerd squad. They're great on technical things, but I can't picture them tramping through the woods."

"I'm having a thought, and you can tell me if I'm being crazy."

"I'm afraid, but lay it on me."

"I was thinking about calling Tom."

"Really? Are things not complicated enough for you already? Your boyfriend is in jail, so you're going to involve your back-up boyfriend in trying to free him?"

"I was just thinking. Tom is a frequent visitor to the homeless camp. If he were to find the guy and talk to him, *he* could report it to the police, and we'd be above suspicion."

Lauren glanced at her.

"All kidding aside, I think you do need to call Tom—and anyone else you can think of."

Harriet didn't say anything.

"I'm serious. People get falsely accused and falsely convicted every day. The longer they have Aiden in their sights, the more committed they're going to be to their case against him, even though it's false."

"That's not very comforting."

"Harriet, this is as serious as it gets. For what it's worth, I think Tom's the kind of guy who will be mad if you *don't* call him."

Harriet sighed and tapped the face of her phone.

✂- - - ✂- - - ✂

"Okay," Harriet said as Lauren parked in the church lot. "It turns out Tom was on his way to Foggy Point on other business. He said he'll get here in thirty minutes or so, and he'll go straight to the homeless camp and start looking.

"We need to have Jessica call him back and tell him exactly where she was when she saw the guy. She could tell him what he looked like, too, on the off chance there's more than one of them in the woods today."

"I wish we didn't have the group dinner tonight," Lauren mused.

"Geez, I forgot about that. We can't miss the big banquet. When do we have to be back here? Six-thirty?"

"Yeah, they figured it gave us just enough time to go home, comb our hair, and come back."

"I better call about Lainie's quilting lesson before we go in." She tapped on her phone one more time and spoke to Cookie Jalbert. They agreed Lainie could come the following evening.

✂- - - ✂- - - ✂

"I know you're all anxious to get home so you can freshen up before the banquet tonight. Our keynote speaker is wonderful, and I'm sure we'll all learn a lot about crazy quilts."

Glynnis Miller from the Small Stitches was standing in front the workshop attendees in the basement meeting room.

"I'll make this brief. As you all know, one of our attendees died earlier this week, someone from our own community—Marine Moreau. Beth Carlson and Mavis Willis contacted her family this afternoon but found they have neither the means nor the inclination to put on any sort of service. As you all have generously donated money toward her memorial, we've decided to go ahead with it. Beth, would you like to tell us the details?"

Aunt Beth went to the front of the room, straightening her lavender cardigan with one hand and squeezing a wrinkled piece of paper in the other. She cleared her throat and began speaking in a louder than normal voice.

"Pastor Hafer has agreed to preside over a small service, to be held here at the Methodist Church on Saturday at one o'clock. I know many of you were already planning on staying through the weekend, and I hope you'll be able to attend. Jorge Perez, the owner of Tico's Tacos will be providing light snacks for a reception to follow in the private room at his restaurant. Thank you all for your generous donations."

She hesitated a few moments to see if anyone might have questions, but everyone was busy gathering purses, bags and coats so they could go get ready for the banquet.

✂ - - - ✂ - - - ✂

When Harriet walked into the basement fellowship hall, it bore no resemblance to the room they'd been in a few hours ago. Quilt racks had been set up along the walls and were draped with a stunning display of crazy quilts. All of the teachers had provided samples of their own work, and the after-dinner speaker had brought examples from his extensive collection—everything from the early dark wool models through brocade silks from Asia and heavily embellished Victorian-influenced designs. The room was buzzing with talk about the quilts.

Aunt Beth moved her purse from the chair beside her so Harriet could sit down.

"Jorge is going to go by your house and take Scooter out when he's on his way to my house and Brownie."

"I'm kind of surprised they didn't ask Jorge to cater this dinner," Harriet said.

Connie leaned across Beth to answer.

"The Small Stitches wanted to share the business around. They have their meetings at Jimmy's Barbecue, so it was natural they would give him the big dinner. And they were generous with Jorge. He got to do the opening reception and that lunch we went to."

Jessica and Lauren arrived, and Lauren set her shoulder bag on the chair next to her roommate before coming over to Harriet.

"Have you heard from Tom yet?"

"No. He said he'd call as soon as he knew anything. I also haven't heard anything from Detective Morse. I'll ask Robin what the attorney said when she gets here."

"She's here," Robin said as she sat down on the other side of Connie. "I told Aiden's attorney about the homeless man. He said he would get a private investigator here and out looking for the guy as quickly as he could. He didn't have anyone with him or know anyone in town, so it was going to be an hour or two."

Harriet clutched the stem of her water glass.

"I wish someone would find the guy."

Aunt Beth pried Harriet's hand off the glass.

112

"Let go, you're going to break that. You need to prepare yourself. Even if they find this fellow, he's likely to be a drunk. The police might not place much stock in what he says."

"If he has the dog, or can show them the dog's corpse, it would support what Aiden said. Besides, it would at least create reasonable doubt." Tears filled Harriet's eyes.

Beth handed her a tissue.

"Oh, honey, I didn't mean to upset you. Aiden will be set free soon enough. I'm just not sure that homeless man is the one who's going be the key."

"Have any of you seen this?" Sharon held up the program that had been lying on her plate. "Bill Volkening is the keynote speaker. It says here he has an extensive collection of crazy quilts. Has anyone heard him before?"

Mavis patted Harriet's hand but looked at Sharon.

"I've heard him speak about his collection of nineteen-seventies polyester quilts. He's very engaging, and he knows his stuff."

Harriet tried to eat what by all accounts was a fabulous barbecue dinner and to listen to what was probably a great talk, but she couldn't stop thinking about Aiden and the homeless man. She'd put her phone on mute, but that only meant she was looking at the screen every five minutes to be sure she didn't miss Tom's call. She was staring at her phone when Aunt Beth poked her in the side. She looked up. Everyone was applauding the conclusion of the keynote speech. Harriet quickly joined in.

"Wow, he was really good," Sharon said. "Of course, I know so little about quilting, he could have said anything and I'd believe him."

"Don't worry," Mavis said. "His talk was based on solid research."

Jessica came around the table to where Harriet was standing.

"That was great. Can we go home?"

Lauren laughed. "How do you really feel?"

"I've been wearing this wig..." She tugged at her hair. "...and these pumps way too long." She lifted her right foot and wiggled it. "I'm ready to get out of this getup."

"Okay," Lauren said. "We need to get home anyway. My landlady is dog-sitting Carter, and she's probably giving him all the treats he doesn't get at home. I need to get him away from her before he decides he doesn't want to leave."

Harriet flicked her phone's ringer back on and looked at the screen for the hundredth time, but there was still no message from Tom.

"Come on," Sharon said. "I'll sit vigil with you at your house. We can stitch on our crazy blocks while we wait."

Robin picked up her coat and purse from the back of her chair.

"I'll check in with Aiden's attorney and see if he was able to get a PI in play this afternoon."

"Thanks for your help," Harriet said. "I don't know what I'd do without all of you."

✂- - - ✂- - - ✂

"We're going to go home and work on our blocks," Sharon told Lauren as they walked to their cars with Harriet and Jessica. She pointed at Harriet's car. "Is that the mysterious Tom?"

Lauren looked. "That would be him. This may take a while. How about you come with us to the coffee shop for a nightcap? We'll drop you back by Harriet's when we're done."

Harriet hurried to her car.

"Did you find the homeless man?"

He ran both hands through his hair.

"Can we sit in your car?"

Sharon paused for a moment.

"I'm going to go get a cup of coffee with Lauren and Jessica." She turned and left, eliminating the need for Harriet to answer.

"Did you just find him?" Harriet asked as she got into the car. "What took so long? Did he tell you Aiden called him? Did—"

He reached over and grabbed her hand.

"Harriet, stop. I found the man's *body*. He's dead. That's what took so long. I had to hang around and be questioned by the police. Fortunately, I'd stopped for coffee and had a receipt establishing what time I'd arrived in Foggy Point. Joyce can back me up on when I checked with her. I guess they could tell by the guy's temperature, too. He was too cold for me to have done it."

"De–dead?"

"They won't know until they do the autopsy, but I heard them say it looks like alcohol poisoning."

Harriet pulled her hand away and leaned her head against the window.

"This nightmare just keeps getting worse. He was Aiden's alibi, and now he's gone, too." She sat back up. "It can't be a coincidence. I mean, someone kills Marine, and now the only guy who can give Aiden an alibi conveniently dies of alcohol poisoning? Just when we're looking for him?"

Tom took back her hand and squeezed it gently.

"He was homeless, and from what Joyce said, he was an addict. He drank and used whatever else he could get his hands on. That's why he wasn't living in the main homeless camp."

"Do they know who he is?"

"I don't think so. When the police arrived, one person talked to me and another one searched his pockets. He didn't have anything on him—no phone, no wallet, nothing. If he's been living in the woods for a while, he probably has a hidey-hole where he keeps his stuff. I'm sure the police will look when it's light."

"Why would some random homeless guy help set Aiden up?"

"Come on, do you really have to ask? The guy was an addict. If—and this is a very big if—he is even the right homeless guy, and if he was part of a setup."

Harriet yanked her hand away and turned to glare at him.

"Are you saying you think Aiden did kill Marine?"

"No, of course not. Doc couldn't kill a spider, much less a person. I'm just saying the homeless man's calling might have been a coincidence. Where would Aiden have been if he hadn't been looking for the guy?"

"He had the morning off because he'd worked the night before. He went for a run, and then he was going to shower, and eventually, he would have gone to work."

"So, all the killer had to do was wait until he went to work. If they were watching him, they'd know once he went down to the clinic he'd be gone for hours."

"Still, I don't believe in coincidence. It's too weird that Aiden is gone on a wild goose chase right when someone is staging a crime at the apartment."

"For what it's worth, I spent quite a bit of time in those woods before I found the guy. If anyone else is living out there, I didn't see any signs of it." Tom shivered and rubbed his hands on his arms. "It was really cold out there."

Harriet turned the engine on and put the heater on full blast. He smiled at her gratefully.

"Well, we aren't going to be able to solve this tonight. How are you doing? Are you remembering to eat? And sleep?"

Harriet tried to smile.

"Sure. I'm busy with the quilt meeting and my houseguest."

"That doesn't answer my question, and I can see from your face, you aren't eating enough, and you're not sleeping. That won't help Aiden. He needs you to be on your A game."

She did smile at that.

"Okay, Dr. Phil. Way to make it about Aiden. But your point is taken. My not eating or sleeping isn't helping him at all."

"I'm just worried about you. Of course, I'm concerned about Aiden, too, but I'm having trouble believing anyone is going to actually prosecute the good doctor for a crime he obviously didn't do."

"Every wrongly accused person sitting on death row probably has had that same thought."

"Let's not borrow trouble. I'm going to be in Foggy Point for a few days. What can I do to help?"

Harriet thought for a moment.

"How would you feel about going to Marine's memorial service? Since her family doesn't have any resources, the quilters took up a collection, and Pastor Hafer said the church would pick up the rest. It's going to be on Saturday. Another set of eyes might be helpful. True crime shows always talk about detectives attending funerals because perpetrators like to show up."

"Well, it must be gospel if it's on TV." Tom laughed. "Seriously. I'd be happy to be your extra set of eyes. Is your roommate staying for that, too? I'd like to meet someone from your old life."

Harriet briefly considered telling him what Jessica had told her about Sharon and the photo album, but *she* didn't want to think about the whole mess, much less involve Tom in it.

"She's just another quilter, so don't get your hopes up."

"I'd better go so I don't keep the Renfros up too late. I have a key so they can go to bed, but they never do. Mrs. R always waits up with a snack for me."

"Thanks for helping today."

He leaned in, took her face in both his hands, pulled her toward him and kissed her on the forehead.

"If you need anything, day or night, call me, and I'll come. Okay? *Anything.*"

With that, he got out of her car and walked away.

Harriet knew Lauren would be still be at the coffee shop, waiting to hear what Tom had said. In any case, it wasn't much out of the way to drive by on her way home.

Sure enough, Lauren, Sharon and Jessica were seated around a table at the Steaming Cup, each with her hands wrapped around a mug.

Lauren flagged her over when she came through the door.

"I went out on a limb and ordered you a cinnamon dulce hot chocolate when I saw you drive up. It'll be ready in a minute."

Harriet slid out of her coat and sat down in the fourth chair. Jessica reached across the table and took her hand.

"Sweetie, I can tell by your face something's happened. Do you feel like talking about it? If you don't, we can just sit here with you."

Lauren and Sharon looked at each other but didn't say anything.

The barista brought Harriet's drink, and she took a long, slow drink.

"Tom found the homeless guy."

"That's great," Jessica said.

"No, it's not great. He found the guy's body."

Lauren sat back in her chair.

"Oh, geez."

Sharon looked at Lauren and back at Harriet but didn't say anything.

"Are you sure it's the same homeless guy?" Jessica asked.

"No, but Foggy Point isn't that big. Most of the homeless people in Fogg Park are in the main camp. It's possible there are multiple people out in the woods, but Tom was out there for an hour before he found the body, and he didn't see anyone else. Besides, like I was telling Tom, I don't believe in coincidences. What are the chances of us needing to find a homeless guy who set Aiden up, and we find a guy in the same area, and he's dead, and then he turns out *not* to be Aiden's guy?"

Jessica's shoulders sagged.

"I was trying to think positive, but you're right. It makes sense that it's the same guy."

Sharon shivered. "That's a scary thought. If he's the same guy, it means whoever killed Marine was willing to kill again to keep Aiden in jail."

"Now, there's a thought," Harriet murmured.

Lauren set her mug down.

"What?"

"Maybe we're looking at this all wrong. I've been thinking it was about Marine, and Aiden was a convenient target because of their past relationship. Maybe it has nothing to do with Marine and more to do with preventing Aiden from doing something. I know he has to testify in a dog hoarding trial. I don't know if someone would commit murder just to prevent him from testifying, or at least to discredit him."

"That seems awfully thin," Jessica said.

"I'm grasping at straws," Harriet said with an attempt at a smile.

"I like it, though," Lauren said. "We need to consider all possibilities and then, one by one, disprove them."

"Please don't quote Sherlock Holmes," Harriet warned her. "I don't think I'm up to a quote."

Lauren looked hurt.

"He wasn't wrong, you know."

117

"He wasn't real, either."

Jessica stood up and took her empty mug and added it to a tub full of dirty dishes on a cart near the bar.

"Okay, you two, I think it's time to go. Our discussion is no longer productive. Besides, I've been in big girl clothes far too long today."

"Thank you for all your help," Harriet told her.

Jessica wrapped both arms around her and gave her a hug.

"You'll get through this. We don't know anything tonight, but maybe the answer will come in the morning." She let go but didn't step away. "And not to get all nun-ey on you, but I'll pray for Aiden before I go to bed, and for you, too."

Lauren stood as well.

"Come on, let's get out of here before somebody starts crying." She put her cup in the busing tub and led the way to the door.

Chapter 20

Sharon was standing in Harriet's kitchen when she returned from taking Scooter out for his evening walk. She hung up the leash and removed her coat. Sharon hadn't moved.

"Can I get you anything?"

"I was wondering if you could recommend someplace I could stay for a few more days." Sharon shuffled her program from the dinner from one hand to the other. "I know you were only planning on having me here through tomorrow afternoon. I'd like to stay for Marine's memorial service and maybe one more day, but I know you've got a lot on your plate right now, and I don't want to impose."

Harriet was quiet for a long moment.

"Here's the deal," she said finally. "You staying here is not a problem, but I can't help thinking you've got another agenda." Sharon started to speak, but Harriet held her hand up to stop her. "You're right. I've got a lot on my mind with what's going on with Aiden. I don't need any distractions, so I'm just going to come out with it.

"The other night when the Threads were here, and you were upstairs working on your embellishments, Jessica went up to look for you. She checked the TV room, and you weren't there, so she opened the next door she came to, which was your room. You weren't in there, either, but she noticed an open photo album on your suitcase. She assumed it would be pictures from your modeling days, so she took a look. I'm not saying what she did was right, but it's what she did."

Sharon went to the kitchen table and collapsed onto a chair.

"She saw the pictures of me and Steve."

"You and Steve 'in compromising positions' was how she put it." Harriet sat down opposite her. "Look, it was a long time ago, and obviously way before I met Steve. I couldn't care less if you and Steve had a teenage romance. He told me you dated briefly, but he said you'd been friends for so long that it felt slightly incestuous, so you both decided you were better as friends. In fact, wasn't he the best man at your wedding?

"What I don't get is why, all these years later, long after Steve is dead, you come to my house packing an album of steamy pictures of you with my husband."

"It's not what you think." Sharon's face had turned red, and her eyes were filling with tears.

"Enlighten me," Harriet said in a hard tone.

"Steve and I started dating in the spring of our junior year in high school. His girlfriend at the time had moved out of state during Christmas break. I'd just had a traumatic breakup with my boyfriend.

"I'm sure you remember how things were at that age—every little thing was a major tragedy. We spent most of our time together commiserating about how much our lives sucked. We were good kids. We didn't drink or do drugs or anything like that. No one in our group did."

Sharon paused, and Harriet got up and brought her a glass of water. She set it in front of her.

"Go on."

"In a moment of terrible judgment, we decided being good wasn't getting us anywhere, so we'd try the other side."

"What did you do?" Harriet asked in spite of herself.

"Steve's parents were going away for the weekend, and of course they didn't give a second thought to leaving him home alone. We were the good kids, after all. I told my parents I was going away for the weekend with a girlfriend. They didn't ask too many questions, so we had the whole weekend and an empty house."

Harriet sat back in her chair, curious now about where this was going.

"So, you got into their liquor cabinet, I'm guessing."

"Yes. First their liquor cabinet, then their bed. When we sobered up, and cleaned up the wreckage, we realized that drinking and having sex were not the answer to anything. We also realized that something that should have been so special when you're with the right person, at the right time, was now ruined forever for us.

"We stayed friends and went to the prom together, mainly because we were sufficiently disgusted with ourselves we weren't ready to date anyone else and didn't want to miss prom."

120

"I guess I'm missing something here, because I'm not getting how that brief, ill-advised interlude in your teen years is causing you to carry a reminder with you here. I mean, everyone makes mistakes in their youth."

Sharon sipped her water.

"Some mistakes carry bigger consequences than others."

Harriet stared at her.

"You got *pregnant?*"

Steve had lied about his illness, but Harriet couldn't believe he'd have omitted having gotten a girl pregnant. He definitely would have told her if he had a child.

Wouldn't he?

"Steve never knew. School was almost out for the summer when I realized. I was in denial at first, but when I missed my second period, there was no doubt. My parents were great. I was already doing modeling jobs by then, so sometimes I'd go away on shoots. My mom told the school I was abroad and would work with a tutor. She took me to her sister who lives on a farm in Middle of Nowhere, Washington. A friend of hers in England would send postcards and letters I'd write back to Oakland."

She paused to sip her water again.

"What happened to the baby?"

"We made arrangements for it to be adopted right from the hospital. I say 'it' because the adoptive parents were in the delivery room. The baby was wrapped in a blanket, I nursed it once; but by previous agreement among all the adults, its gender was never mentioned. The new parents took the baby away to another room, and I was moved to a different floor where there weren't mothers or babies."

Tears began to slide down Sharon's perfect face.

Without thinking, Harriet reached across the table and took her hand.

"That sounds so sad. I can't imagine how you coped."

"Like I said, my mom was great. We stayed on for another month in Washington. She took me to a therapist daily at first and continued it when we got back to California. They kept me on antidepressants until I'd made peace with the situation. I came back during Christmas break as if nothing had happened. If the others noticed I'd changed, they chalked it up to my modeling in Europe."

"And you never thought Steve would want to know he had a child?"

"Later, yeah. When it was too late. My mom and the therapist kept really close tabs on me. I was in my senior year when I came back, and I was getting more and more modeling jobs. I threw myself into my career and never looked back."

"What changed?"

"The easy answer is—my accident. I'd like to think I'd have gotten to this point even if I hadn't been in the accident, but being in the hospital brought back memories and gave me ample time to think. I used it reflecting on the mistakes I've made. Steve's dead, so I can never fix that mistake. When I saw the quilting event and saw the opportunity to come stay with you, I guess I figured telling you would be the next best thing."

"So, when were you going to tell me?"

"After I got here and spent time with you, I decided it wasn't fair to make myself feel better by unloading all this on you. I wasn't going to tell you."

"And yet here we are. What I still don't understand is why the pictures? They have to be a painful reminder."

"They aren't, strangely enough. I don't have a single picture of my child, so those are the only things I have to remind me that it was real. Steve and I were together, and we created a child."

"Are you still seeing a therapist?"

"I am. Not the same one, of course. That's another reason I wanted to come to Washington. It turns out attitudes have changed about adoption. Both birth parents and adopted children are finding it beneficial to connect. And before you say anything, I've talked a lot with my therapist, and I know not every child wants to find their birth parents and vice versa. I also know my child might not still be alive, and I've been warned he or she might not have had the ideal childhood I've imagined for him or her. And he or she might blame me, if that's the case."

"But you're going to try and find your baby?"

"I am. The adoption took place in Washington, so I was going to find an investigator while I'm here."

The two women sat in silence until Scooter jumped into Harriet's lap and settled.

"I may be speaking out of turn, and we'll have to ask Lauren first, but she works with a group of computer people who might be helpful. They're programmers, not real investigators, but they can find things through the internet no one else can."

"Should I ask her, or do you need to talk to her?"

"I better talk to her first. And you're welcome to stay here while you get things set up."

"I'm really sorry. You don't need my drama on top of everything else."

Harriet set Scooter on the floor.

"I'm going to go upstairs and pretend to sleep. Help yourself to a snack or tea, if you want."

Sharon groaned. "I may never eat again after this week. I think I'll go up—I need to refresh my manicure." She held her right hand out, fingers spread. "It probably seems silly, but for so many years when I was working, we had to keep our nails neat and prepped with clear nail polish so we'd be ready on a moment's notice. It's just habit now."

"I hear you about the food. And there are worse habits than keeping your manicure tuned up." She looked down at her dog. "Come on, let's get on up to bed." She looked back at Sharon. "See you in the morning."

Chapter 21

The sky was gray when Harriet took Scooter out for his morning walk. With luck, the clouds would clear off before Marine's funeral tomorrow.

Sharon came out of the house through the studio door. She was wearing tan slacks and a pink silk blouse and looked every inch the former model she was. She also had a spring in her step that had been absent until now.

"I slept the whole night through for the first time in forever," she said.

"Oh, good. I'm glad we talked last night. And I'll ask Lauren about what we discussed when we see her at the breakfast buffet. I'll be ready as soon as I get this little guy settled." She looked down at Scooter with a smile.

Sharon's look turned serious.

"I'm going to drive *my* car today. I called my doctor about my headaches, and he called in a different prescription for me. I've always had headaches, but not as frequently as I have lately. And it's not just the stress—I've had some tough therapy sessions, and it hasn't triggered anything.

"Anyway, he called my prescription to the pharmacy out by the highway. I stuck a cereal bar in my purse, and I thought I'd skip breakfast and go by this morning before class."

"Okay, I guess I'll see you in class or at morning break. By then, I should have an answer from Lauren."

✂ - - - ✂ - - - ✂

Lauren was at the buffet table loading a bagel with cream cheese and smoked salmon when Harriet arrived.

"I need to talk to you privately," Harriet said as she passed by on her way to the beginning of the line.

"I love it when we sit in the corner and tell secrets."

"This is serious," Harriet scolded.

"Isn't it always?"

Harriet rolled her eyes and turned her attention to the bowl of cut fruit in front of her.

"Where are your aunt and Mavis this morning?" Lauren asked when she arrived with her plate and glass of juice.

Harriet set her food down and pulled out the chair opposite her friend.

"They'll be a little late. They're going by the florist to arrange for flowers for the service tomorrow. They're going to hit up the rest of us Threads for donations when they figure out how much it's going to cost."

Lauren took a bite of her bagel.

"I don't have a problem with that," she said when she'd finished chewing. "It's kind of sad that Marine didn't have anyone to put on a funeral for her."

Jessica came to the table.

"Is this a private party?"

Lauren looked at Harriet.

"I can go sit over there," Jessica indicated with her napkin-wrapped silverware, and then looked from Lauren to Harriet.

Harriet indicated she should sit down.

"Are you sure? I don't want to intrude."

"It's fine, really. This sort of involves you. I'll trust your discretion. What I'm going to tell you is someone else's secret."

"Of course I won't tell anyone. It's part of my previous professional training."

"I confronted Sharon about the book of pictures." She went on to tell them the story Sharon had told them. "Part of the reason she came here was to find an investigator to find her baby." She looked at Lauren. "I told her about your nerd herd. I don't know if they do this sort of thing, but I thought they might have more luck than a random investigator in digging through electronic records."

"Are you suggesting they could hack into records that a licensed investigator couldn't or wouldn't?"

"No."

Lauren tilted her chin downward and looked up at her.

"I'm supposed to believe that?"

"Okay, it did occur to me they might be able to access records that weren't quite public."

"Only because I know they can get into and out of the level of records we are speaking about without leaving a trace will I even consider asking them to help. What's in it for them?"

Harriet took a bite of her roll and chewed thoughtfully.

"I didn't ask, but I'm sure she's willing to pay them for their time."

Glynnis Miller came hurrying up to the table; her usually neat bun had wisps hanging down to her collar on one side.

"Harriet, I'm so glad I found you. Could I impose on you to drive over to the screen-printing shop?"

"Sure, what's happening?"

"We're putting together the goodbye goodie bags, and the printer made a mistake on the logo. We discovered it yesterday, and they printed a new batch for us, but I'm afraid the rest of the Small Stitches are tied up with the funeral arrangements. We're having trouble finding some of Marine's family and friends. I spoke to Beth, but she and Mavis and Connie are busy getting flowers, and Robin and DeAnn are printing up a program. She suggested you or Lauren. I hope you don't mind."

"It's no problem. Is the printer in that industrial park down by the docks?"

Glynnis handed her a piece of paper.

"I wrote down the address and what the printing on the bags should say. I'm sure they're fine this time, but please check them while you're still there."

"I'll go right now."

Glynnis thanked her two more times before she bustled off to deal with whatever the next crisis on her list was.

"Shotgun," Lauren called out the moment Glynnis was out of ear-shot. "I don't think this is a good time for any of us to be driving to sketchy neighborhoods alone."

"It's fine down there during the day when the businesses are open. It's nighttime that's the problem."

Lauren crumpled her napkin onto her plate.

"I'm coming with anyway."

Jessica looked from Lauren to Harriet and back to Lauren.

"Me, too?"

Harriet sighed. "Sure, why not. We'll make it a party bus." She glanced at the time on the face of her phone. "Come on. If we hustle we won't miss much of our morning session."

✂ - - - ✂ - - - ✂

Jessica leaned forward from the middle seat of Harriet's car.

"Hey, is this the wrong side of the tracks Foggy Point style? I didn't think this town had a bad part."

Lauren looked back at her.

"Every town has a bad part. And Harriet's quite familiar with this one."

"Thanks for reminding me of an unfortunate chapter in my life in Foggy Point," Harriet said with a laugh.

"You can't leave me hanging like that," Jessica said. "Come on, spill."

Harriet sighed. "I was looking for a young woman who might have some information I needed. She was in hiding, and I came down here to the apartment she'd been living in. She wasn't home, but someone else was there and was unhappy to see me. I took a little side trip to the hospital, but as you can see, I'm fine, so it all worked out in the end."

"It's hard to imagine a young person, especially a girl, living down here and surviving for very long." Jessica mused, looking out the window at the peeling paint and broken windows on the rundown apartments they were driving past.

"Aunt Beth told me the Foggy Point Redevelopment Committee has been trying to clean up this area for years. The trouble is, a number of the larger buildings are owned by absentee landlords in Seattle. They're not very invested in cleaning up Foggy Point. They get tax concessions for offering low-rent apartments. No one in the city cares that they're slums."

"That's sad. Can't you do anything about it?" Jessica asked.

"The committee is working on them one at a time," Lauren said with a smug smile and looked at Harriet.

Jessica looked from one to the other.

"What?"

"Let's just say a certain computer expert we know is making sure the landlords are following the letter of the law."

"Something they're not used to doing, I might add," Lauren said.

Harriet abruptly slowed the car and turned left down a side street.

"What?" Lauren said but then looked where Harriet was pointing as she made a U-turn and pulled to the curb facing the main through road.

"It's Sharon's rental car. She's supposed to be picking up a prescription downtown. What's she doing here?"

Jessica leaned through the two front seats from the back again.

"We're going to wait and see, right?"

"Of course," Lauren told her. "We're with Harriet. We never pass up an opportunity like this."

Harriet settled back in her seat.

"Hopefully, whatever she's doing will be quick. She'll be needing to get back as much as we do."

They didn't have long to wait. A door that was almost hidden between an exterior staircase and a boarded-up storefront window opened, and two women came out.

"That's definitely Sharon in the front," Harriet said. "But who's the other one?"

The other women was older and had obviously lived more. She was thin, wearing tight, faded jeans and canvas tennis shoes. Her hair was pulled back in a stiff, strawlike ponytail.

"I don't recognize the woman," Lauren said. "But you can tell by the body language there's no love lost between them."

Harriet hit her palm against the steering wheel as she watched Sharon look up and down the block before getting in her car and driving away.

"After last night, I thought she'd come clean about her agenda in Foggy Point. Clearly there was more."

"Maybe this doesn't have anything to do with you." Lauren offered. "As I've reminded you so often in the past, the world doesn't revolve solely around you."

"I'm with Harriet," Jessica said from the back. "How many agendas can one big city woman have in a small place like Foggy Point."

"I know," Lauren said. "I was just hoping this wasn't going to get more complicated than it already is. I should know better."

"Chances are this has something to do with finding her child." Harriet said. "We didn't talk about what she's done already in her search. I can just imagine how many people there are out there ready to take advantage of people like Sharon." She started the car again and pulled back out onto the main road. "With everything going on with Aiden, I really didn't need this. A small part of me wants to ignore what we just saw."

"But…" Lauren said.

"Now that I know Sharon and, more important, my dead husband have a child out there somewhere, I can't ignore it. And okay, I can't in good conscience have her possibly being taken advantage of by who knows who and not do something to help her."

Lauren sighed again and looked toward the heavens.

"I was afraid you were going to say that."

"Come on, tough girl," Jessica said from the back. "You wouldn't be at Harriet's side for all this stuff if you didn't want to be."

"My life was pretty ordinary before Harriet moved back to town."

"Don't even try to sell me on that one," Jessica said with a laugh. "I'd be willing to bet nothing in your life has ever been ordinary. Don't forget, I've seen some of the names on your speed-dial list."

The rest of their trip was blessedly uneventful, and Sharon's rental car was in the church parking lot when they parked.

"I can't thank you enough for picking these up," Glynnis told Harriet when she'd opened the first box and inspected the replacement bags for herself.

"We were happy to do it."

"I told your teachers you were doing an errand for me. All the groups are having work time so everyone can get as far as possible before the final show-and-tell."

Harriet handed Glynnis the receipt from the printer.

"We'd better get going so we can get to work."

"Thank you again, ladies."

✂- - - ✂- - - ✂

Most of the students made considerable progress on their crazy quilt blocks. Harriet's stitching looked so bad she ended pulling half of it out. She couldn't stop thinking about Aiden, locked up in a cell. She was thankful he wasn't in the general population, but that would only be true as long as they had space. It was a nightmare without end, and it wasn't even happening to her.

Aiden had been through a lot in recent years. He'd told her stories about his time in Uganda, how hard it was just to survive daily life. And then his mother died right after he returned to Foggy Point. She could feel tears burning her eyes.

A wrinkled hand pressed a tissue into her hand. She glanced to her side and saw Mavis, busily clipping a thread on her block.

"Thank you," she whispered.

"Let me see your block. You've got a bit of a snarl going on there." Mavis took her block and finished removing a piece of lace Harriet had misapplied. She repositioned it and deftly sewed it into place. "There, that's better." She handed the work back to Harriet.

"Fretting about that boy sitting in jail isn't going to help anyone. He's tougher than you think, and we're going to get this thing figured out and get him home before you know it."

✂- - - ✂- - - ✂

Glynnis and the Small Stitches went all out for the final lunch—they had gotten The Smuggler's Cove restaurant to cater the event. Harriet had met the owner-chef when she'd first moved to Foggy Point, and she and James

129

had gone on to become friends when she'd filled in for his sister at the wiener dog races earlier in the year.

Aunt Beth was saving places for the Loose Threads at a long table near the front of the dining room when Harriet joined her and Mavis.

"I'm going to go see if James is here," Harriet said. She set her purse and quilting bag on her chair and headed for the kitchen. She found him in his white apron standing at the big industrial stove. He was cooking burgers, and his assistant was plating them on homemade buns along with baked sweet potato fries, lettuce and tomatoes.

"Hey, how's our favorite race dog?" she asked.

"He's still in the game. I think he's going to make it all the way to the big show."

"Tell Cyrano that Scooter and I are pulling for him."

"I'm sorry about Aiden. As you can imagine, everyone who's been in the restaurant in the last few days has been talking about it. No one believes for a minute he killed that woman."

"Unfortunately, there are a few people who don't believe he's innocent. Most importantly—the district attorney. We all know innocent people are wrongly prosecuted. Maybe not every day, but it happens."

"If there's anything I can do, just say the word. Otherwise, you need to go sit down and prepare to have the best burger you've ever tasted." He bowed at the waist and pointed toward the door.

"Thanks, you're the best."

"I bet you say that to all the guys who ply you with chocolate."

Harriet smiled as she turned and went back to the dining room.

"James is making us burgers and baked sweet potato fries. They smell wonderful." she said.

Lauren leaned toward Jessica.

"James could make cardboard taste delicious."

"Not to change the subject from our wonderful lunch, but does anyone know when we finish up today?" Jessica asked.

"Lunch is followed by a show-and-tell, and then I think Glynnis will make some closing remarks," Connie told them. "Mainly she's going to ask people to fill out a questionnaire. I heard them talking in the bathroom. They're trying to figure out whether they should repeat crazy quilting again or if they should do a different type of quilting next time."

"Are we going to have an after party?" Mavis asked. "My guest is going home as soon as we're done."

Connie put her napkin in her lap.

"Mine scheduled themselves for a spa afternoon, so I'm free."

"I've got Lainie coming over to sew quilt blocks," Harriet told them.

Servers began setting plates of food in front of the quilters, interrupting the flow of conversation.

"Why don't we meet at Harriet's?" Beth suggested when the food had been delivered.

"Fine with me," Harriet said around her first bite of burger. "Mmmm," she moaned as she chewed.

No more conversation was possible until everyone was finished eating.

✂- - - ✂- - - ✂

"So I hope you'll all fill out your questionnaires about what you're interested in, and I hope everyone will mark the yes box to say you'll be back again next year." Glynnis told everyone when the show-and-tell was over.

Three women, including Beth's roommate, made their way to the front of the room and presented a large floral bouquet to Glynnis and smaller bouquets to each member of her executive committee. They thanked the committee on behalf of the attendees, and with a final round of applause, the workshop was over.

Harriet stood up and put her coat on.

"Will four o'clock work for everyone? That'll give me some time to work with Lainie alone before you come. Carla's going to bring a movie Lainie and Wendy can watch upstairs while we're talking."

Sharon came up to Harriet and Lauren.

"I'll see you back at your house," she said and turned to go.

"Hold on," Lauren said. "Harriet told me you might need a little help with a research project. Can I get some information from you when I come over? I can get my guys going, and we should know quickly if it's going to be something we'll be able to help with."

Sharon pressed her hand to her heart, hope plain on her face.

"That would be great."

Chapter 22

Cookie got out of her car and followed her niece to the studio door. "Lainie said she was staying until six o'clock, is that right?" she asked as they came into the studio.

"Yes, the Loose Threads are coming over after we sew, and Carla's bringing Wendy. I asked Lainie if I could hire her to sit and watch a movie with Wendy in my TV room while we have our meeting."

"That's fine. We always have takeout and watch movies with the kids on Friday nights."

"I hope you don't mind a movie double header," Harriet said to Lainie. The girl grinned.

"As long as the boys don't choose the same movie Wendy and I watch."

Cookie laughed. "I can guarantee the boys won't choose anything a toddler girl would like."

"We can bring her back if you want. Connie has to head your direction when she goes home, and if she's not going straight home, I don't mind bringing her. She's really helping us out."

"That would be great, thank you."

Cookie left, and Harriet hung Lainie's coat over the back of a chair before leading her to the sewing station she'd set up.

"Knock-knock," said Sharon from the connecting door. "Mind if I join you?"

"I thought you might want to work on your patchwork quilt, so I set up a second machine for you."

The next hour passed in a flurry of cutting, stitching, pressing and stitching some more. Lainie cried the first time she had to rip a block apart, and amazingly, Sharon made the same mistake a few minutes later. They laughed together, and Sharon's stock went up a little in Harriet's eyes.

✂- - - ✂- - - ✂

Harriet glanced at the face of her phone.

"The group is about to arrive, so we'd better finish up the pieces we're working on. One more day of making blocks, and you should be ready to start sewing them into rows."

Lainie handed her last block to Harriet to press.

"Can I call my brother?"

"Sure, there's a phone in the kitchen," Harriet told her.

She pulled a cell phone with a sparkly purple case from her sewing bag.

"Mom let me use one of her phones."

Sharon looked up from her block.

"How many phones does your mom have?"

"Three. Because of the kind of people she works with at legal aid, she has extra phones so her clients don't accidentally talk to me or Etienne. She said they also can't find out where we live. She let my brother and me each take a phone while we're staying at Aunt Cookie's and Uncle Marcel's. We have to give them back when we get back to Uncle Aiden's house."

"She must trust you a lot," Harriet said.

"That's what she said. She said if she finds out we're making prank calls or talking to our friends when we're supposed to be doing homework she'll take them back."

"Are you being good?" Sharon teased.

Lainie sighed. "I'm always good."

Aunt Beth came into the studio without knocking. She held a glass baking dish in one hand and a reusable grocery bag looped over her opposite arm.

Harriet reached for the dish.

"What have we here?"

Aunt Beth swung away from her.

"Go get my stitching bag from the car, and I'll tell you."

Mavis drove up while Harriet was leaning into her aunt's silver Beetle.

"You guys must have talked," she said when Mavis got out carrying another glass baking dish.

"We knew you were going to be busy sewing, so we put together a plan. I know we had a big lunch, but that was hours ago."

Harriet took Mavis's sewing bag as well and followed her into the house. Aunt Beth was setting her dish into the microwave when they came into the kitchen.

"Now will you tell me what you brought?" Harriet asked as Sharon filled the teakettle with water and set it on the stove.

"This is pizza dip," Beth said and gestured to her dish with a flourish. "It has all the things you'd put on a pizza, only it's in a dish instead of a crust. When everyone gets here, I'll warm it a little to melt the cheese." She pulled a bag and a box from her grocery bag. "We have pita bread cut into little triangles and crackers for people to dip with."

"And I brought chocolate lasagna," Mavis said.

"That sounds deadly," Harriet said. "Tell me more."

"It's simple. Crushed-up chocolate sandwich cookies, then a layer of cream cheese mixed with sugar and whipped topping followed by chocolate pudding and more whipped topping and then mini chocolate chips."

"I'm not even hungry, and it sounds heavenly," Sharon said.

"Do Wendy and I get some, too," Lainie asked. She'd been so quiet, Harriet had almost forgotten she was there.

The rest of the Loose Threads arrived over the next fifteen minutes, including Carla, who took Wendy and Lainie up to the TV room. She'd brought a selection of Disney movies for the girls to choose from. Harriet was reasonably sure Lainie had seen them all, but she could hear her discussing the finer points of princesses vs. mermaids with Wendy as they went up the stairs.

It took a few minutes more, but eventually the Loose Threads were seated around the dining room table along with Sharon and Jessica.

"This dip is so good," Carla said. "Can you teach me to make it?"

"Of course, honey," Beth told her.

Carla's ears turned pink, but she maintained eye contact with Beth. She was definitely growing up, Harriet thought.

"Raise your hand if you're going to finish your crazy quilt," Lauren said.

Four people raised their hands.

"I'm making my square into a pillow," Lauren continued.

"I was thinking a wall hanging," Robin said.

"Did you ever find Marine's mom or other family members?" Harriet asked Lauren.

"Way to bring the party down," Lauren said.

"I hope you had better luck than we did," Mavis said.

Lauren shot a meaningful look to Harriet before speaking.

"As a matter of fact, I did. Some of my associates made contact with her this afternoon; she'll be at the funeral. I had them give her some money to buy a black dress, but I have no real hope she'll use the money for that. They did tell her they would give her more money if she showed up in the dress."

"That was clever," Beth noted.

"The 'good' sibling was easy to find. I'm not sure she'll show, but she has the information, anyway. The brother will be there, if only to see if there's anything for him in it."

Jessica high-fived her roommate.

"Way to go," she said.

The discussion was interrupted by knocking on the studio door. Carla jumped up.

"I'll get it."

She returned with Detective Morse in tow.

"I should give you your own key," Harriet said.

"I'm sorry to interrupt, but I was looking for your aunt and I thought I'd check here on my way out to her house. None of you are answering your phones, so I guessed you were meeting."

"No problem," Aunt Beth said. "We've gotten in the habit of silencing our phones when we meet."

"I'm not knocking it. It's a great idea."

"How can I help you," Aunt Beth said in her sweetest "I'm just a little old lady" voice.

"I was hoping you got hold of Marine Moreau's mother, Francine Moreau. We believe she goes by Frankie."

Mavis scooped a serving of pizza dip onto one of the saucers Harriet had set on the table. Beth added a few pita wedges and handed it to Morse.

"Mavis and I didn't have any luck, but Lauren managed to run her to ground."

"Really?" Morse said. "Do I want to know?"

"I'll tell you later, but I assure you, it was all above board."

Harriet scooped a bite of dip onto a cracker, popped it into her mouth and chewed thoughtfully.

"She'll be at the funeral tomorrow, if we're lucky. Have your people not spoken to her yet? I hope…" She paused. "…Lauren wasn't the first person to tell her about Marine."

"She definitely knew about Marine," Lauren said in a hurry. If Morse noticed, she didn't say anything.

"We spoke to her other daughter when we couldn't find her right away, and she assured us she could contact her. No, this is something else."

"Anything we can help with?" Harriet asked.

Morse sighed and sagged in her chair.

"I suppose you're going to find out soon enough anyway. Just please promise me you won't talk to her before I do."

135

"That's not likely," Robin said dryly.

"We identified the body Tom Bainbridge found in the park." She paused for effect. "It's Lucien Moreau."

The group was silent.

"Lucien Moreau," she repeated. "Marine's stepdad Luc."

"Whoa," said Carla.

Harriet sat erect in her chair.

"Oh, my gosh, That's crazy. *He* was the one who distracted Aiden so someone could kill Marine in his house?"

"If that's, in fact, what happened." Morse reminded her. "With this new development, we have to consider the possibility someone is out to get the Moreau family. With the other brother being in jail, someone could be killing his family for payback."

"Wait, Tom said he died from alcohol poisoning," Harriet said.

It was Morse's turn to take a bite of dip before answering.

"That was the assumption when the paramedics arrived. He was drunk when he died, but that wasn't what killed him."

The Loose Threads stopped chatting and turned toward her as one.

"Wow, do you practice that move?" Morse said and laughed. "I'm sorry. Cops tend to find humor in strange places. This will be out in the media soon enough, anyway. Mr. Moreau was hit from behind with an as-yet unidentified blunt object."

"From what we know of that family, it's hard to believe that killing the abusive drunken patriarch, who by all accounts was long estranged from his family, would be much of a payback for anything," Robin observed. "If I were trying to hurt any of the family, I'd go for the college sister. I'll bet they were proud of her, in their own way."

"It does make more sense if he were killed to keep him quiet, if he did help set up Aiden," Morse said. "I'll give you that."

Mavis took a sip of her tea and set her cup down.

"It's hard to imagine any parent could sink so low as to participate in their own child's murder."

"Once people spiral into addiction, drugs or alcohol become more important than family or anything else. Unfortunately, we see it all too often. People will sell their own children if it gets them their next fix." Morse said.

"That's just sad," Beth said.

Harriet stood up

"On that depressing note, I think we need some chocolate."

She went to the kitchen for the dessert.

"I'll get plates," Sharon said and went with her.

Jessica followed them into the kitchen, got dessert for the kids and took it upstairs.

"So, where does this all leave Aiden?" Harriet said as she returned and started cutting the chocolate lasagna into pieces and handing them out.

Mavis and Aunt Beth both took sandwich bags that held precut triangles of fabric and several pre-threaded needles from their purses. They quietly began hand-sewing the pieces together.

Jessica returned to her place at the table.

"They were "letting it go" at the top of their lungs when I got there. I'm surprised we didn't hear them.

Robin slid her legal tablet and pen from her bag.

"The way I see it, there are two possibilities. One, we figure out who did kill Marine, and/or two, we come up with evidence to show that Aiden didn't do it."

"Whatever forensic evidence they have has to be rigged, but without access to the material, we may have a hard time proving it," Lauren said.

Carla twirled her fork in her dessert.

"Has anyone looked for security camera footage around the vet clinic or around the back of Fogg Park?"

"I went door to door in the neighborhood behind the park," Jessica told her. "The first row of houses looking into the woods, at least. Not everyone was home, though. I made a list of the addresses when they were. No one fessed up to having a security camera."

Robin made a note.

"So, we could follow up on that. Has anyone looked for cameras around the clinic?"

Morse took a bite of her chocolate.

"This is really good," she said when she'd swallowed. "Let me check and see if they've pulled the footage around the crime scene. They should have. You need to tread lightly around the detectives assigned to this. They're aware that Harriet and you all have upstaged the FPPD in the past, but more important, they're well aware of Harriet's relationship with Aiden. I think canvassing in the neighborhood is a good idea, though. The officers assigned to the case are spending most of their time trying to prove Aiden did it. I doubt very much they're spending any time verifying his alibi."

"So, what about Marine's family?" Lauren asked. "Is there any chance one of them knows anything?"

"Given tonight's revelation about her dad, I'd think there's a good chance they know something," Harriet said.

"Surely, one of them was close enough to her to know what she's been up to lately," Aunt Beth said.

Mavis sipped her tea.

"You know, one of us should probably talk to Michelle. Marine was staying at her house."

Carla cleared her throat.

"Yes, dear?" Mavis said.

"I noticed Marine used to talk to the kids' tutor in French. Michelle said Marine's family lived in the same town in France her mom came from. Marine's mom is a lot younger than Aiden's and Michelle's parents, but I think they knew Marine's grandparents. That's why Avanell let Marine stay with her when her own mom wouldn't let her come home, back when Aiden was in Uganda."

"You know, honey," Beth said, "you're right. I remember Avanell saying something about that at the time."

Carla looked down at her plate and blushed.

"Marine was born here," Beth continued, "but her family probably spoke French at home because of the grandparents."

"Do you know how to get hold of the tutor?" Harriet asked Carla.

"I don't, but I'm pretty sure she's still going over to Marcel's and Cookie's to give the kids their homework assignments, so they probably have her number."

Robin wrote "talk to tutor" on her paper.

Connie raised her hand.

"I'm taking Lainie home tonight, I can ask Cookie then. I'll call the tutor and see what she has to say."

"We should talk to whichever relatives show up for the memorial service, too," Robin said and wrote each of the relatives' names down.

Lauren scraped her nearly empty plate with her fork.

"It's possible the mom or siblings will know of other friends. We need to be prepared to grill them, too."

"Too bad you don't know who her dealer is," Jessica said with a smirk. "That's where I'd be looking for leads."

Harriet picked up her teacup.

"Marine hasn't been in town long enough to be in the kind of trouble that gets you killed. And she did seem to be either out of money or genuinely trying to kick her habit."

Lauren looked at her.

"So, you think someone killed Marine to send a message to...who? Her mother? Her brother? If her mother wouldn't let her live with her, would she be swayed by someone threatening to kill her daughter and then carrying out the threat?"

"No, it doesn't fit," Harriet agreed. "Marine's family *isn't* much to work with, but it's almost all we've got."

Morse had been sitting quietly while the conversation ran on.

"If you talk to her family, and it sounds like you will, be very careful. These are not your average Foggy Point neighbors. If they talk to you, they'll be trying to figure what's in it for them. Using people is a way of life for that type of people.

"Don't talk to them alone, stay in pairs. And don't let any of them talk you into going anywhere with them away from the church. Not even the college sister. She may be what she appears—the one that got away., but she might still feel allegiance to her family. Just be careful. And if you find out anything at all, call the police. Either me or one of the other detectives."

"Yes, Mama," Lauren said with a salute.

"I'm serious," Morse said.

"We'll be careful," Harriet assured her. "I hope you can understand that we can't just sit and do nothing."

Morse sighed. "Unfortunately, I do. I know I sound like a broken record with you ladies, but you've been very lucky so far."

Harriet crumpled her napkin and dropped it on her plate.

"If we don't do anything, Aiden will go to jail for a crime he didn't commit. I can't live with that."

"I'll do everything I can to prevent that from happening," Morse said. "In the meantime, I've got to go back to the station to do some research on my cold case."

Connie stood up, too.

"I'd better get Lainie back to Marcel's. I'll get Wendy ready, too."

Carla picked up her plate and started gathering the others in a stack.

"Wendy isn't going to be happy when she finds out Lainie isn't coming to Connie's with us."

Aunt Beth packed her stitching back in the small bag and dropped it into her purse. She pushed back from the table.

"Okay, then, I guess I'll see you all tomorrow at the funeral."

Chapter 23

Saturday dawned clear and sunny. Harriet walked Scooter to the end of the driveway and back before breakfast. It was a long walk, given his small size, but he was going to be in the house for a longer than normal stretch, given the funeral, the church's cookie-and-coffee reception and then the gathering at Jorge's restaurant. She would take him on another long walk before they left for the service.

Sharon was in the kitchen when they got back in the house.

"Who are you going to talk to at the funeral?" she asked.

"I'm going to attempt to talk to all of them. You never know which one of us any one of them will relate to, so several of us will have a go at them."

"I'll try to listen to all of them," Sharon said. "Since I'm not from here, people will likely ignore me. I'll wear minimal makeup, and I didn't bring black pants; but I have gray pants and a gray sweater. I've had lots of practice from my modeling years. No one ever wants the models to talk. We're the classic example of 'be seen but not heard.'"

"I can't believe anyone ignores you when you walk in a room."

"They notice, but in the way you notice a new piece of furniture. They look and then comment about you to someone else, like you're deaf, and then you're just part of the background."

Harriet dispensed pet food to Fred and Scooter.

"Interesting. I'd never thought about it, but now that you mention it, you don't hear models talk very often."

Sharon smiled. "Watch, you'll see."

"We should probably get to the church a half-hour early. Meantime, I've got to put a client's quilt on my big machine and get started stitching."

"Would it bother you if I worked on my blocks while you're doing that?"

Harriet smiled. "Not at all. I'll enjoy the company."

The Loose Threads gathered in the foyer of the Methodist church thirty minutes before the service was to begin. Beth entered carrying a large vase of flowers.

"Harriet, will you unload the rest of the flowers? I parked right in front." She set her vase on a large table to the right of the double doors that opened into the sanctuary. Someone else had placed a sign-in book on the same table.

"Sure, how much have you got?"

"There are two big baskets that go on either side up front and a long flat piece that goes on the table in front of the choir area. And a small arrangement that goes by the piano."

Lauren came over.

"I'll help. I'm surprised they were able to rustle up the choir on such short notice."

Beth turned to her. "It's not the full choir. Several of the Small Stitches sing, so they volunteered. And Glynnis's youngest daughter is a soloist, so she's going to do a few songs. Mavis's hairdresser plays piano, and he's going to come from Angel Harbor," She paused. "I think it's going to be a nice service."

Harriet didn't know what to say to that. It would have helped Marine more if all these people had taken this much interest in her when she was alive. Still, she had to admit, if she'd known her before and knew she was involved in drugs, she would have thought twice before attempting to help her. She decided she'd have to reflect on that a little more when she was back at home.

Sharon helped carry flowers in, too, and when they brought them into the sanctuary, they found Jessica helping a woman Harriet didn't know attach large black bows to the end of each pew.

Lauren moved up behind Harriet.

"Okay, the bows are a bit over the top, if you ask me."

"Yeah, I was just thinking about how much effort we're putting out for Marine now that she's dead. You wonder what would have happened if the same amount of attention had been paid to her when she was still alive."

Jessica was close enough to hear the last comment.

"It wouldn't have made a difference. Probably. When people are fighting an addiction, they have to want to change. Usually as a result of hit-

141

ting bottom. Only when they themselves get so tired of being an addict that they're willing to do the work will they get better."

"Do you think she might have been trying to set Aiden up herself? Could she have been trying to do some sort of 'if you don't help me, I'll kill myself' scam?" Lauren asked Jessica.

"I suppose it's possible."

Harriet moved a couple of the flowers in the basket to the right of the podium.

"Aiden says he hadn't talked to Marine. If she were going to do something like that, it seems like she would have talked to him." She squeezed her eyes shut then opened them. "It's just so impossible. Aiden is going to end up in jail for something he had nothing to do with, and we're never going to know why."

"Come on," Lauren said and led the way back to the foyer. "We'll figure it out. We're missing something, but her family is going to reveal something to us that will get us on the right path."

"They better."

"Oh, my goodness," Jessica said and pointed to the parking area through the front window, effectively cutting off Harriet's negative spiral downward. "Lainie is coming to the funeral."

Lauren looked out the window, too.

"That's Michelle for you. She probably didn't want to come alone, so she brought the kids—never mind how stressful it might be for them."

Aunt Beth and Mavis came back into the foyer from the office hallway.

"Let's go ahead in and save a couple of pews for the rest of our group."

✂- - - ✂- - - ✂

Mr. Max played "Just As I Am" on the piano when everyone was seated, and the service began. Pastor Hafer delivered a sermon around a passage from First Corinthians and led the group in prayer. Mr. Max played "Rock of Ages" and Glynnis's daughter Trista sang "Amazing Grace" and there wasn't a dry eye in the house.

Max finished with "When the Saints Go Marching In" and "Shall We Gather at the River?"

Given the circumstance, Glynnis decided asking the quilt group to do a eulogy would be insincere and asking her family would be too unpredictable. So, they left the speaking to Pastor Hafer and told the family remembrances could be done at the reception in the fellowship hall after the main service.

Marine's family, followed by the quilters and then a group of church members who attended all funerals held at the church, left the sanctuary pew by pew. Francine was wearing the black dress the groups had paid for. The dress was a classic cut, but it was a little too tight through the hips and much too short. The overall effect was more barfly than grieving mother.

"I thought that went well, all things considered," Lauren said as she and Harriet walked down the aisle. "Now the fun begins."

"Can we postpone it for just a few minutes and swing by the ladies room?" Jessica was behind them with Sharon.

"We'll meet you downstairs in the cookie room. I want to get up close and personal with the family and see what we see."

Lauren turned on the faucet at the sink and was washing her hands when Harriet came out of her stall and joined her.

"Do you want to work the family together?"

"I know that's what Jane Morse said to do, but I'd rather take them one-on-one. I'm afraid they'll become defensive if two of us gang up on them. If we stay in the same room, we should be okay."

"I think you're right. Just don't go out of the fellowship hall."

Harriet held her three fingers up beside her face.

"Scout's honor."

"Okay, let's do this."

Aunt Beth and Mavis were standing with Marine's college-student sister by the coffee urn when Lauren and Harriet arrived. Glynnis was talking to Marine's mother, so she was out of play for now. Harriet surveyed the room for the brother. He was on the opposite side of the room, eating cookies and scanning all around, much as she and Lauren were. He was clearly weighing options.

Their eyes met, and he set his plate of cookies down on the table.

"I got brother," she said to Lauren and crossed the room. "Hi, my name is Harriet Truman," she said when she'd reached her target. "I'm very sorry for your loss."

"I know who you are. You're that chick that sticks her nose in police business. I read about you in the paper."

Harriet didn't know what to say to that, so she kept her mouth shut.

The man stuck his hand out.

"I'm Jules, nice to meet you." He had the same dark good looks as his sister but, like her, looked older than she knew him to be.

She shook his hand.

"Were you and your sister close?"

Jules laughed.

"Not how you're probably thinking. I guess you know we weren't your conventional family. We called each other when we needed something, but

143

that's about all. Foggy Point's a small enough town that we shared the same 'contacts,' if you know what I mean."

Harriet guessed he was referring to drug dealers but could only imagine.

"I had heard your sister was trying to clean up her act." She was fishing but felt no obligation to be completely honest.

Jules laughed again, but the humor didn't reach his eyes.

"Is that what she was telling people? She was in a court-ordered diversion program that made her to go to rehab a couple of months ago. I talked to her when she got out. She was looking for drugs. She did what she had to do to avoid jail."

"That's sad."

"No, that's genetics. You can't fight science. We come from bad stock. All of us were born to be addicts. When both of your parents are druggies, you're pretty much doomed. Nature or nurture, take your pick. My mom started doing drugs with us boys when my brother was thirteen and I was twelve. I'm pretty sure she slipped something into our food when we were even younger than that."

"What about your sister who's in college?"

"She's a different story. We all have different dads. Aimee's dad hooked up with our mother when he was young and she was turning tricks. His buddies took him down to the docks for his birthday. He was in a rebellious phase—or as rebellious as rich kids ever get. He had money, so she didn't have to work the streets and that amused her for a while.

"He was naive, thought she loved him, realized she was using him for his money. The old, sad story. She got pregnant, and when a paternity test proved he was the baby-daddy, his family took over. They kept us in a nice apartment with a nice companion who made sure Mom stayed off drugs and even got her GED. We went to school and had clean clothes.

"As soon as Aimee was born, they took the baby, gave Mom a fat envelope of cash and six additional months in the apartment, minus the companion. She chose not to take the opportunity. She went back to her old life, and we went with her."

"I'm sorry."

He attempted a smile.

"Don't be. I learned a long time ago this is my lot in life. Things got a lot easier when I quit trying to be something I'm not and will never be."

"Do *you* have children?"

This time he really did laugh.

"As soon as I was physically mature enough for the procedure, I went to a doctor and had that possibility eliminated. It's kind of funny, but when

I asked how much money I had to have, and I told him why I wanted the surgery, he told me he'd do it for free, and he did. My life may not amount to much, but my one gift to the world is pruning this branch of our family tree. There will never be another me."

Harriet didn't know what to say. Jules wasn't at all what she'd expected.

"Huh," he said, more to himself than her. "I hadn't thought about it, but now Marine can't have kids. My older brother Alex will be in jail long enough that he probably won't have kids. Maybe there is hope for our family after all."

"It's sad that Marine didn't have a choice in the matter. Do you have any idea what happened to her?"

"I can tell you what didn't happen. The animal doctor didn't kill her."

"Do you know who did?"

Jules leaned in and whispered in her ear.

"What's in it for me?"

She stepped back away from him.

"Really? Your sister is dead, and my boyfriend is wrongly accused, and you want to know what's in it for you?" Her voice got louder as she spoke.

He looked around to see if anyone had overheard.

"Hey, keep it down. There are cops here."

Harriet started to walk away, but Jules grabbed her arm.

"Hey, if you mistook me for a guy with a conscience or something just because I know how I got where I am, that's your problem. I'm a user in every way. Are you going to let a good man go to jail because you can't accept that?"

She removed his hand from her arm with her free hand, but she didn't move away. She looked at the floor.

"I don't believe you."

He leaned back and looked at her.

"Have I misjudged you? Are you not willing to do anything it takes to save the young doctor?"

"I'm willing to help Aiden. I'm not willing to negotiate with a con man. If you really had information that would solve your sister's murder, I think you'd tell somebody. The fact that you're trying to con me tells me you don't really know anything. When you're ready to tell me whatever it is you think you know, come find me."

Now it was Jules who looked down at the floor. It was clear he was used to women being so charmed by his good looks and apparent honesty they gave him whatever he asked for.

"Okay, you got me," he finally said. "What I really want—"

Harriet didn't get to hear what Jules wanted. Not then, anyway.

"Get away from me!" Sharon screamed from across the room.

He brushed past Harriet and pushed through the crowd to reach the action. She looked in time to see Marine's mother standing toe-to-toe with Sharon and screaming back at her.

"Oh, should I just tell all your new friends who the high-and-mighty Sharon really is? Is that what you want? They all think you're this tragic figure, but I know who you really are. You're no better than me. You just have nicer threads and a better car."

Jules reached the two women and forced himself between them.

"Come on, Mom. Time for you to go home. Let's not make a scene. Marine wouldn't have wanted that."

He stayed behind her, his arms wrapped around her, frog-marching her toward the exit doors.

She tried to break free.

"Wait, we didn't get the money. They told me they took up a collection for us. We need our money."

"Not now, Mom."

Francine looked back over her shoulder, searching the crowd to find Sharon.

"We're not done here."

"I'm sorry," Jules said, a look of embarrassment on his face. Harriet almost believed him—except for the extortion scheme he'd just tried on her moments ago.

The Loose Threads quickly gathered around Sharon, preventing any onlookers from approaching her.

"Are you okay?" Harriet asked.

Sharon shuddered.

"I'm fine." She looked at Harriet as she spoke, challenging her to argue. "I have no idea what that woman wanted from me."

Francine clearly had something on Sharon, and after Sharon's earlier revelation, Harriet felt sure she knew what it was.

Marine's mom knew about Sharon's pregnancy.

"I think we'll go powder our noses," she told the group.

Jessica started to follow them.

"I got this," Harriet told her and led Sharon out into the hall.

She bypassed the restrooms just outside the fellowship hall and continued on upstairs to the ladies room next to the sanctuary, where there would be less chance of funeral goers eavesdropping on their conversation. When the door was shut behind them, she turned to Sharon.

146

"You don't have to say anything, but based on my interaction with Marine's brother, I'm guessing Mom just tried to blackmail you."

Sharon hung her head.

"This is a nightmare that won't end."

"If you don't want to talk about it, we can leave. There's a door at the end of the hall, and my car is outside."

"I think it's a little late for that, don't you?" She sighed. "That family has been onto me since I got here. Marine must have told her mother my name, or maybe her mom saw the class list. We all received a list of class members before we got here, so people who lived within driving distance could carpool if they wanted."

"I didn't think she was that close to her mom. She was staying with Aiden's sister, after all."

"She couldn't stay with her mom, but that doesn't mean they didn't talk. In the end, it doesn't matter. Somehow, Francine found out I was coming, and she was ready."

Harriet leaned against the sink.

"How does Francine know who you are, much less have any information to blackmail you with?"

"One giant stroke of bad luck. That small town I retreated to, where my aunt lived, it also contained the rock Francine crawled out from under. I don't know how she ended up there, since I now know her parents were in Foggy Point, but it doesn't matter.

"My aunt took me to a small clinic in town. They also ran a free clinic, and Francine was a regular customer. When a pregnant teen shows up in a town like that, only to leave seven months later, it doesn't take a genius to figure out what's going on. I assume she saw my modeling work in an ad somewhere after that and filed it away as a future opportunity."

"Do you think she's that bright?" Harriet asked.

"Clever is more like it. People like her can be really stupid in most facets of life, but when money's involved suddenly they're Einstein."

"So, she saw your name, remembered you as an unwed teen turned successful model, and guessed you wouldn't want the world to know about your past."

"That's it in a nutshell. She told Marine and had her approach me. Foolishly, I gave them some money, thinking that would be the end of it."

"And of course, it wasn't?"

"Not even a little. Once Marine was gone, mommy dearest contacted me directly."

"That was her, yesterday morning?"

147

"I thought I saw your car, down in the industrial area yesterday morning. Yes, that was her, and I gave her more money and told her that was it."

"For someone like her, no amount is ever enough."

"I know that. I do. I don't care anymore if people know I had a child. My career is virtually over. My fear is...and I realize it's irrational...is that Francine knows who my baby is and where it is."

Harriet stood up straight.

"Has she said that?"

"No. She's taunting me with her threats to tell the world I had a baby. I just can't be sure she doesn't know more."

"But you've no reason to believe she does."

Sharon turned to look directly into Harriet's eyes.

"I can't have my child find out about me from some horrible drug addict."

Harriet put her hands on Sharon's upper arms.

"It won't come to that. We'll figure something out."

Sharon's face turned a blotchy red, and tears slid down her cheeks.

"It's so unfair," she sobbed. "One weekend. I've followed the rules all my life except for that one weekend so many years ago, and it just won't end. Everyone else makes crazy mistakes in their teens, and they move on. I'm a good person. I give money to charity, I serve meals at the homeless shelter at Christmas. Now all everyone is going to remember about me is I got pregnant in my teens and hid it from the public. They'll know all my fresh-faced teen modeling shoots were a lie." She sagged against the counter, the agony etched into her face.

"I don't think it will be as bad as all that. If people had found out when you were still doing those teen magazine shoots it might have been news for a few minutes, but it was years ago. It's unlikely to make the national news, and your child probably has no idea who you are, in any case."

"What if Francine knows the adoptive parents? What if she tries to blackmail them? She could demand money for her silence."

"Let's not borrow trouble. I doubt Francine is that clever. Did the adoptive parents ever come to the clinic where you did your prenatal care?"

Sharon sniffled. "No, they took the baby from the hospital; I never saw them."

"Then Francine doesn't know who they are, either."

"She might know if someone adopted a baby in the area."

"You're assuming the adoptive parents lived in that small town. They could have come from anywhere. Are your parents or your aunt still alive?"

148

"My mother and my aunt are. My dad passed away a few years ago. But they've never talked about it. I came back to Oakland, and it was like it had never happened. Except in my dreams. My mother changed the subject whenever I asked. My therapist told me to leave it in the past and forget about it."

"Maybe it's time to get some answers from them. Time may have changed them, too. Your mom might like the idea of knowing more about her grandchild. And you aren't a scared teenager anymore. You can demand answers. Even if they don't know the adoptive parents personally, they probably know if they were from the area or not, and they can tell you who the adoption agency is. If it was a private adoption, they probably arranged it in Oakland. They could be in California."

Sharon swiped at her tears. Harriet waved her hand in front of the towel dispenser and then caught the sheet it spat out and handed it to her roommate.

"Come on, splash a little water on your face while I use the restroom, and we can go back down before someone comes looking for us."

✂- - - ✂- - - ✂

Things were back to normal when Harriet and Sharon returned to the fellowship hall. Francine and Jules were gone, and people were standing in groups of two or three eating cookies and drinking coffee and lemonade.

Harriet found her aunt with Mavis and Connie by the silver coffee urn.

"What did I miss?"

Jessica came up and edged Sharon away from Harriet.

"Are you okay? Would you like some coffee or lemonade?"

Sharon indicated coffee, and Jessica poured and then walked her away to a quiet corner where she was partly concealed from the room by a potted palm. Beth watched them go then turned to Harriet.

"We should be asking you that. I assume you know what's going on."

Harriet pressed her lips together.

"I do, but I'm afraid it's not my story to tell. I can say this. Sharon shares a history with Marine's mother, and being the fine upstanding citizen she is, Mom has been blackmailing Sharon."

Lauren joined them while they were talking.

"You know Sharon better than we do. Is there any chance she offed Marine to stop the blackmail?"

Harriet thought for a moment.

"If she did, it didn't solve the problem. Mom was hitting her up for more money yesterday morning."

149

"Seriously," Mavis said. "*Could* she have killed Marine?"

"It doesn't make sense, but I really don't know. It would have made more sense to kill Francine. And I'm not sure how or why she would have set Aiden up."

"But it's not impossible." Lauren persisted. "She was home getting over a headache the morning Marine was killed, if I remember right."

"You be sure and lock your bedroom at night, just in case," Aunt Beth cautioned Harriet.

"Does my room have a lock?"

Beth looked at her.

"What do you think those big keyholes are for? The keys to all the bedrooms are in the top left drawer of the sideboard in the dining room."

"Good to know. I'd never have looked there. I figured the keys were long gone."

"Every lock in the house works, and there are two keys for each of them. Lauren tugged on her lower lip.

"Have we stayed long enough yet?"

Harriet glanced past her to the rest of the room.

"I'd like to go talk to the college sister before we leave."

"Knock yourself out," Lauren told her.

<hr />

"I'm sorry for your loss," Harriet told the young blond woman after she crossed the room and joined the cluster of women around her.

Aimee Plummer reached out and shook Harriet's hand.

"Thank you. It's so generous of your community to give my sister such a wonderful memorial."

"I didn't know your sister well, but it's very sad to see anyone pass on before their time."

Aimee looked at her without speaking for a moment while the other women drifted away. They looked relieved to have escaped. Aimee tried to swallow a smile. She finally laughed.

"I'm sorry. Those poor women were trying to say nice things about my sister." Her expression became serious again. "I actually haven't known Marine that long myself."

Harriet didn't say anything, hoping her silence would encourage the young woman to unburden herself.

"My father didn't want me to meet my mother. He'd told me about her and my half-brothers and sisters when I was younger. He said the reality was not as pleasant as I was probably imagining, and of course, he was right."

150

"You're lucky you lived with your father."

Aimee sighed. "I've always wondered why I got to be the one to get away. I mean, I didn't do anything different than Marine or Jules or any of them, yet my life was privileged in every way while they always wondered where their next meal was coming from."

"Oh, sweetie, you can't take responsibility for the choices Francine made or the results of those choices," Harriet counseled her. "All you can do is be the best you can be."

"I've been trying. And I've been to a counselor. She says I have survivor's guilt, even though I didn't go through any of the bad stuff they did."

"Would you like something to drink?" Harriet asked her.

Aimee smiled gratefully at her.

"Some coffee would be nice."

Harriet went to the food table and poured a cup of coffee. She put two cookies on a paper plate with a napkin; she noticed as she was walking back that Michelle had entered the fellowship hall with Lainie and Etienne in tow.

Aimee took the offering. She sipped the coffee and then nodded in Michelle's direction.

"Who's that woman?"

"No one of consequence," Harriet told her.

"No, really. Who is she?"

"Her name is Michelle Jalbert."

"So, that's the infamous Michelle." Aimee looked her up and down before speaking again. "I'm working on my bachelors in social work and want to get my masters, too. You have to have practical experience to get into a good graduate school, so I volunteer at a drug treatment program." She lowered her voice. "My dad doesn't know this, but after I met Marine when I was eighteen, we stayed in touch. I told her about the place I was working, and I guess they'd already planted the seed when she was in the court-mandated program. She decided to give it a try.

"She'd been clean and sober for a month when her friend there..." She gestured with her coffee cup. "...came and took her away to live with her in Foggy Point last week."

"Michelle's been working with a legal aid group. Maybe she was working on a legal case for Marine and needed her to be close at hand." Harriet wasn't sure why she was defending Aiden's sister. "Marine lived with Michelle's mom for a while at one point when Francine wouldn't let her stay at home. Apparently, Michelle's mom knew Marine's grandparents in France."

151

"I didn't know that." Aimee said. "Other than Marine, I know very little about my maternal roots."

Harriet was staring across the room, listening to Aimee's story, when she noticed Lainie waving to her. She waved back, and Lainie skipped across the open space to stand beside her.

Aimee smiled at her.

"Aimee, meet Lainie. Lainie, this is Aimee. She's Marine's little sister."

"I'm sorry for your loss," Lainie intoned formally. Clearly, she'd been prepped for this event.

"Thank you, honey. It's very sweet of you."

Lainie stood quietly and fidgeted for a moment.

"Harriet, can I come work on my quilt?"

"You're a quilter?" Aimee asked.

"Harriet's teaching me." Lainie looked at Harriet, watching for approval while she spoke. "I'm making a four-patch quilt."

"That's right, and you're a very good student. You can come today if your mom says it's okay."

Lainie dashed back to her mother's side to seek the required permission.

Aimee took a bite of her chocolate chip cookie.

"She's a cutie," she said when she was finished.

"That she is." Harriet watched Lainie negotiate with her mother then turned back to Aimee. "I better go nail down the details. Again, I really am sorry for your loss. It was very brave of you to come here by yourself today."

Aimee blushed. "Not that brave. My dad is parked just out of sight down the road, waiting for me to call for rescue."

"Hey, it never hurts to have a back-up plan. Are you and your dad coming to the gathering at Tico's Tacos?"

"My dad doesn't want to see my bio-mom, so no," she said, chuckling. "He only agreed to bring me to this part when I told him Marine had been coming to the program I was working at. He didn't want the people there to think we were awful."

"Under the circumstances, I can understand why he doesn't want to cross paths with Francine."

"You and the quilters have been more than kind. I'm glad I came."

Aunt Beth and Mavis came over as Aimee went to Glynnis Miller to make her final goodbyes. Beth reached out and patted Harriet on the upper arm.

"Are you doing okay?"

"I'm fine."

Mavis followed Aimee with her eyes.

"The sister seems nice. I didn't talk to her much, but she seems to have escaped the family curse."

"I learned something interesting," Harriet told them. "Aimee is getting a degree in social work and is volunteering at some kind of rehab program. Marine was in her program until Michelle came and got her out."

"That *is* interesting," Beth said thoughtfully.

Mavis turned her attention back to Harriet and Beth.

"Michelle is doing legal aid work now. Marine might have needed to come back for legal reasons. I wonder if Lauren can look that up on her computer."

"Look what up on my computer?" Lauren had joined the group while they were talking.

Mavis explained, and Lauren assured her it would be easy enough.

Harriet glanced at the time on her smartphone.

"I'm going to run by the jail before I go to the reception at Tico's. Visiting hours are limited, and today is Aiden's day for visitors."

"Do you want company?" Lauren asked.

"I'm not sure how many visitors he can have at a time, and in any case, he has to have put you on his visitors' list first."

"Okay, then, I guess we'll see you at the reception."

Chapter 24

*H*arriet felt like *she* was the criminal by the time she was finally led to the visitors' room; she'd been searched, lectured and had all her possessions put in a locker.

Aiden was sitting at a table in the small cafeteria-like room. Vending machines lined one wall, and windows facing onto a cement patio filled the opposite side. The remaining walls were painted cement blocks. A guard sat on the far side of the room reading a newspaper.

She couldn't see his face. His head was down, his elbows on the table, hands on either side of his head. She came over and sat opposite him. When he finally looked up, she could see what he'd been hiding. One eye was swollen nearly shut, and he sported a neat line of stitches on his cheekbone.

"Oh, Aiden," she cried. "What…?"

"It's nothing. They put us all outside together. One of Marine's drug dealer friends is in here. Believe it or not, he looks worse than I do."

"You're right. I find that hard to believe."

"Uganda was a very harsh place. Because we had drugs with us for the animals, we were targets. We took self-defense classes stateside before we left, and then we took more classes once we got there. These clowns only think they're tough. They wouldn't last a week in Africa."

"Will they keep you by yourself now?"

He laughed. "Naw. This is like any group. You have to establish yourself. I won't have any problems now."

"That's not very comforting. How do you know the next guy won't have a knife or something worse?"

"This is jail, not prison. Besides, there are a couple of bikers in here who were clients; I've patched their pit bulls a time or two. After the dealer came to, they told him he better not try anything like that again."

"Does your lawyer have any good news?"

"He has investigators digging into Marine's background, but nothing yet."

"I talked to Marine's half-brother Jules at the funeral. He says he knows something, but he wanted me to pay him for the information. I told him no, but maybe I should have said yes."

"Knowing that family, he's blowing smoke. They're all users, in every sense of the word. I'd guess he's trying to take advantage of my misfortune."

"Did they tell you the homeless guy who called you was Marine's step-dad?"

"I take it your use of the word was means he's dead."

"Tom was searching the woods and found his body."

Aiden was silent for a moment.

"I wonder what that means."

"Either someone was setting you both up, or he set you up for somebody and that somebody was eliminating loose ends."

Aiden's normally angular face was drawn and pale with the exception of his eye. For all his bravado about his fighting skills, Harriet could see that sitting in jail was taking a toll on him.

"Did you know Marine's brother, or her dad when he was alive? Back when you were in high school or anything?"

"Her dad, no. Her brother Jules, yes. I actually liked him. He always seemed a little sharper than the rest of the bunch. The other brother, the one who's in jail, was always in one sort of trouble or another. Everyone always said he'd end up in jail."

"Do you think Jules could have killed her?"

"No, those kids were loyal to each other. With the mother they had, they had to stick together. I could see Francine being involved before I'd believe either of the boys did anything. And before you ask, I don't think Francine was involved. I can't see her being able to plan and execute such a detailed plan. Someone, somehow, got my saliva and hair and put them on Marine's body."

"I'll see if Detective Morse is able to tell us how much saliva was found."

Aiden sat up straighter and looked at her, alert now.

"What're you thinking?"

"I'm just wondering if someone could have taken a soda cup or something from your garbage."

He reached across the table and put his hand over hers. The guard looked at them over the top of his paper then went back to reading.

Aiden sighed. "I'm trying really hard to stay positive, but the longer I'm in here, the more I wonder if they're going to find the real killer. What if they convict me? They've already suggested to my attorney they would consider charging me with voluntary manslaughter or something less if I'd plead guilty and save them the expense of a trial."

"But you didn't do anything," she protested.

"I have to be realistic. If they go forward with the first-degree murder charge, I would get life in prison. My lawyer doesn't think they can come up with special circumstances that would bring the death penalty into play, but I didn't think they could charge an innocent person with murder, so I have to consider the possibility."

"Please tell me you aren't considering pleading guilty to something you didn't do."

"Harriet, I have to be realistic. For voluntary manslaughter, I could get as little as ten years. Twenty would be the worst-case scenario."

"But you'd lose your license."

He gave a sharp laugh.

"I think that would be the least of my problems. I can go back to Uganda. They don't care if you have a license or not."

"Oh, Aiden. I can't believe you're even thinking about it."

"I'm thinking about how I would survive spending the rest of my life locked up."

Harriet pulled her hand back from his.

"I'm going to have to figure out who really killed Marine before you have to make a decision."

Aiden's lips twitched up at the corners.

"I do love you." He paused for a moment. "But please...promise me you won't do anything crazy."

She smiled at him.

"Me? Never."

They both stood up. Aiden looked over at the guard.

"We done?" the man asked. He followed Aiden out one door and when the lock clicked, the other door opened and a different guard ushered Harriet out.

✂- - - ✂- - - ✂

The Loose Threads and a few of the Small Stitches were already seated at the big table in the back room at Tico's Tacos. Lainie came skipping up behind Harriet as she took her coat off.

"Mom said to tell you she's dropping Etienne off with me and you should ask Tom to take him to Mr. Renfro's house when we're done here."

Harriet glanced in the direction Lainie had just come from, and there, at a side table, sat Etienne, drawing in a sketchbook and dipping corn chips into a bowl of warm queso.

"Does Tom know about this plan?" she asked.

Lainie made an exaggerated shrug.

"I don't know."

Sharon got up from the table and came over.

"Do you want to come sit by me? We need to make a plan for our quilting session."

Lainie's face lit up, and she began chattering to Sharon about her plan for her next quilt.

Harriet looked around the room, but Tom hadn't arrived yet.

Aunt Beth pulled out the chair beside hers.

"Here, sit down before you fall down. You look terrible. What's wrong? I mean, besides all this." She gestured at the assembled group.

"I stopped by the jail to see Aiden. He'd been in a fight."

"Oh, honey, is he okay?"

"Physically, yes. Emotionally, not so much. He's talking about taking a plea deal to a lesser charge because he's afraid he'll be convicted and get life in prison."

Mavis leaned in from Beth's other side.

"Surely we aren't to that point yet. It hasn't even been a week yet."

Harriet slumped into her chair.

"For Aiden, I'm sure it feels like years. And the police get to lie to him. They can tell him anything. His lawyer is probably telling him not to panic and not to listen to them, but I know Aiden. He's obsessing twenty-four-seven."

"Did you set him straight?" Mavis asked.

"I told him we'd figure this out. We know he didn't kill Marine. We just have to find out who did."

Aunt Beth looked past her to the front door.

"Francine is coming."

Lauren was standing across the room on the other side of the table. Harriet gestured to catch her attention and pointed at Francine. Lauren jostled Jessica and, when she had her attention, glanced at the door and then back at Sharon.

"Hey, guys, how about we go on over to Harriet's and start working on those quilts?" she said.

She got Sharon up and grabbed Lainie's coat and bag. Jessica collected Sharon's purse and coat and handed them to her as Lauren led them toward the kitchen.

Jessica turned sharply and went to the side table where Etienne was still drawing pictures in his book. She gathered book and coat and hustled him toward the rest of the group.

"We're going to take a little tour of the kitchen on our way out," Harriet heard Lauren say as they disappeared.

"I'm surprised Francine showed up here after that scene at the church." Mavis whispered.

Glynnis went over and asked Francine if she could get her something to drink.

"Have you got any beer?" the woman asked in a loud voice.

"I'm not sure we have alcohol available," Glynnis told her, blushing.

"No beer? What kind of Mexican place is this?" Francine went on.

Jorge came out of the kitchen with two bottles of beer in one hand and a frosty glass in the other.

"Señora, would you care for Mexican or American?"

Francine grabbed both bottles.

Jorge herded her to the table and pulled out a chair for her.

"Let me get you some food to go with that." He went back to the kitchen and returned with a large plate of nachos. When she was settled, he came around the table and sat down beside Harriet.

"This is the best I can do," he told her and Beth in a quiet voice. "A couple of beers and a belly full of food, and she should settle down."

A look passed between him and Aunt Beth.

"Thanks. We were just saying it was surprising she showed up here after the scene at the church," Beth said.

"Lauren told me what was going on as she and the others sneaked out through the kitchen. I put lots of beans and cheese on her nachos—lots of calories. Wait till she's on her second beer, and then you can talk to her and see if she knows anything."

Harriet looked up at him with appreciation.

"Aren't you the sly one."

"We can't let Aiden sit in jail any longer than he has to. I talked to him on the phone, and he's not doing well."

"I know," Harriet told him. "I went to see him before I came here. He didn't look good."

"He sounded very down. He was talking about plea deals," Jorge said.

"I told him we were going to figure out who really did it so it wouldn't come to that."

Jorge smiled. "I told him the same thing." He looked over at Francine. "I've done what I can. See what you can get out of that one."

He picked up two empty plates and took them back to the kitchen.

Mavis, Aunt Beth and Harriet made their way around the table, stopping and talking to Glynnis about how the retreat had gone along the way. When Francine was on her second beer they approached her. Aunt Beth sat down in the chair next to her.

"Are you doing okay?"

Francine looked up. Mavis stood by her shoulder.

"Can I get you anything?"

"I wouldn't mind another cold brew." Francine gave her a weary smile. "It's been a long day."

Mavis headed for the kitchen. Harriet sat down next to Aunt Beth but kept silent.

Aunt Beth reached out and patted Francine's shoulder.

"It's always sad losing a child." She paused. "It must be especially hard with her just having come back to town after being away for so long."

Francine's eyes were red, but Harriet suspected it was more from the beer than from tears.

"You know my Marine was an actress. She played the maid on *The Edge of Tomorrow*."

"Yes, I'd heard she was an actress," Harriet said.

Francine picked up her beer glass and sipped at it, seemingly unaware it was empty. She set it down on the table and looked toward the kitchen.

"You know, the reason she came back to town was so she could play Elvira in *Blythe Spirit*. Did you know? Michelle Jalbert hooked her up with the director. She's had a little trouble, my baby, but she was making a comeback. She said Elvira was the lead role. And now…"

A tear slid down her cheek, and Aunt Beth handed her an unused napkin. Francine stared across the room. Mavis came back from the kitchen carrying a bottle of beer. Harriet was sure her friend had been listening over the intercom and had waited for Francine to stop talking before bringing another drink.

"We're all very sorry for your loss," Aunt Beth said as she stood up. She patted Francine on the back and moved back around the table. Harriet followed with Mavis, and they gathered their purses and coats and headed to the door.

Harriet paused and put her palm to her forehead.

"What?" Aunt Beth asked her.

"Tom never showed up. I'm supposed to pass Etienne off so Tom can take him to the Renfros'…or something. Michelle passed instructions through Lainie, and I don't know if Tom is in on it or not."

Aunt Beth opened the door to the parking lot.

"That's easy enough to solve. Call the man."

Harriet pulled out her phone and dialed Tom's number. When he didn't answer, she left a message asking him to call and let her know if he planned on picking up Etienne and offering to drop him at the Renfros' if this was the first he was hearing about the plan.

✂- - - ✂- - - ✂

"Can anyone join this party?" Harriet asked when she came through her studio door. Sharon and Lainie were sitting at the two sewing machines, stitching four patch blocks together. Lauren was ironing seams for them, and Jessica sat at the cutting table with Etienne drawing quilt patterns on graph paper and coloring them with colored pencils.

Lauren looked up from the ironing board.

"You can join if you fetch some snacks for the two hoodlums. It seems they escaped Tico's without filling their bellies."

Harriet crossed to the kitchen door.

"Let me take Scooter out; then I'm sure I can find a dry bread crust or something."

Lainie looked up, her eyes big, checking to be sure Harriet was joking.

"We already took the little rat out. Carter's in the kitchen with him if your cat hasn't eaten them both." That got a giggle from the kids. "You think I'm kidding? Fred's a tough customer."

"I'll let you know," Harriet said over her shoulder as she disappeared through the door.

The phone machine was beeping when she came into the kitchen. She pressed the button and heard Connie's voice.

"I have some information for you. I have to go to the store later, and I can drop by on my way home."

She raised her eyebrows. It must be something interesting if Connie felt she needed to deliver it in person.

Harriet greeted the two dogs, who were dancing around her feet. She noticed that, contrary to Lauren's expectations, Fred had, in fact, helped the little dogs get into trouble, having opened one of the kitchen cabinets and knocked several granola bars onto the floor. The dogs had ripped through the packing, leaving a trail of oats, nuts and torn paper in their wake.

For his part, Fred had found the butter dish Harriet had left out, pushed the lid off and eaten half a stick of butter.

"I hope you have a cleansing experience after all that grease," she told her delinquent cat.

Fred sat on the counter in dignified silence.

Harriet cleaned up the mess before digging in her snack cabinet and pulling out the box of ginger snaps. She poured two glasses of milk and got a plate for the cookies before returning to the studio. Lauren took the cookies from her and filled the plate, setting it on the cutting table and pulling up a chair for Lainie. Harriet put a cup of milk at each place.

When the kids were settled, the women went to the reception area by the door and sat down.

"Anyone want tea or coffee?" Harriet asked them.

Jessica held her cup up. "We all helped ourselves, so just fix yourself some and tell us what Francine said.

Lauren had pulled two wheeled chairs up opposite the two wingback chairs, and when Harriet had her drink fixed, she sat down.

"I already knew Francine was a bit of a wreck, and she didn't do anything to change my opinion, so I'm not sure how reliable anything she said is."

"Okay, we'll factor that in," Jessica told her. "What did she say?"

"The most interesting thing is, she claims her daughter came back to Foggy Point because..." Harriet lowered her voice to a whisper, keeping her eyes on Lainie and Etienne to see if they were listening. "She said Michelle had arranged for Marine to have a lead role in the play that's coming up at the Foggy Point Theater."

Sharon straightened in her chair and pulled her eyebrows together.

"Do you believe that? She had a minor, barely-a-speaking role on a soap opera. Somehow, I can't see her qualifying for a lead role in anything."

Jessica sipped her tea, holding her cup with two hands.

"Especially in the shape she was in."

Lauren also glanced at the kids and then spoke in a whisper.

"I find it hard to believe Michelle arranged anything for someone other than herself. I mean, I know we're all supposed to buy the new Michelle, and I could believe her doing legal aid work for Marine, because that helps her get reinstated with the bar, but doing something purely for the benefit of someone else? Never happen."

Everyone drank their tea in silence while they thought about the new information.

Lainie came over to Harriet, interrupting their quiet.

"Can I use my phone to call the Renfros for Etienne? He wants to know what time he's supposed to go there."

"Do you have the number?" Harriet asked.

She nodded, using her whole body in the motion. Harriet smiled.

"Okay, I guess you can call them. Let me know what they say, okay?"

Lainie skipped back over to the cutting table and said something to Etienne they couldn't hear, but he dug in his pocket and brought out a wrinkled card he handed to his sister. She looked at it and started pressing buttons on her cell phone.

"Isn't she a little young for a phone?" Jessica asked.

"I thought so," Harriet said. "She said her mother is letting her use a spare one just while they're staying with Uncle Marcel. She says she has to give it back when she returns to Aiden's."

Lainie set her phone on the cutting table when she'd finished talking. She turned toward the tea drinkers.

"They said they talked to Tom, and he'll come pick Etienne up in an hour. I'm supposed to go over there with them."

Harriet looked at the stack of blocks beside her machine.

"Finish a few more blocks, and we can sew some strips."

A soft tap sounded on the studio door, followed by Connie entering.

"Did you get my message on your machine?"

"I did," Harriet told her. "I'm very curious to hear your news."

"Would you like tea?" Jessica asked her.

Connie smiled at her.

"Yes, please." She slipped her jacket off and hung it on the back of the chair Sharon wheeled over to her then sat down. She took the cup of tea from Jessica, dunking the teabag up and down a few times before wrapping the bag string around the cup handle. Like the others, she glanced at the kids before speaking.

"I got the phone number for the tutor from Marcel's wife. It took a few tries, but I finally got a call back from the woman. I fibbed a little. I told her we were helping Detective Morse gather evidence to try to find out who killed Marine."

"You go, girl," Lauren said.

Harriet glared at her.

"Sorry," she whispered.

Connie continued. "She was reluctant at first, but once she started, I couldn't get her to stop talking."

Jessica leaned forward in her chair.

"What did she say?"

"I asked her if she and Marine had talked much. She said Marine confided in her almost as soon as she got here. Marine said she thought she was making a big mistake. She said she was involved in a program in Seattle and was getting her life together, but she'd wanted to be an actress since she was a little girl. Michelle told her she could get her a lead role in the next play at the Foggy Point Theater."

"So Francine was telling the truth," Sharon said.

"Do we think Michelle could really do that?" Harriet asked.

Connie shrugged. "That's what she asked the tutor when she got to Aiden's. The tutor said she wasn't around Michelle enough to know for sure. Like us, her observation says no, but she said she was usually in a room on the third floor, so she didn't hear phone calls or anything like that. She said the nanny would know. She doesn't know if Marine ever talked to the nanny. She gave me Madame du Cloutier's phone number, and I left her a message. I haven't heard back yet."

Lauren pulled her tablet from her bag and started tapping on it. Connie sipped her tea and wiped her mouth with a napkin.

"The tutor told me it was clear Marine had started using drugs again, although she said it seemed like she was trying not to use. Marine would be real shaky and sweaty, she'd go for walks and take showers, and eventually, it would be clear she'd taken some sort of medication."

"Are you finding anything?" Harriet asked Lauren.

"If I'm reading this right, the three leads in the upcoming play are already cast. They're from Seattle."

"Is it *Blythe Spirit?*" Connie asked.

"That's what it says here. They have a casting call for some of the other roles."

Harriet looked at the kids again, but they were engrossed in their respective projects.

"Maybe Michelle could get her into one of those and overstated its importance."

Sharon set her teacup back on the drink table.

"Could you ask her?"

Connie, Lauren and Harriet started speaking at once, each explaining why that would never happen. They laughed.

"That was a no," Harriet said finally.

Lainie stood up and came over to the reception area.

"I'm ready to sew blocks together now."

"Okay," Harriet told her and went over to the sewing machine. Sharon got up.

"I guess I might as well sew some more of mine together, too." she said.
Lauren put her tablet back in her bag.
"I'll take the dogs out again."

✂- - - ✂- - - ✂

Lainie had completed three strips made up of seven six-inch blocks each
when Harriet's phone signaled she had a text. She glanced at the message
and then read it out loud.

"It says Tom is leaving his meeting and will be here in about fifteen
minutes. Time to clean up."

Connie came over and held up two of the finished strips.

"Oh, *mi'ja*, these are wonderful."

Lainie's cheeks turned pink, and she smiled. Harriet put her arm around
the girl's shoulders and gave her a quick squeeze.

"See, we'll make an expert quilter out of you yet."

"I'm going to show my strips to Mrs. Renfro when we get there," Lainie
said as she carefully folded her quilt pieces and packed them in her quilting bag.

✂- - - ✂- - - ✂

Etienne and Lainie were sitting in the wingback chairs, coats in their laps
and bags sitting on the floor beside them, when Tom knocked on the studio door.

"Has anyone seen two lost children?" he said in a loud voice as he came
in. He strode past the children in the chairs and made an exaggerated show
of looking under tables and around corners. Lainie and Etienne followed
him, giggling.

Jessica grinned and stood with her hands on her hips.

"I haven't seen any children, have you, Connie?"

Etienne tugged on Tom's jacket pocket.

"Here we are," he said.

Tom whirled around. "Where have you been hiding?" He tickled the
boy, which sent him into gales of laughter. When they finished tussling,
he stood up straight again. "Harriet, can I talk to you and Lauren in the
kitchen for a moment?"

Connie and Jessica looked from Harriet to Tom and back again.

"Can you entertain the kids for a bit?" Harriet asked.

"Of course," Connie said.

✂- - - ✂- - - ✂

Harriet closed the door behind her and turned to Tom.

"What's wrong?"

He reached out and squeezed her arm.

"Nothing. I mean, nothing bad. I heard a piece of information from Joyce. I just didn't want to talk about anything else in front of the kids. Etienne has been talking to Mr. Renfro. He and Lainie don't understand why they're still living at Marcel's and why they've barely seen their mother."

"So, what did Joyce have to say?" she asked.

"I took some canned goods out to the camp, and while we were loading it into the storage boxes, I was asking her about Marine's father. She said he'd been living in the woods for a while. He was an alcoholic, but Joyce thinks his real problem was dementia. Chances are he was homeless and drinking because of that."

"So, whoever got him to call Aiden probably tricked him into it."

Lauren sat down at the kitchen table.

"Maybe they offered him money or shelter. Depending on how far his dementia had progressed, he might not have remembered he'd sold out his daughter after he'd done it."

Harriet paced across the kitchen.

"That still leaves us with the big question of who. Who would want to set up Aiden? Who knew Marine's father had dementia? And who had access to Aiden's saliva?"

"The real question is: Who even knew that guy was Marine's father?" Lauren pointed out.

Tom sat down opposite her at the table.

"Maybe that part was coincidence. Whoever was setting Aiden up needed someone to make a false call. It wasn't important who. I suspect the perpetrator was as surprised as anyone in this town to discover the relationship between Marine and the drunk in the forest."

Harriet joined them.

"That's interesting, but I'm not sure it gets us anywhere." Tom's shoulders sagged, and she reached over and put her hand on his. "Thank you for telling us. I'm sure it will make sense when we know more."

"It has to be someone close to one or both of the families," Lauren said thoughtfully. "I wonder if someone from the French community is involved. I can look and see who else in Foggy Point is French. Don't they have some sort of local association?"

"There's a French-American School of Puget Sound," Tom said. "Aiden's mother was involved in founding it and was a regular donor. It was started twenty years ago."

Harriet and Lauren stared at him.

"Don't look at me like I just grew a second head. I did the plans for an addition they made to the school some years ago."

"Hard to imagine what could have happened at the school that would cause someone to kill Marine and blame Aiden," Harriet said with a sigh.

"I know," Tom said. He stood up. "I'm grasping at straws like everyone else. I better take the kids to the Renfros. Let me know if you need anything, or if you hear anything."

Lauren and Harriet followed him back to the studio. He took the kids and left.

"Did he have earth-shattering news?" Connie asked when the door was shut once again.

Harriet recounted Tom's news.

Connie shifted in her chair. "Interesting, but it doesn't really help, does it?"

Harriet ran her hands through her hair.

"We're missing something."

"Well, we aren't going to solve it sitting around here," Lauren looked at Jessica. "You ready to head to the homestead?"

Jessica picked up her purse.

"Can we get in our jammies and watch old movies?"

Lauren rolled her eyes.

"Whatever." She went to the kitchen door, called Carter, and followed Jessica to the door.

Connie followed suit and gathered her things.

"Can I give you the nanny's phone number to follow up with? I have Carla and Wendy coming over tonight. I think we should try calling again, but I told Wendy I'd watch the princess movie with her, and it'll be too late for me to call if she doesn't fall asleep right away."

"Sure, no problem." Harriet crossed to her desk and got a piece of paper and a pencil.

"I'm going to go upstairs and take a bubble bath," Sharon announced.

"Okay, I'm going to work a little on my customer quilt," Harriet told her as she handed Connie the paper.

Connie wrote the information and gave the paper back.

"Let me know if you hear anything."

Chapter 25

Scooter was curled up on his bed under Harriet's desk sleeping; Harriet had been stitching for an hour. Her customer wanted a dense stitching pattern that took all of her concentration.

It was a relief to be by herself, not thinking about Aiden or anyone else. She felt a little guilty when she stopped to stretch her back and realized that, while she had the liberty to take a mental break from it all, Aiden had to live it without relief.

She was lost in thought when her dog went flying off his pillow to the studio door, barking for all he was worth.

"Scooter, hush." The dog redoubled his efforts. Through the cacophony, she heard someone tapping. She picked Scooter up and went to the side window to see who was on her doorstep.

"Jules?" she said through the window.

He leaned from the doorstep toward the window.

"Can I come in?"

"What do you want?"

"Let me in, and I'll tell you what I know. I promise."

Harriet looked away from the window. Sharon was upstairs watching TV after her bath. She'd probably come down if she heard loud voices. Harriet decided she'd let him in but take him to the kitchen to be closer to Sharon's hearing range.

She stepped to the door and opened it.

"Come in." Scooter was still barking for all he was worth, wriggling and twisting. "Let's go to the kitchen."

Jules reached out and patted Scooter's head. The dog fell silent and started wagging his tail.

"You little traitor," Harriet whispered to him. "Would you like something to drink?" she said in a louder voice.

He went to the table and sat down.

"Water would be good."

Harriet got a glass and filled it from the refrigerator dispenser. She set the glass in front of him and sat down.

"Why are you here?" she asked in a flat voice.

He studied her face for a moment.

"I'm sorry about earlier," he started and then watched for her reaction. "I shouldn't have said I would sell you what I know. I'd like to think I wouldn't have taken your money."

"I'm supposed to believe you now? That's a bell you can't unring." A cloud of musky men's cologne shrouded him. Harriet turned her head to the side and took a deep breath.

"I'm not the bad guy here."

Harriet supposed the sort of women he spent time with were impressed by the big blue eyes, leather jacket and trendy cologne. She was not. She rubbed her face and then looked at him.

"I've had a long day. For that matter, I've had a long week. I don't really care if you're a misunderstood hero or Jack the Ripper. If you have something to say, spit it out. Otherwise, please leave."

"So much for the small talk." He sat back in his chair. "I think you're looking in the wrong direction. In this town, my family is the scum of the earth, and the high and mighty Jalberts can do no wrong. I know my mom and dad have, or had, problems, but they would never do anything to hurt one of us kids."

Harriet stared at him and wondered again why he was really here.

"Okay, I know my dad had problems. He was a longtime drug user and alcoholic. If you live long enough with both of those habits, you develop health problems. Dad had alcoholic neuropathy and anemia, and lately it became clear he had dementia.

"He was never much of a father, but he was my dad. I hadn't seen him in years, but when he surfaced again and it was obvious what shape he was in, I started seeing him. I took him his iron pills and made sure he was eating. And I know it probably wasn't the best thing for him, but I'd take him a fifth of bourbon. I mean, he was never going to really get better at this point, so what was the point in trying to detox him."

He stopped and sipped his water.

168

"Anyway, a week or so ago, I went to find him in his favorite little clearing in the woods, and I heard him talking to someone besides himself. I stepped behind a tree and waited to see who came back out." He paused to make sure his audience was paying attention. "It was Michelle Jalbert."

Harriet let out the breath she hadn't realized she was holding.

"Oh, my gosh." Her head was literally spinning.

"I'll bet if you listen to the messages on Marine's phone, there'll be one from Michelle setting her up."

"That would be great—if I had Marine's phone."

"What are you talking about? It's sitting on your desk in the other room."

"The only phone I have is the one Michelle's daughter left."

"Black with purple sparkly nail polish all over it? Marine did that to every phone she ever owned. She borrowed my phone once, and when she gave it back it was covered with that junk. I never could get it all off. I'm telling you, that's her phone. Go get it, you'll see."

He followed Harriet into her studio, and when they got to the table, he picked it up and typed in the unlock code. The phone chirped to life.

He held it out to Harriet.

"See, it opened with Marine's code."

Harriet took the phone and pressed the contact button; the file contained only one number—Aiden's house. She tried messages, emails and the calendar. If there had been data in any of these, it had been wiped.

"Michelle supposedly has three phones—two of them for her legal-aid clients to contact her. Lainie is using one of them while she's staying at her uncle's. It would make sense for the legal-aid phone to not have any other data on it. And we don't really need to bring in the code breakers to figure out one, two, three, four as the password."

"I'm telling you, this was my sister's phone. I've seen it before."

Harriet turned it over, but all she could see was poorly shaped stars painted in purple glitter nail polish.

"I'll hang on to this until we sort things out. You've given me a lot to think about. I'm not a fan of Michelle, but I have a hard time believing she would kill Marine and set up her own brother. She's annoying, but a killer?

"I need more proof than her talking to your father and her daughter having a phone that looks like Marine's. There are reasonable explanations for both of those things. She works for legal aid; your dad could be one of her clients. I've explained the phone. Marine was at Michelle's for several days. She could have painted one of Michelle's phones."

Jules held his hands up in surrender.

169

"I knew you wouldn't believe me. But at least you know. Do with it what you will." He turned toward the door.

"Wait." She reached out and grabbed his arm, and he turned back. "Thank you. You didn't have to come back and talk to me, and I do appreciate that you did."

Jules looked at his feet.

"I'm not really a bad guy. I just don't live in the same world you do. Spending time with my dad in the shape he was in has had me thinking about the future. Maybe it's not too late for me to make some changes."

"I think plenty of people would say it's never too late to change." Harriet thought for a moment. "Look, I'll follow up on what you've told me. Tell me the phone number for Marine's phone. I'll have a friend check out the cell phone records. If the phone was Marine's, and it's been wiped, there will still be call records."

"Will tell me what you find out?"

She handed him a paper and pen.

"Write down your contact info, too, and I'll let you know either way."

He handed her the numbers and let himself out. Harriet watched at the window until she saw his headlights go down her driveway and turn onto the street. She shot the deadbolt on the door and went into the kitchen,

She punched Lauren's phone number into her house phone.

"Jules just paid me a visit," she said when they'd gotten through their greetings. "He decided to share his information gratis." She repeated his story about seeing Michelle with his dad and ended with his insistence that Lainie's phone was actually Marine's.

"Do you know anyone who can access cell phone records?" she asked when she'd finished the explanations.

"That would be hacking," Lauren pointed out.

"I know that. The question was—Do you know anyone who can do it for us?"

"I might. It will mean I'll owe someone I'd rather not owe."

"I can give the information to Detective Morse tomorrow."

"You should do that in any case, but I didn't say I couldn't get my guy to do it. I just will have to pay the piper at some point in the future."

"I don't want you to do anything that's going to cause you problems."

"Nothing I can't handle. Give me the number."

Harriet gave it to her.

"Should we get together for coffee in the morning?" she asked.

"Probably a good idea. If it turns out to be Marine's phone, we may have some things to talk about. We need to see if we know why Michelle was in the woods with Dad, too. I suppose it's possible she was doing legal aid work for him."

"That's what I said to Jules. He didn't seem to know one way or the other. I wonder if Robin has any friends in that world who could shed some light on that?"

"You call Robin, and I'll get my guy going. Let's meet at the Steaming Cup at nine."

"See you then."

Harriet called Robin and her aunt and Connie. They agreed to call the rest of the Loose Threads. Finally, she left a message for Detective Morse, letting her know that it was possible she had Marine's phone.

She sat for a moment lost in thought and then picked up her phone one more time.

"Tom?" she said when he answered. "I may be paranoid or just holding a past grudge, but..." She explained how Jules had suggested Michelle might have something to with his sister's death. "Even with all she's done, I can't believe she'd do that to Aiden. Just in case I'm being naive, do you think the Renfros could come up with a reason to keep Lainie and Etienne for a few days? If Michelle is questioned by the police, even if she's cleared, it would be better if the kids didn't have to see it."

Tom assured her the Renfros would be thrilled for any excuse to keep the kids. She thanked him and told him about the morning coffee gathering.

"Come on," she said to Scooter when she'd hung up. "Let's go update Sharon and see if there's any mindless TV we can watch before bedtime."

Chapter 26

*H*arriet woke with a start at six a.m. She'd been dreaming. Having a nightmare, really. Square after square of satin, silk and velvet were floating down from the sky like snow, burying her to her neck. She'd had to fight to keep her head above the growing pile of crazy quilt fabric.

She must have called out in her sleep, because it was the only explanation for Fred being awake and head-butting her that early.

"Sorry, Fred. I was having a nightmare." He meowed his understanding. She fluffed her hair with her hand. "Now what are we going to do?" She looked over the edge of her bed to Scooter's bed. All that was visible was a pile of fleecy blankets. "Let's go for a walk," she said. Fred meowed again, but the dog bed was silent. "Okay, *I'll* go for a walk, you can stay in your bed."

She dressed in her running tights and T-shirt and pulled her gray hoodie over the top. She quietly closed the door and went downstairs, stopping to feed Fred on her way outside. After a few stretches, she jogged slowly down her drive and onto the roadway.

Running gave Harriet time to think about the previous week's events. For Michelle to have killed Marine, she would have to have gotten Marine's dad to call Aiden and get him out of the apartment. She would also have had to kill Marine, plant evidence on her body, and then be seen driving around town looking for Marine at the same time.

She focused for a minute while she watched traffic and then crossed the busy intersection at the bottom of her hill. Michelle would almost have to have had an accomplice—if the time of death was right.

She ran on, pondering that thought for a mile. Although she'd become closer with Sharon, it was hard to ignore the fact that Sharon was the one with no alibi at the exact time Marine had died.

She looped around and headed back up her hill. If you took a step back and looked at Marine's death without the prism of knowledge about the individuals, her killer should be someone from the drug world, or her family. She ran on. Nothing else presented itself on the steep run except a charley horse in her calf.

⬚ ⬚ ⬚ ⬚ ⬚ ⬚ ⬚ ⬚

Harriet got a cup of hot cocoa at the counter of the Steaming Cup. She carried it to the large table where the Loose Threads were assembled.

"Hi, all," she said and sat down between her aunt and Lauren.

"You took your sweet time getting here," Lauren said.

"Sorry. I woke up early having nightmares about our crazy quilts. I decided to go out for a run, since I was up, and after I showered…never mind, it doesn't matter. What did you find out?"

Lauren pulled out her tablet.

"The phone is a burner."

Aunt Beth set her cup of coffee on the table and leaned toward Lauren.

"What does that mean?"

"The actual name is 'prepaid cellular.' That means you buy the phone at Walmart or any other store that has them and, at the same time, pay for a preset amount of minutes. In a normal prepay, you can reload it as many times as you want. In the world of drug dealers, they don't reload. They use the phone until its minutes are gone and then throw it away. If the phone was purchased with cash, we have no way of knowing who bought it."

Harriet sipped her chocolate.

"So, does that mean we can't access the call records?"

"No, it doesn't mean that. Records can be gotten as to what number the phone called, but without knowing who owns the phone, it's not very useful." Lauren pulled a paper from her bag. "It turns out this burner received a number of calls from Michelle on the day in question. More interesting is the pattern of this phone calling Aiden. If this was purchased by Michelle as a second phone, and was used by Lainie part of the time, then this call pattern is completely innocent."

"What if the burner was Marine's?" Mavis asked.

Lauren looked down at her paper.

"Then we have to wonder why Marine was calling Aiden so often before she died."

"He swears he didn't call her and she didn't call him," Harriet said.

Robin got out her yellow legal tablet.

"I checked with my friend in legal aid. First, they've been happy with Michelle's work for them. Not germane to the issue at hand, but points for Michelle. Anyway, Luc Moreau is not one of their clients and further checking does not show him having any open legal cases in any of the local courts. He could have contacted her, or Marine may have asked her to help him. She may have been doing something for him off the books, but there's no way of knowing that."

Connie stirred a packet of sugar into her cup.

"So, that means Michelle had no reason to be talking to Marine's dad."

"That we know of," Robin corrected.

"I heard back from the nanny," Connie said. "She told me she needed her job and did not want to do anything to offend Michelle. From her tone, I gathered there were things she could say if she wasn't worried about her employment."

"Michelle was sort of mean to the tutor and the nanny," Carla said in quiet voice. "I think they stayed because they felt sorry for Lainie and Etienne."

Detective Morse came into the coffee shop.

"Wow, the gang's all here," she said. She went to the counter, ordered her coffee, and came to the table to sit while she waited for it. "I got your message about the phone. It's a burner, but I'm guessing…" She looked pointedly at Lauren. "…you already know that."

Lauren shrugged but kept her mouth shut.

"The detectives working on Marine's murder aren't interested in pursuing other possible suspects because they have an ironclad case against Aiden. Unless you can find clear, overwhelming evidence that someone else planted his hair and saliva on Marine's body, they don't care. If you had unimpeachable evidence he was somewhere else at the critical time that might do it. I'm not trying to be mean or to upset you, but you need to be prepared. If nothing changes, Aiden will be tried and very likely will be found guilty."

Harriet sucked in her breath. Connie put her hands over her face.

"*Diós mio*," she whispered.

"Anyone could have planted the hair," Harriet said. "People shed hair lots of places. We need to figure out how they got his saliva."

"Has he been to the dentist lately?" Mavis asked.

Carla looked up from her tea.

"He just got a reminder in the mail for his six-month checkup. Maybe a week ago. He hasn't gone for that yet, so probably not."

"The likely suspects are the least likely to have access to his spit," Aunt Beth said.

Detective Morse stood up.

"I've got to get back to the station. I'm sorry I didn't have better news for you. Let me know if you come up with anything I can help with."

The group watched her leave in silence.

"Do we know if the police searched Michelle's room when they were at Aiden's?" Harriet asked.

Carla straightened and leaned in toward the table.

"They didn't search *any* of our rooms. They looked in Aiden's rooms and the library and parlor. They looked in all the public rooms and bathrooms. Michelle had a lawyer there, and they talked a lot about exactly what the warrant said. They said something about sugar bowls. I don't know why that was important, but they weren't allowed to search them."

Robin laughed. "Sorry, it's not funny, but sugar bowls refers to a legal maxim describing a fourth amendment limit on search and seizure. It's often stated 'If you are looking for televisions you can't look in sugar bowls.' People searching are limited to the locations where the item they're searching for might reasonably be.

"I'm sure Michelle's attorney was trying to make sure they didn't tear the house up. Sometimes, when people don't find what they're looking for, they take their frustrations out on the property they're searching."

"Hold on a minute. Which rooms *didn't* they search?" Harriet asked Carla.

"My room, Michelle's room…I don't think they went up to the third floor at all. Like I said, they spent their time going through Aiden's bedroom and sitting room. They asked where he kept his veterinary drugs, and I told them he didn't bring them in the house because of Wendy. He kept that stuff in the dog kennel building behind the house. I think they looked out there, but he usually keeps his doctor bag in his car."

Mavis set her mug down.

"What are you thinking?"

"I was thinking we have to consider all the possibilities. Marine's family doesn't have access to Aiden's saliva—that we know of. If anyone does, it's most likely to be the people who live with him. I'm not sure how, yet, but maybe Michelle or someone else in the house." She turned to Carla again. "Not you, Carla, but there were a lot of people staying there, what with the nanny, the tutor and Marine herself. Maybe one of them put something in his drink that caused him to spit it back into his cup or something. I don't know how that sort of thing works. Maybe his saliva was mixed with that liquid, but all the police look for is spit."

"That may be," Aunt Beth said, "But how does that help us? Do you think the person would keep the evidence lying around for someone to find?"

Harriet tore her napkin into shreds.

"I don't know. Checking out the rooms the police didn't search would give us something to do besides sitting around watching Aiden grow old in jail."

"Michelle's bedroom is the only one in the house that's locked all the time," Carla told them.

"What?" Harriet and Mavis said at the same time.

Carla cheeks turned pink. "She's really paranoid about it. I'm not allowed to clean it or anything. Even the kids are only allowed in her sitting room. She puts her sheets out in the hall."

"Do you know where the key is?" Harriet asked.

Carla's face turned from pink to red.

"I know where she hid a spare. She didn't know I was home when she hid it. It's under the rug in her sitting room. I was behind the sofa on my hands and knees polishing the wood floor edges, and she came in and hid it. She never knew I was there."

"Are you sure it's her room key?" Mavis asked.

"I know I shouldn't have, but I was curious," Carla stammered. "When she was gone, I took the key and tried it. I swear, I didn't go in, I just checked to see if it worked."

Beth looked at her and smiled.

"You did fine, honey. It's all very weird if you ask me. Locking her room. Hiding a spare key." She shuddered. "I suppose you want to go look in her room," she said to Harriet.

"I think we have to."

Robin slid her pad and pen back into her bag.

"I'm not saying it's a bad idea, but I can't be there. Let me know if you find anything. And don't touch anything."

"Do we know when Michelle will be out of the house for sure?" Mavis asked.

"The only place she goes on a schedule is legal aid," Carla said.

Harriet drained the remains of her cocoa, and Beth gathered up her purse.

"I'll swing by Jorge's and pick up more plastic gloves."

176

Mavis shrugged into her jacket.

"I'll be part of the distraction team if it becomes necessary. Carla and I can be stitching on our quilt blocks downstairs after she lets us in. Beth, you can search with Harriet and Lauren."

"I'll call Jessica," Lauren said. "She can sit in her car outside legal aid. No one in town knows her, and her rental car is average looking."

"Is all this cloak-and-dagger necessary?" DeAnn asked, speaking for the first time.

Harriet looked down the table to where she was sitting.

"It probably isn't. We likely won't find anything, Michelle will be at legal aid, none the wiser, but we will feel a tiny bit better for having done something…anything."

"Fair enough," DeAnn said. She stood up. "I have to go get the kids ready for church."

Harriet's shoulders drooped.

"Are we being silly?" she asked her aunt.

Beth patted her back.

"What you told DeAnn is correct. We need to do something besides sit here. Come on. I don't want Michelle to be tied up in this anymore than you do, but we need to find out."

"Does Michelle work on Sunday, though?" Mavis asked Carla.

Carla smirked. "Yeah, and she hates it. They make her come in and research cases. She said they make her come in Sunday afternoons because she went to school with the guy who does the schedule, and he doesn't like her because she turned him down for prom when she didn't even have another date."

"When does she leave?" Harriet asked.

Unless she has something else to do along the way, she leaves at one-forty-five," Carla reported. "She's usually late for everything she does, but she has to be on time there because they keep records and report it to the court. She can't mess up if she wants her license back."

Mavis put her purse over her arm.

"Shall we gather at Aiden's at two?"

Harriet finally stood and put her coat on.

"That works for me. You know, if Michelle turns out to be involved in this, Aiden is going to be crushed. He's had such a hard time dealing with all her shenanigans trying to keep us apart this last year. They were finally repairing their relationship."

Aunt Beth picked up their mugs and carried them to the bussing station then returned.

177

"You'll to be there for Aiden, no matter what happens. We're going to figure out who killed Marine and get him out of jail. Then we can all support him as he recovers. He listens to Jorge. He'll talk to him, too."

The group trickled out to the parking lot. Lauren stopped by Harriet's car.

"Do you care if Jessica and I come over and stitch for an hour or two before we go to Aiden's? It'll give us a chance to mull over the possibilities."

Harriet opened her car door.

"Sure. I'll make us something for lunch."

✂ - - - ✂ - - - ✂

Lauren and Jessica arrived as Harriet was putting the finishing touches on chicken Caesar salads. Sharon was making iced tea.

"We're in here," Harriet called when she heard them come into her studio. She set the large bowl of salad on the table. "I hope it's okay we're eating in the kitchen."

"Hey, it's fine," Lauren told her. "If I don't have to cook, I'll sit on the floor with Scooter it that's what it takes."

Harriet laughed. "We won't be that casual."

"Just suppose," Jessica said, gesturing with her fork when they were seated around the table, "you find a jar of saliva marked 'Aiden' on Michelle's dresser. How do you get the police to find it? And then how do you get them to believe Michelle used it to set him up?"

Lauren chewed thoughtfully and swallowed.

"I'm reasonably sure the police can get a search warrant based on an anonymous call. Probable cause can be a phone call, if I remember right."

"Are you a lawyer?" Sharon asked her.

She laughed. "No. Let's just say some of the computer work I do for my clients involves sensitive situations."

Jessica was still using her fork as a pointer.

"So, you or Harriet call the police and tell them there's saliva that could have been used to implicate Aiden. Is that enough?"

"That's the question," Harriet said. "Let's hope we find more than just a jar of saliva."

Lauren stabbed a piece of chicken but hesitated before putting it in her mouth.

"She's right—we need a plan."

Harriet thought about it.

"If, and this is a big if, we do find Aiden's spit, or drugs from his vet bag, or anything else that convinces us Michelle is guilty, we might be able to use Jules Moreau."

"Go on," Lauren encouraged.

"You know how he offered to sell me information about Michelle being in the woods? What if we had him go to Michelle and tell her he saw her go into Aiden's apartment with Marine, and he saw her come out alone a few minutes later. He could say he knows it was at the critical time."

Jessica set her fork down.

"Would he lie for you?"

"Not for me," Harriet told her. "But I think he would for his sister."

Lauren stabbed another piece of salad.

"Okay, I like this plan better now. We may have a chance."

Harriet sighed. "This all depends on us finding something in Michelle's room."

Jessica started eating again.

"Oh, I think you'll find something," she said between bites. "Nobody locks their bedroom all the time in their own home unless they've got something to hide. And I'm guessing it's something big."

The women finished their lunch and cleaned up the dishes.

"Shall we stitch for an hour and try to calm our nerves?" Harriet asked.

"Would it be okay if I ride along with Jessica in the observation car?" Sharon asked. "After all this, I'm not sure I can sit home and wait."

Jessica smiled. "I'd be happy for the company."

With that settled, they made their way to the studio to embellish their crazy quilt pieces for the next hour.

Chapter 27

Carla had called Harriet to tell her when Michelle was gone. Lauren and Harriet waited up the road from Aiden's house until they got the call from Jessica that Michelle was in the legal aid building. Mavis had gone ahead into the house before Michelle left, since she was supposed to be there helping Carla with her crazy quilt block.

"It's show time," Lauren said when Carla answered the door. "Jessica and Sharon have eyes on Michelle's car, and she's inside her building."

Aunt Beth handed out pairs of one-size-fits-all plastic food-handling gloves.

"Put these on," she instructed.

Carla led them to Michelle's sitting room and went to the corner by the window. She flipped the edge of the rug up. As she had reported, a shiny key lay on the rug pad.

"Let me pick it up, dear," Beth told her. "We don't want your finger-prints anywhere they shouldn't be." She picked it up with her gloved hand. "Well, let's see if this fits." She crossed the room to the bedroom door, slid the key into the lock and turned the knob. The door opened.

Weak light filtered into the room through the sheer lace curtains. Beth looked on the wall beside the door and found the switch. The room was bathed in yellowish light when she pushed the old-fashioned button switch.

Harriet followed her aunt into the room and was quickly joined by Lauren.

"Well, not quite as messy as I'd hoped," she commented.

Lauren looked around. Michelle's desk had a small note cube and one pen. Her dresser had a crocheted scarf and a painted glass lamp.

"I didn't expect the surfaces to be quite so devoid of…everything."

"Let's not make any judgments here. And be sure you don't leave any-thing out of place," Beth told them. She began opening dresser drawers one at a time.

The women worked in silence for a few minutes.

"This is curious," Beth said finally.

Harriet looked up from the desk.

"What?"

Beth pulled a large blue plastic bag from the bottom drawer.

"This looks like an electric blanket. How very curious."

"What's the problem?" Lauren asked her.

"First of all, as cold as it still is this time of year, if you had an electric blanket, you would be using it."

"Maybe she doesn't like them," Harriet countered.

"You're right," Beth continued. "But if she didn't like them, this house is so big and has so many closets, you'd put an unneeded blanket in a linen closet. Her dresser is crowded with clothes. This…" She pointed at the bag she was holding up. "…is out of place."

Harriet stood silently for a moment.

"If Michelle killed Marine before we saw her driving around looking for her, she could have kept her body warm with that blanket. After she saw us, she could have gone back and taken the blanket off the body."

Lauren turned away from the nightstand she was examining.

"I wonder if she was tracking Aiden."

"Wouldn't she have to have help?" Beth asked.

"Not really," Lauren told her. "All she'd have to do is tape a cell phone to his bumper and use the track-my-phone function on her own phone. When he was a couple of miles away, she could take the blanket off, go back to her car and take off. Marine would measure as warm as toast, lead-ing the medical examiner to believe she'd just passed."

Harriet turned back to the desk.

"There are more sophisticated time-of-death tests, but I doubt anyone did any of them because they originally thought she was a drug overdose." She pulled open a deep file drawer to the right of the knee well on the old oak desk. "Bingo," she said and pulled out a stack of smallish white boxes.

Aunt Beth looked at the stack of boxes as Harriet placed them on the desktop.

"What have you got there?"

Harriet set each box down so she could read the labels.

"Remember a month or two ago when I was digging up all those pho-tos for Lainie and Etienne? They were working on a school genealogy project." She held up one of the white boxes. "They sent their DNA to one of those services that analyzes your sample and tells you what country or countries your ancestors come from."

Lauren stopped what she was doing, holding a notepad in her hand. "And the punch line is?"

"You send them saliva samples," Harriet said. "There are five boxes here. There should be four—one each for Lainie, Etienne, Aiden and Michelle." She started opening lids. "I'm betting one of these boxes still has its vial inside." In the third box, she hit pay dirt. She carefully eased the stoppered tube from its foam cutout in the box. It was half full of liquid. "She sent in two vials of her own saliva and kept Aiden's. I've seen the report. It doesn't tell gender because presumably you know that already. It only tells you countries and percentages. She's been planning this for a while."

Lauren set the pad she'd been scanning back in the nightstand. "So I guess that seals the deal for Michelle."

Harriet carefully replaced the vial in its box and put the boxes back in the drawer. For the sake of completeness, she opened the shallow center drawer on the desk.

"Hello. I found the stash of burner phones." She pulled the drawer wide. Four phones were side-by-side, sticky notes on their tops identifying them by number.

Aunt Beth had struggled to push the blanket back into the dresser drawer, then finished looking in the other drawers, finding nothing else of interest.

"Do we have enough? I mean, to convince ourselves Michelle is involved. Isn't this when we should call Detective Morse?"

Harriet explained what she and Lauren and their roommates had discussed at lunch.

"So, we need to tell Detective Morse, but I think we need to get Jules to help us set a trap."

"Let's finish up in here and get out. We can call Morse when we have this place locked back up."

✂ - - - ✂ - - - ✂

"Detective Morse said she can meet us in a half-hour at the coffee shop." Harriet slid her phone back into her pocket.

"Has anyone called the watch team?" Aunt Beth asked.

Mavis picked up her coat and bag.

"We can call them from the car. I know they're watching, but it still makes me nervous being in Michelle's house. Especially if she really is capable of killing someone." She shivered. "I hate to even think about that."

Harriet turned to Carla.

"Can you come with us?"

She touched her phone screen to see the time.

"Wendy's going to be playing at DeAnn's for another hour, but I'll take my own car, in case Detective Morse is late."

At the Steaming Cup, Detective Morse picked up her coffee at the bar and joined the group, who were once again seated around a large table.

"Your message was pretty cryptic. Do I want to know what you think you know?" She sat down across from Harriet and looked at each one of them. No one smiled at her comment. "Okay, something has you spooked. Who wants to tell me what it is?"

No one spoke at first, then Harriet began.

"We came across some information that Aiden's sister was seen talking to Marine's dad. We were reviewing the evidence we knew about. We know Aiden didn't deposit his saliva on Marine." Morse started to speak, but Harriet stopped her. "Let me get this all out at once, or it won't make sense."

"Fair enough," Morse said.

"We figured the people in Aiden's house are the most likely to be able to get his saliva. We know it wasn't Carla."

Carla's cheeks turned pink, but she didn't say anything. Morse leaned back in her chair.

"We asked Carla where the police searched when they executed their warrant on Aiden's house, and she mentioned that Michelle kept her bedroom locked at all times."

Harriet sipped her tea and set her cup down again. Mavis took up the story.

"We were getting antsy sitting around doing nothing. Carla, here, knows where Michelle hides her spare key, so we decided we'd take a peek in her room. We figured we wouldn't find anything, but at least we could eliminate her as a suspect."

Morse ran her hand through her short hair.

"What did you find?" she asked.

"A couple of things," Harriet said. "First of all, I was looking in her desk, and I found the boxes from the genealogy test kits Aiden, Michelle and the kids did a few months ago. There should have been four kits. I remember when the kids were doing their ancestry project for school; they only talked about testing themselves, their uncle and their mother.

"Anyway, I looked in all the boxes. Four had empty foam and papers. One box had a vial half full of saliva. We have no way of knowing, but my bet is Michelle sent in two vials of her own spit, since she and Aiden would have the same heritage. She kept Aiden's actual vial for her own purposes."

"Don't forget the blanket," Aunt Beth reminded her.

Morse drank a sip of her coffee.

"There's more?"

"I found an electric blanket in her dresser drawer. This is out of our realm, but we're wondering if Michelle could have used it to keep Marine's body warm while she came to ask us if we'd seen her, then took it off before Aiden got back to find the body."

Detective Morse looked thoughtful.

"It's possible, I suppose. But you know there are problems with your illegal search of her room. I mean, I can go see if blanket fibers were found on her clothing or body, but even if you call in an anonymous tip about what's in her room, it's not going to take a genius to figure out it was one of you, and probably Carla will be accused of illegally entering her locked room."

Harriet's mouth lifted on one side in a half-smile.

"Oh, no. Here it comes," Morse said.

"We have an idea about getting Michelle to confess," Harriet told her. "Marine's half-brother was the one who told me he saw Michelle talking to his dad. He runs with a rough crowd.

"I haven't talked to him about this, but I'm willing to bet Jules would go to Michelle and tell her he saw her and Marine going into Aiden's apartment at the critical time. He could say he was trying to find Marine and was waiting for Michelle to leave so he could talk to her. He could claim he went up to the door when he saw her leave, and no one answered. Then he can ask her for a payoff to keep quiet."

"We assume you could wire him for sound?" Aunt Beth added.

Morse sipped her coffee thoughtfully. The Loose Threads stared at her intently. She set her mug down and sighed.

"You guys never make it easy, starting with the fact that it's not my case."

"But you can help?" Mavis persisted.

"Let me do some checking. I can find out about the blanket fibers. What color was the blanket, by the way?"

"Blue," Aunt Beth said.

"I can talk to the genealogy company and see if they can tell us the gender of the samples sent by the Jalbert family. For your part, give Jules my number and ask him to call me. If it goes that far, and the detectives assigned to the case agree, we can set it up. In the meantime, are you sure you didn't leave any sign that you were in Michelle's room?"

They all nodded.

"Stay away from Michelle. We don't want to spook her. I know you all think you're Miss Marple but trust me, you're not, and if you see her, there's a good chance at least one of you will act different enough to tip her off."

"I asked Tom to get the Renfros to make an excuse to keep Michelle's kids," Harriet told her. "I'd like to think she wouldn't hurt her own kids, but I'm not positive."

"It's sad to say, but I think that's a good idea. If she *is* guilty, she's sick and sick people sometimes do terrible things."

Mavis rested her hand on the back of Carla's chair.

"Honey, whenever this all goes down, I think you should go stay with Connie. I'll call her, but I'm sure it'll be okay."

"That's also a good idea," Morse said. "If she realizes we're on to her before she's arrested, it could be dangerous for anyone around her." She finished her coffee and crumpled her napkin. "I'd better get going. I'll check with the crime lab and see what they've got."

"I'll call Jules and see if he's willing to go along with our plan."

Aunt Beth stood up.

"Let us know what he says." She picked up her purse. "We better get going."

✂- - - ✂- - - ✂

Sharon and Harriet put their purses and coats away and went out to the grassy area by the driveway with Scooter.

"What will you do if Jules refuses?" Sharon asked.

"Well, it wouldn't be optimum," Harriet told her. "But we'd have to figure out another one of us to confront her and claim we'd seen her go in the apartment with Aiden."

"Can I do anything to help?"

"I'm going to call and see if he'll come by. I have to admit it'd make me feel better if you stayed within earshot. I think he's okay, but I've only met with him twice, and one of those times he was trying to extort money from me."

"I wondered."

"I guess I'd better make the call," Harriet said and led the way back into the house.

Chapter 28

*H*arriet dialed the number Jules had given her, and the call went straight to voicemail. She did as instructed, saying only that she needed to see him. An hour later, he still hadn't called back.

"I'm going to work on my customer quilt out in the studio," she told Sharon. "We'll give Jules another hour, and if he doesn't make contact, I'll call Lauren and my aunt and see what they think."

"I'm going to sit in the TV room and stitch on my crazy quilt block, if that's okay with you."

"Sure, no problem," Harriet told her.

Forty-five minutes later, Harriet's stitching was interrupted by a quiet tap on her studio door. She crossed the room and opened the door. Jules stood on her porch, hands in his pockets and a toothpick in the corner of his mouth. His jaw was dark with five o'clock shadow.

"Are you going to invite me in?" he asked.

She held the door wide to admit him and indicated her reception area. He flopped into the nearest wingback chair.

"Yesterday, you barely had the time of day for me. Now you want to see me. We both know you could have left a message with what you found out. So, what do you want?"

Harriet had the grace to blush.

"I did follow up on what you told me. The phone turned out to be a burner. It had been used to call Aiden a bunch of times, even though he says Marine and he didn't call each other."

"Why am I here, Harriet?"

"Okay, I'll cut to the chase. My friends and I searched Michelle's room and found what looks like a vial of saliva—Aiden's saliva, if my guess is right. We also found an electric blanket bagged up in a dresser."

"I'm going to guess Michelle didn't give you permission to search her room."

"Umm, it's a little worse than that. Her room was locked."

Jules sat up.

"You broke into her bedroom? I like it."

"We didn't break in; we used a hidden key."

"So, the police can't act on what you found because you didn't find it legally, right? Is this where I come in to it? You think I'll be your pet criminal?"

"I went to the police. I told Detective Morse what we found and what we thought happened. She's going to check to see if blanket fibers were found on Marine, but as you said, she can't get a warrant to search Michelle's room based on our illegal search. My friends and I had an idea."

"And you don't want to get your hands dirty."

"Look, you came to me and tried to extort money for information, so don't try to play Mr. Innocent now. You cast yourself as a bad guy. I do give you credit for coming back and telling me what you know—if that is, in fact, all you know. It doesn't matter now. You want to know who killed Marine, I want Aiden out of jail. Can we stop with the verbal sparring and get to the plan?"

"Please, enlighten me."

"First, if you agree to do this, you have to call Detective Morse. It will all be legal and aboveboard. The police will wire you, and you'll go to Michelle and tell her that, on the day she died, you were trying to find Marine. Maybe you could say Marine wanted you to bring her drugs or something."

"Because, of course, I'm that kind of guy."

Harriet glared at him.

"Sorry, continue."

"You tell Michelle you saw her go into Aiden's apartment with Marine and then come out alone. You waited until she left then knocked on the door. No one answered. You found out later Marine had been found dead at Aiden's. If Michelle would like you to keep this piece of information to yourself, she needs to pay you. It's just another extortion scheme. You should be a natural."

"What if she decides to just kill me instead? Did you think of that."

The color drained from Harriet's face.

"Guess not, huh? I'm expendable."

"Of course not. I'm sure Detective Morse will have undercover people near you all the time. You could wear a Kevlar vest."

"Oh, yeah, 'cause that wouldn't look suspicious at all."

"Okay, so, maybe it wasn't such a good idea, after all." Harriet sat back in her chair. "It all sounded so simple when we talked about it."

"Things like this are always simpler when it isn't your hide on the line."

"We'll have to think of something else."

"I'll do it." Jules said.

"But it's too dangerous. You said so yourself."

"I didn't say too dangerous. I just pointed out the risks. If Michelle killed my sister, she probably killed my dad, too. Someone needs to stop her."

"Detective Morse is going to check on the blanket fibers, and check with the genealogy company and find out if she sent in two of her sample and none of Aiden's. She thinks they can tell male versus female. There was one too many test kits in Michelle's desk drawer, and one of them still had the spit sample in it, and it wasn't full anymore. If it all checks out, she'll talk to the detectives in charge of the case, and if they agree only then will she bring you into it."

"Maybe I'll find Michelle and take care of things myself," Jules said.

"What happened to 'I'm not a bad guy'? You killing Michelle makes you no better than she is."

Jules sighed. "I know you're right, but she killed my family. They may not be much, but they're my blood. Can you understand that?"

"I do understand the impulse, but you can't act on it."

He blew out his breath.

"I know. I'll call your cop and hope she does the right thing."

"She will. She's one of the good guys." Harriet wrote Morse's number on a piece of paper and handed it to him.

He looked into her eyes.

"If you say so." He took the paper and then hung his head.

She looked at him, studying what she could see of his face. He was pale under his day's growth of beard, and she could see fatigue lines etched into his face.

"You look tired."

He swiped his hand over his face.

"I'm fine. I've been working the midnight shift at the factory."

Harriet tried to keep her face neutral. She felt ashamed of the assumptions she'd made. After Jules had tried to extort her, she'd just assumed he made his living selling drugs or scamming people or both. Maybe he did all of those things, but he also had a regular job; and she had to at least consider that he might not do any of those other things. She hadn't bothered to find out.

"Do you want a cup of coffee or something? I mean, as long as you're here."

His mouth curved up on one side.

"Oooh, are you inviting the bad boy into the inner sanctum?"

"My roommate is on the other side of the door." She hoped she was telling the truth. She was pretty sure she'd heard Sharon shuffling around in the kitchen shortly after he had entered. "I also have a ferocious watchdog."

Jules laughed. "Yeah, we've met. Now I'm scared."

Sharon must have been listening at the door. When Harriet led Jules into the kitchen, she was pouring water into the coffeepot and had an array of pods out on the counter. She had also gotten the box of ginger snaps from the cabinet and had a plate out to put them on.

Scooter wagged his tail and, when Jules sat down, jumped into his lap and attempted to lick his face.

Jules pulled his cell phone from his pocket.

"Let's see what the good detective has to say for herself." He tapped in the number Harriet had given him. He identified himself, stated his willingness to help, and then listened.

"Call me when you're ready," he said and tapped his phone off.

Harriet and Sharon had stopped what they were doing and stared expectantly at him.

"She wants to check a few more things, but she said there were blanket fibers on my sister's clothes. She'll call about the DNA tests tomorrow, but she ran into one of the detectives in charge of the case, and he's going to talk to his partner about the sting, but he was pretty sure they were going to go along with it. He told her they had nothing to lose. If she confesses, good, but if she doesn't, they still have Aiden."

Harriet set a cup of coffee in front of him and sat down opposite him with her own.

"Somehow, I don't find that very comforting."

Jules looked up as Sharon slid a plateful of cookies onto the tabletop between them.

"The more we talk about it, the more convinced I am that Michelle killed my sister. It never seemed right that she would go get Marine out of her sobriety program and bring her to Foggy Point to go to a quilting class. I mean, no offense, but...quilting?"

189

"I have to admit, I was a bit skeptical about Marine being a quilter when I saw her."

"I know Michelle's mom was very good to my sister, but I never got that same vibe from Michelle. Unless she's changed from when we were younger, Michelle never does anything that doesn't benefit Michelle."

Sharon sat down at the table, and Harriet introduced her to Jules. They talked about California and modeling and anything else but the murder.

"I better go," Jules told them. "I have to be at work at midnight, and I need to go home before that."

Harriet walked him to the studio door.

"Thank you for doing this."

"Don't thank me until I get Michelle to talk."

He reached for the doorknob, and Harriet stopped him with a hand on his arm.

"Jules, I'm sorry. For the way I've treated you."

"Don't be. I may not be the villain you thought I was, but I'm nobody's hero, either. I'm just a guy from the streets trying to get along."

"Thank you for doing what you're doing. Even if it doesn't work, thank you for being willing to try."

He looked away from her.

"I gotta go."

Harriet dropped her hand, and he went out the door.

✂ - - - ✂ - - - ✂

"How do you feel about pizza?" Harriet asked Sharon. "It's eight o'clock, and I'm sick of cookies and coffee drinks."

"Pizza sounds really good right now."

Harriet put food in Scooter's dish on the kitchen floor and set a dish of dry food on the counter for Fred.

"Let's go."

Chapter 29

The opening notes of the song "Jane" by Jefferson Starship sounded on Harriet's phone as she reached her driveway the next morning at the end of her run. She stopped and keyed her phone on.

"Hello?"

"It's Morse. I talked to the DNA people. You were right. Michelle sent two female samples. I went to the case detectives, and they're on board. I also talked to your friend Jules. He worked last night, so we're going to let him sleep a few hours before we have him approach Michelle. That'll give us time to get Carla and Wendy out of the house. Are the kids still stashed at the Renfros'?"

Harriet assured her they were.

"Stay out of the way, and I'll let you know when it's over."

"Thanks for letting me know."

"And Harriet....you can't say anything to Aiden about this. It'll be over soon enough, but until we have the evidence, you can't tell him."

"I hate it that he has to suffer for another day."

"I know. But you have to realize that, for him, it will only be trading one pain for another. It's going to be real hard when he finds out his sister was willing to let him go to jail for life—or worse."

"I'm assuming she did all this as yet another ploy to get her hands on her mother's house and money," Harriet told her.

"This will end all that. If she killed Marine and her dad, she's going away and never coming back."

"I feel sorry for her kids."

"I'll call Cookie Jalbert. You probably know she's a clinical psychologist. She can be trusted to keep her mouth shut until it's over. But she can also be figuring out the best way to help the kids through this. It wouldn't surprise me if she and Marcel ended up with them. I've heard some things about Michelle's ex."

"That's nice of you to think about them."

"Yeah, it seems like the children are the ones who suffer most in these situations."

"Let me know what's happening when you can."

They said their goodbyes, and Harriet put her phone back in her pocket.

"Sharon," she called as she came into the kitchen from the studio.

"What's up?" Sharon answered, coming down the stairs.

"Morse called as I finished my run. They're going to have Jules do his thing this afternoon. We need to let the Threads know."

"I can call people while you shower, if you want. Don't we need to let Carla know so she can make herself scarce?"

"Detective Morse said something about getting her out of the house. I imagine they'll plan the meeting in some public place for Jules's safety. Assuming Michelle takes the bait, they probably have to wait until she delivers the money to him before they can arrest her. If she goes back to the house, Carla probably shouldn't be there. We should touch base with her just to be sure she knows. I think she and Connie already talked about it, but still...."

"Give me the numbers of whoever you want me to call."

"If you just call my aunt, she can let Carla and Connie know. There's a card with all the Loose Thread numbers on it by the phone in the kitchen. And thanks."

✂- - - ✂- - - ✂

Harriet came back downstairs forty-five minutes later. Sharon sat at the kitchen table drinking coffee.

"Did you have any trouble getting hold of my aunt?"

"No. She said she'd take care of things."

"I was thinking maybe we could drive over to Sequim today. They're having their annual tour of homes and gardens this week. I've heard they're stunning."

Sharon stood up.

"Don't you want to be here while all this goes down?"

Harriet poured water into the coffeepot and clicked a pod into place.

"Of course I'd like to be here. That's exactly why we need to go somewhere else. I thought we could call Lauren and see if she and Jessica want to come with. Besides, I feel like Lauren and I should do something touristy for you two before you go home. Somehow, I'm guessing trying to clear someone of murder charges wasn't on your agenda when you came here."

"On the other hand, I've already told you I came here for reasons other than quilting, and Lauren is helping me with my search." Sharon put her cup on the counter beside the coffeemaker.

"Well, I think we should go to Sequim anyway. I've been warned over and over again to keep out of police operations. I'm trying to do as they asked."

"Okay, if you say so."

"I'll call Lauren."

✂- - - ✂- - - ✂

"That fairy garden was amazing," Jessica said as she settled in beside Sharon in the middle seat of Harriet's SUV.

Sharon buckled her seatbelt.

"I have to admit, I was skeptical about going on the garden tour with everything that's been happening, but, Harriet, you were right. It was a great distraction."

Lauren turned in her seat so she could see everyone.

"I told Jessica I would take her to Annie's Coffee Shop before she leaves. Is everyone up for a hot beverage?"

They all nodded.

"Good. There's a chance some of my...friends will be there. Besides, Annie makes the best cinnamon twists in the universe, bar none."

"I'm never one to pass up a cinnamon twist; even a mediocre one works for me," Jessica said.

Harriet pulled her car from its parking spot and headed back to Foggy Point.

"Annie's, here we come."

Lauren pulled her tablet from her bag and tapped on its screen.

"Do you know what time they were going to have Jules talk to Michelle?"

"Morse just said 'afternoon.' He has to call her and set up a meeting time and place, and then they have to meet and arrange for the payoff, if it gets that far."

"So, it could be anytime and anywhere."

"Pretty much. Morse will call when she can. Meantime, we stay out of the way and wait."

"Who are you, and what did you do with my friend Harriet?" Lauren asked.

"What?"

193

"We never sit on the sidelines. There's always a plan."

"I told Morse we'd stay out of the way. Besides, I don't want to do anything that might jeopardize Aiden."

"It doesn't seem right for us to be going to gardens and sipping coffee when all the action's happening."

"Morse is right, though. We've been lucky in the past that none of us has been seriously hurt. She said to leave the police work to the police, and I intend to do just that. Michelle may have killed two people, and she knows who we are. I don't want to give her any reason to look my way."

"Yeah, whatever."

✂ - - - ✂ - - - ✂

Harriet parked in front of the Pins and Needles Quilt Store.

"We can cut through the alley to get to Annie's, and if you want, we can make a last shop on our way home." She looked back at Sharon and Jessica. "Marjory has a secret stash of embellishment stuff in the attic. Usually, only locals get access to it, but I think you guys have earned the right to a trip upstairs."

"Oooh, that sounds exciting," Jessica said. "My crazy block needs something to give it a little pizazz. It's not quite right yet."

Sharon crawled out of the middle seat.

"Where are those best-in-the-universe cinnamon twists?"

"Follow me," Harriet said as she clicked the doors locked.

✂ - - - ✂ - - - ✂

Lauren held the back door to Annie's open for the other three to pass into the coffee shop.

"Annie used to be a librarian, in case you can't tell."

Bookshelves lined the walls. In addition to serving coffee drinks and pastries, the shop had an unofficial library that ran on the honor system. People brought in books they no longer wanted, and anyone could borrow or even keep a book, if they wished. An old wooden library table had been converted into a service counter.

Lauren went to the back of the room to a table for four and set her bag down while the rest of the group ordered. Harriet ordered cinnamon twists for everyone and mochas for Lauren and herself.

"Thank you," she said when the food and drinks were delivered to the table.

Jessica grabbed a twist and took a bite.

"Yummm!" she said when she'd swallowed the first bite. "These are every bit as good as—" She froze, her mouth open. "Isn't that...?" She made a small gesture with her twist toward the door. "Don't turn around," she said to Lauren and Sharon.

"Oh, my gosh," Harriet whispered. "It's Michelle."

"So, she didn't take the bait?" Lauren whispered back.

Michelle scanned the room, and when she saw Harriet, she waved. Harriet raised her hand in a halfhearted acknowledgment.

"Hey, what are you doing here?" Michelle asked as she walked up to their table.

"Our guests are going home, and they hadn't tasted Annie's cinnamon twists yet," Harriet told her. "We're going to the quilt store from here."

She wasn't sure why she'd shared that. She thought about Morse telling her to stay away from Michelle because she couldn't avoid tipping her off and clamped her lips shut.

Michelle looked at Sharon and Jessica.

"I hope you enjoyed your visit to Foggy Point." She was looking at the door before she even finished speaking. "I better go get a table. I'm meeting a friend."

There weren't many other people in the shop. Harriet recognized a guy sitting near the window wearing a gray sweater and sporting black-framed glasses. He was one of Lauren's nerd herd. She didn't know the people working at the counter, but that wasn't too surprising. Both of the coffee shops in town turned over their barista staff several times a year.

Lauren scooted her chair closer to the table and leaned in.

"Do you think we should leave?"

Jessica took a sip of her latte and set it down.

"That would draw more attention to us. I mean, we just got our pastries and drinks. I think we should just keep our heads down, eat our food, and then casually leave."

"I think she's right," Sharon whispered.

"Oh, no," Harriet groaned.

"What?" the other three said at almost the same time.

"Jules just walked in. Michelle's here because it's going down—here and now. She must have made him wait a couple of hours."

"I wonder why?" Lauren said. "She wasn't scheduled to work today."

"I'm not even going to ask how you know that," Harriet hissed. "Look natural, everyone."

They picked up their cups in unintended unison and brought them to their lips. Their eyes met, and they laughed, and Sharon and Harriet put theirs down.

195

"Morse probably has people watching the front and diverting people," Harriet said, keeping her voice low. "I guess they didn't think about the back alley entrance."

She watched as Jules took his time going to the counter, flirting with the cashier and ordering his drink. She glanced at Michelle, who was now sitting two tables away. She was at right angles to Harriet, tapping her spoon nervously on the table.

Harriet took another bite of her twist, keeping her eyes on Michelle the whole time. Michelle slipped a hand into her pocket and came out holding something small.

"Jessica. Don't stare, but can you see what's in her left hand?"

Jessica picked up her cup and sipped, looking over the rim as she did.

"It looks like a vial with liquid in it."

Jules finally came to Michelle's table and sat down. He ignored Harriet and her friends completely.

Harriet looked at each of her friends.

"Does anyone here read lips?"

They all shook their heads. Michelle leaned toward Jules and smiled. Jules's face was hard. He finally got up and went to the counter, returning a few moments later with a cup of coffee. Michelle talked and smiled more. Harriet had spent enough time around her to know the amount of smiling she was doing was not natural.

Jules said something, and Michelle leaned back in her chair. She lifted her mug, sipped and made a face. She set it down and said something to Jules. He sighed and got up, taking her cup back to the counter.

Harriet had almost looked away, but the quick motion caught her eye. Michelle pulled the vial from her pocket, unscrewed the top and upended it over Jules's cup. She dropped the empty vial back in her pocket and leaned back, re-crossing her legs.

Jules came back to the table, set Michelle's cup on the table in front of her, and sat down in his own chair.

"She's poisoning him," Harriet hissed. "Jessica, follow my lead. I'm going to the restroom," she announced loudly. "Anyone want to join me?"

She got up without waiting for an answer, Jessica hot on her heels. She took three quick strides toward the restrooms by way of Michelle's table, where she brushed too close to Jules and pretended to stumble. Jessica toppled into her, pushing her onto Jules's lap. Harriet reached out to the table as though to break her fall and grabbed Jules's cup in the process, spilling hot coffee on both of them.

He hastily slid his chair away from the table, pulling Harriet with him.

"Oh, I'm so sorry," she said from his lap. She brought her face close to his as she struggled to stand up. "Don't drink or eat anything," she whispered in his ear. He made eye contact briefly.

"I'm so sorry," she said. "I must have tripped. Let me get you a fresh cup. Coffee?"

"Me, too," Jessica added. "I mean, I didn't trip. I was following too close behind, and when Harriet tripped I couldn't stop."

The female barista came over with a white mop rag and began sponging the table. Harriet took Jules's empty cup to the bar.

The other barista met her at the counter. She slid the cup toward him; but before she could ask for a plastic bag to put it in and figure out how she was going to explain it, he picked it up and whispered, "I'm with the police. I'll get this to the detectives."

At the same time, he handed her one already filled with coffee to take back to Jules.

"I'm really sorry I'm so clumsy." She set the mug in front of Jules and turned to Michelle. "I'm so sorry I interrupted you."

Michelle glared daggers at her. Harriet smiled at her and continued on to the restroom.

✂- - - ✂- - - ✂

Lauren wadded up her napkin as Harriet returned to their table several minutes later.

"I think it's time for us to go."

"I think you're right," Harriet agreed.

The four women picked up their bags and coats and made their way out the front door of the coffee shop. Harriet was surprised no one stopped them as they walked to the corner.

"We're going to have to go around the block, since we came out the front door," she told the two visitors.

Lauren led the way.

"We can use the extra walk after eating all those cinnamon twists."

Detective Morse was waiting in Pins and Needles when they arrived, leaning against a table of sale fabric. She looked at Harriet and Lauren and then down at her feet.

"I don't even know what to say."

"Complete coincidence," Lauren told her.

Jessica smiled sheepishly.

"We did go out of town today."

Harriet stood in front of the detective.

"We went to the garden tour in Sequim and decided to go get cinnamon twists at Annie's on our way here. You said you were going to let Jules sleep a few hours then have him call Michelle. We figured this would be all over before we got back."

"You thought wrong. That being said…" Morse paused. "…it appears you saved Jules's life. Michelle was going to eliminate him before he even got to set a price. We have to test the coffee mug, but I think we know what we're going to find." She held her hand to the tiny receiver in her ear. "Okay," she said to someone not in the room. "Thanks, I'll be waiting to hear."

"She took the bait," Morse said. "He gave her until tomorrow morning to deliver the hush money."

"I hope you're going to take better care of Jules this time. As you said, it appears we were the ones to save his life. And we stumbled in there by chance."

Morse turned her head away.

"Let's just say my team members were less than enthusiastic about our plan. Until this drama went down, they were still convinced Aiden was their killer. They were only cooperating because the captain told them they had to."

"And Jules almost paid the price. You know, he believes people who live on his side of the tracks don't get treated the same as the rest of us. I'm starting to think he's on to something," Harriet told her.

"Yet Aiden's name and money didn't keep him out of jail," Morse pointed out. She paused and listened. "Okay." She stood up. "Jules and Michelle are both clear of the area, so I'm done here."

Harriet walked with her to the door.

"Can you let us know when you have her in custody?"

"I will. And we'll have someone watching Jules overnight, just in case she tries anything else."

Morse went out, and Harriet went to the back classroom to find Marjory.

"Do you mind if Lauren and I take our workshop guests up to look at the trims in the attic?"

Marjory laughed. "If any of you are interested in that stuff, I'll give you a really good deal."

"Thanks, you're the best."

Chapter 30

avis tapped on the studio door and let herself in.

"Whoa. Looks like you ladies had fun in Marjory's attic."

Lauren, Jessica, Sharon and Harriet were sitting at the four sides of the big cutting table, each with a pile of ribbons and lace in front of them. A larger collection of embellishments was piled in the middle.

"Marjory made us a deal we couldn't refuse," Sharon told her.

Jessica looked up. "After this week, we know what to do with all this stuff. More is better, as my teacher said."

Aunt Beth came in as Mavis was digging through the center pile; she now had her own assortment next to Harriet's.

"What on earth are you all doing?" Beth asked.

"Marjory gave them a deal on a bunch of stuff from the attic," Mavis explained. "There's plenty for all of us."

"I'll look after you're all done. Jorge is coming in a few minutes with dinner."

"He's here," he said as he came in behind her, insulated bags in each hand.

Harriet stood. "Do you need any help?"

"Sure," he said over his shoulder as he continued on to the kitchen. "You can set your dining room table and help me find two big platters and a bowl."

Harriet got him the requested serving dishes and set the table.

"Have you talked to Aiden today?"

"I did. I hope this is over soon. He is too sensitive to be locked up with criminals."

"Unfortunately, getting out of jail is only going to be the beginning of his troubles. I'm not sure how much my aunt told you, but it looks like Michelle murdered Marine and her father. The police wired her brother, and he met with her and told her he saw her go into Aiden's apartment with Marine and come out alone. She's supposed to pay for his silence tomorrow. Morse said we can't tell Aiden or anyone until they have Michelle in custody."

"*Diós mio!* It's going to kill him when he finds out."

"Jail was hard enough. Getting out is going to be worse."

"He will be hurt, but we will all support him. After the initial shock, he has to know things were never going to end well with his sister. She was trouble from the start. Their parents gave her every kind of therapy and counseling money could buy. They spent time with the girl, too. It wasn't like they neglected her or let other people raise her." He shook his head. "I think some people are just born bad."

Harriet sighed. "I hope he's strong enough to get through all this."

✄ - - - ✄ - - - ✄

Jessica pushed away from the table.

"That was amazing. If you're all eating Jorge's cooking every week, I don't understand why you don't weigh a million pounds."

Harriet smiled. "It's the main reason I run."

"I'm blessed with a good metabolism," Lauren told her.

Sharon set her fork on her plate.

"The raisins were unexpected in the picadillo."

Jorge blushed. "I have to surprise these ladies once in a while."

Beth poked him in the shoulder.

"Admit it, you've been showing off for our visitors."

"I have a reputation—"

Jorge was interrupted by the front doorbell ringing. Harriet and Aunt Beth looked at each other.

"No one comes to the front door," Harriet said.

"Someone better go answer it," Lauren suggested.

Harriet slid her chair back and stepped out into the entryway. She opened the small spy door at eye level that allowed her to see who was on her porch.

"Michelle?" she said, then, louder: "What do you want?"

"Can I come in a minute? I need to talk to you."

She held a packet of papers in her hand and was bouncing up and down on her toes. Harriet decided she didn't look immediately dangerous.

She turned to call back toward the dining room, "It's Michelle". She took a deep breath and opened the door. "Michelle, come in. How can I help you?"

"I have to go help a friend in Seattle, and I need to leave tonight. I couldn't get hold of the Renfros to talk to the kids, and Marcel isn't taking my calls. Here." She shoved the packet of papers into Harriet's hand. "I'm not sure how long this will take. This is a temporary medical power of attorney for each of them and their passports. It's not a big deal—we do this whenever they spend a weekend away. Tell them I'll be in touch when I can, but I don't know how long my friend will need me."

"Do you have a name or number where we can reach you?"

"You've got my cell number, I'll keep it on. Look, I gotta go." She turned and all but ran out the front door. Harriet watched as she crossed the porch, descended the steps and got into Aiden's Bronco.

Harriet leaned against the front door, her hand to her heart. Lauren and Aunt Beth had rushed into the entry.

"Oh, my gosh," she told them. "She's making a run for it."

Lauren pulled her phone from her pants pocket.

"We need to call Morse."

Aunt Beth took Harriet by the arm and led her back to the dining room to her chair.

"Come on. Sit down." She handed Harriet her glass of water. "Don't you think the police have her under surveillance?"

"Call Morse," Harriet said. "Michelle's driving Aiden's Bronco, so I'm guessing she had a plan B—and it worked."

"Call me right away. Michelle was just here." Lauren looked up at the group. "It went straight to the machine."

"Call nine-one-one." Harriet said.

Lauren complied, but from her side of the conversation, it didn't go well.

"Well, apparently, Michelle isn't on any sort of wanted list, and no one they talked to knew anything about her. The operator said she'd contact the detectives on call and have those guys get in touch with us."

"What did she give you?" Mavis asked.

Harriet opened the packet Michelle had handed her.

"She said it's the kids' medical power of attorney and their passports." She leafed through the papers. Looks like that's what it is."

"Surprising she was that thoughtful." Lauren said.

"She is a narcissist, and I can't say she's been the most thoughtful mother, but she does make sure their basic needs are taken care of."

Jorge came from the kitchen carrying a tray with dishes of flan.

"We might as well have our dessert while we wait for a call back."

Harriet was eating her last bite of flan when her phone rang.

"Yes, Michelle came to my house and gave me her kids' passports and said she had to go to Seattle," she said when Morse identified herself. "She's driving Aiden's Bronco...About ten, fifteen minutes ago. Lauren called you right after she left." Harriet keyed her phone off. "Bye," she said to the dead screen.

The rest of the group was watching her.

"She was in a hurry. She did say everyone should stay here in case Michelle gets spooked and decides to come back."

Lauren went to the studio and returned with her tablet.

"Who wants to take bets on whether Michelle gets into Canada before they catch up to her?"

Aunt Beth looked at her watch.

"Ten minutes to the highway and another ten to the ferry terminal, if she drives fast. If a ferry is sitting there, and she walks on...." She looked at the ceiling in what Harriet knew was her counting-in-her-head mode. "She might make it."

"Touch and go whether she makes the last ferry," Lauren said when she'd pulled up the schedule.

Harriet scraped the last bit of caramel sauce from her plate and licked it off her spoon.

"Even if she gets on the ferry, it takes—what?—two hours to cross the strait. That should give the police enough time to alert the guys on the other side to grab her."

"So, now we wait." Mavis said.

"Now, we wait," Harriet agreed.

✂- - - ✂- - - ✂

It was midnight when they finally heard. Jorge was making decaf coffee in the kitchen when Scooter ran to the studio door, barking as he went.

"I'll get it," he called to the group in the dining room.

Detective Morse followed him into the dining room and sat down; he returned to the kitchen to get her a mug of coffee.

"I figured it would be easier to come tell you in person," she said.

"Did you catch her?" Harriet asked.

Jorge came in and set a dish of flan in front of Morse.

"Your coffee will be ready in a minute, but you can start with this."

She looked up gratefully.

202

"The detectives in charge were busy getting their teams set up for tomorrow's meeting with Jules. No one thought she'd bail, so they hadn't warned dispatch...and you know the rest of that story."

Harriet stood up and began to pace.

"Please tell me she's in custody."

Jorge carried in a steaming cup of coffee for Morse. She took the mug and sipped it, closing her eyes in appreciation.

"You're killing me here," Harriet hissed.

Morse opened her eyes.

"Sorry, it's been a long night. And dinner wasn't part of it. Yes, Michelle is in custody. She's currently in Canada, but she's being held and will be returned in the morning. This option was one she'd given some thought to. While she was making the crossing, she went into the bathroom, cut and colored her hair and came out dressed as a boy, complete with a forged passport that included a picture that matched her new look."

"Wow," Mavis said. "She *must* have planned that more than a day or two ahead."

Jorge appeared with a plate containing a burrito and a scoop of fruit salad.

"You need to eat." he said and set the plate in front of Morse.

Morse ate a bite before continuing her story.

"Michelle managed to get off the ferry and walk to the car rental place, which is about ten minutes away on foot. She tried to rent the car with cash, and that made the customer rep suspicious. He wanted to call a supervisor, so Michelle offered to use a credit card. She pulled out one of Aiden's—apparently, he has one he leaves at home in case Carla needs to pay for something big. She figured out where he kept it and took it with her.

"The rep found the whole interaction a bit too suspicious, so she stalled and went into a back room and called the police. Then she dragged out the process of checking out the car until the police got there and were able to arrest Michelle without incident."

Harriet sat back down.

"What a relief. I was afraid she'd figure we were on to her and come back here."

Aunt Beth waited until Morse had eaten another few bites of her dinner.

"Did it turn out Michelle did try to poison Jules?"

Morse's mouth twitched as she tried to suppress a smile.

"It would seem Jules does owe you his life. Once again, everyone had underestimated Michelle. She was supposed to negotiate with him and then, when she brought him the money the next day, they were going to arrest her in the act. They would confront her with the taped agreement that she'd done something that required payment to keep silent, and she would confess.

"No one expected her to poison him, and they certainly didn't expect her to run. Our psychologist says she's a narcissist, and that narcissists believe they are smarter than everyone else. Running didn't figure into her profile."

"We really were there by chance," Lauren said. "We've been promising our visitors a visit to Annie's for cinnamon twists, and it never occurred to us the meeting between Michelle and Jules would take place there."

"Michelle suggested it," Morse said. "I guess she likes the cinnamon twists, too."

Harriet ran her hands through her hair and sighed.

"I think I know why she tried to kill Jules, and why she ran."

"Why?" Mavis and Beth said at the same time.

"She can't put her hands on any cash to speak of. That's why she's always tormenting Aiden. Their parents set Michelle's portion of the inheritance as an annuity that's controlled by a banker. She gets periodic disbursements for spending, but her ex-husband pays for the kids' expenses as they come up, and the bank pays for Michelle's rent and therapy appointments.

"Now that she can't practice law, her personal income is minimal. She gets a little from legal aid, but she spent more than she made when she had a big income. Her legal aid money wouldn't even cover her spa bills. I hadn't thought about it before, but she just didn't have the money to make the payoff."

Morse chewed thoughtfully.

"I guess with her coming from such a prominent family, no one considered she wouldn't have access to cash."

"When will Aiden get out?" Harriet asked.

"I'd like to say tonight, but unfortunately, the detectives on the case are still in Canada questioning Michelle, and anyway, the people who need to process him out work day shift. He'll be out as soon as they get the paperwork to the jail. I'll follow up and make sure it happens as quickly as possible."

"I'd like to pick him up. He doesn't have his car." Harriet thought for a moment. "Do you know where his car is?"

Morse put her fork down.

"Michelle left it in the parking lot at the ferry landing in Port Angeles. She wiped it down for fingerprints and left the keys under the mat. She obviously put much thought into her plans and had lots of options."

"I wonder if she wasn't planning to head out of the country all along," Beth said. "She had contacts in France from her parents, and she'd clearly been prepping her kids, what with the French nanny and the French tutor. They speak French like natives. So does she."

"You're probably right," Morse told her.

"She needed to wait to get control of Aiden's money," Harriet said, continuing the thought. "That's why she didn't just kill him. If he was in jail, he'd have handed over the keys to the castle. She's been working on him. She's made all her counseling appointments and has been polite to both Carla and me. We were starting to believe her."

Aunt Beth sipped her coffee.

"Makes sense. Aiden has the money from his grandma as well as his share of his parents' estate. She could go to France or Belgium or Luxembourg or any other French-speaking nation and start with a clean slate. Being sanctioned by the bar association must really bother someone like her."

Mavis sighed. "That girl never could figure things out. She's bright and good-looking. She has two beautiful children. She had all the advantages, but it was never enough for her. She always wanted more, and she didn't want to have to work to get it."

Jorge picked up Morse's empty plates and carried them to the kitchen. When he returned, he stood behind Aunt Beth, his hands on her shoulders.

"We aren't going to be able to understand Michelle or what she did if we talk all night. Harriet is safe, so maybe we should let her get some sleep so she can go pick up her young man in the morning."

"Good idea," Lauren agreed. "I have a teleconference with a client first thing tomorrow myself."

She and Jessica went back to the studio to gather their quilting supplies. Mavis and Beth followed when they'd cleared the rest of the table.

Morse stood up.

"I'll make some calls. I think we can get Aiden out as soon as the day crew gets to the jail. If you were to be there at eight tomorrow morning, I don't think you'd have to wait long."

"Thank you. I know this hasn't made your situation at work any easier."

"The younger guys on the force are fine. There are a couple of older guys that will never completely accept a woman detective, but I can't spend my time worrying about them. I have to do what's right, no matter," She smiled, "Besides, they're going to either retire or have heart attacks long before my career is over."

"I'm glad you've got a good attitude about it."

Morse patted her on the back.

"I'll talk to you tomorrow." With that she went to the kitchen and on through the studio and out.

Chapter 31

arriet was sitting in the jail's reception area at seven-thirty. She checked the time, the weather and the news on her phone. The story about Michelle hadn't hit the news yet, but that wasn't unusual, given how far away from Seattle Foggy Point was.

It was five minutes after eight when the receptionist smiled at her.

"I hear the locks," she said.

"Do I look okay?" Harriet asked her nervously.

"He's going to think you look just fine."

Moments later, Aiden came through the last door. Harriet hesitated a moment. He looked terrible. The bruises around his eye were changing color. His chiseled face looked skeletal. He was wearing the clothes he'd worn to their dinner a week ago. She felt tears sting her eyes.

He stopped and waited for her to come to him. She paused a moment more, and then he opened his arms slightly, and she closed the distance and wrapped her arms around him. He pulled her to his chest and rested his chin on her head, his arms tight around her.

"I've missed you," he groaned.

Harriet looked up at him.

"Me, too."

She caught sight of the receptionist out of the corner of her eye. The woman was standing by her desk, her hands clasped over her heart. She was smiling at them.

"Can we get out of here?" she said, suddenly self-conscious.

Aiden sighed. "I know this isn't very romantic, but could we go to the Pancake House before we do anything else? All of a sudden, I'm starving."

There was no restaurant called The Pancake House in Foggy Point. If someone used the name, they were talking about a restaurant called Seabirds. It was located on Pirate's Cove, at the marina.

Jessica was sitting at a booth when they walked in.

"Hi," she called to them and waved. "Join me if you want, but I totally understand if you want to be alone."

They looked around the restaurant. The other tables were full.

"I can put our name on the list if you want privacy," Harriet told him. He shook his head.

"No offense, but I need good food more than privacy right now."

Jessica smiled and spread her arms.

"I'm happy to have you join me. I'm Jessica, by the way. I'm staying with Lauren. I was here for the crazy quilt retreat, and Lauren invited me to stay a few more days. She's having a teleconference this morning, so I took myself to breakfast. I'm sorry, I'm talking too much."

Aiden smiled. "Not at all. I'm happy to hear a female voice, to tell the truth." He stretched his arms out. "I need to eat, and then I need to sleep for about a month."

The waitress took their orders, raising her eyebrows as Aiden ordered two people's worth of food.

"Tell me about your workshop while I eat," he said as the waitress brought drinks and then their food.

Jessica looked at Harriet and raised her left eyebrow, watching to be sure Aiden didn't notice.

"I'm going to go powder my nose," she said. "Can you show me where it is? I have a terrible sense of direction. Without a guide, I might never get back."

Harriet followed her to the ladies room. Jessica whirled around as soon as the door was shut.

"Has he mentioned his sister?"

"No, it hasn't come up. He's just been going on about how hungry he is, and how much he appreciates the blue sky and grass and stuff like that."

"Something's not right. I mean, he should be more upset about his sister killing two people just to get her hands on his money."

"You're right. I expected him to be…I don't know what, but not this. He's Mister Merry Sunshine."

"Do you suppose no one's told him why he's free?" Jessica wondered.

"It's starting to look that way. You know, I think I'll call Jorge. I don't know if Lauren told you Aiden's history, but his dad died when he was young, and Jorge took over as father figure. Jorge's son Julio is Aiden's best friend."

She called Jorge, who was at his restaurant, and explained the situation. He told her what he thought, and she hung up.

"He says bring him to the restaurant. He agrees he needs to be there when he finds out."

"That sounds better than telling him over his first good meal in a week."

They returned to the table as the waitress was delivering Aiden's second breakfast. He'd eaten eggs and bacon in the first round and was chowing down on pumpkin pancakes with caramel syrup when they returned.

Harriet's French toast was cold, but she wouldn't have tasted it if it had been perfect.

"Jorge called while I was in the bathroom, and he insists we stop by the restaurant on our way home."

Aiden groaned. "I just want to go home and take a shower before falling into bed, but I get he wants to see me with his own eyes."

"Exactly," she said.

✂ - - - ✂ - - - ✂

"*Mi'jo*, it is so good to see you," Jorge said and clapped Aiden on the back before pulling him into a bear hug. "You are a sight for sore eyes."

"I'm happy to be out of there. I hope I never have to see the inside of a jail again." Aiden told him.

"So, what happened?" Jorge asked. Harriet stood back and let him handle the situation. "Did the detectives say why they let you go?"

Aiden stopped smiling.

"Actually, now that you mention it, they didn't. They came to my cell early this morning and told me to pack my things—I was checking out. I didn't think to ask why. I was busy taking what passes for a shower and changing into my own clothes. I had to be checked by the doctor who looked at my eye originally, too, so they could document that they'd given me proper care.

"I know I should care who killed Marine, and maybe next week, I will. For now, I just care that everyone knows it's not me."

Harriet was biting the inside of her cheek. Aiden's optimism was painful to watch.

Jorge put his arm around Aiden's shoulders and guided him into the big back room. He nodded to Harriet, indicating she shouldn't follow.

"There's something I need to tell you," she heard him say as the door closed.

Aunt Beth and Mavis were waiting in her studio when she got home.

"Oh, honey," Beth said. "Jorge called me and told me he was going to tell Aiden about his sister." She put her arms around Harriet and pulled her into a bear hug. Tears filled Harriet's eyes and slid down her face. Mavis handed her a tissue and patted her back.

"Let's make you a nice cup of tea," she said as Aunt Beth steered her to the kitchen.

"He's going to be so hurt," Harriet said when she'd cried as much as she could and pulled herself together again.

Mavis handed her the cup of tea.

"There's nothing for it. His sister did something terrible, and he's going to have to mourn the loss of the relationship that was probably always one-sided. When he gets that sorted, he'll have to figure out how to move on."

Scooter jumped into Harriet's lap and started licking her face.

"I know, you're trying to help," she told him as she moved him away from her mouth.

Aunt Beth sipped her tea then set it down.

"He's going to need some time today. It wouldn't surprise me if he hid from the situation by sleeping."

"He did say he wanted to go home and sleep. And that was before he knew about Michelle."

Mavis handed Harriet a chocolate cookie from a bag she pulled from her purse.

"Chocolate might help."

"Before Jorge called, Glynnis said the Small Stitches were having a meeting about the crazy quilt event and wanted to know if we wanted to come. She said they were going to do a show-and-tell for anyone who's worked more on her block," Aunt Beth told her. "Would you like to go? It might take your mind off things. We can take two cars so you can leave if Aiden calls."

Harriet popped the rest of her cookie into her mouth and chewed thoughtfully.

"I guess I could do that," she said finally. "I'm probably too distracted to stitch on my customer quilt, and I have plenty of time to finish it."

"I'll call Lauren and see if she and Jessica want to come. Can you check with Sharon?"

"Sharon's available," Sharon said. "I wasn't eavesdropping, I promise. I was coming down the stairs and heard just the end of what you were saying."

"Honey," Mavis told her, "you've been a good guest. And with everything that's been going on, Beth and I have appreciated the fact that Harriet hasn't been alone these last few days."

✂- - - ✂- - - ✂

Harriet walked to the parking lot of the Methodist church with her aunt and Mavis.

"Wow, the Small Stitches are ready to do it all again. If I never go to a crazy quilt retreat again in my life it will be too soon."

Mavis patted her on the back.

"Well, honey, I think once you separate the quilting from all the other stuff, you'll appreciate all the techniques you've learned."

"I'm not holding my breath on that one."

Beth held her phone to her ear and spoke in a voice too quiet for Harriet to hear. She slipped the phone back into her purse and turned to her niece.

"That was Jorge. He said Aiden is going to stay with him for a few days. He can't face going back to his house and seeing reminders of his sister. Julio is coming from Seattle for a few days, too.

"He said Aiden is pretty upset. They talked, and he was able to get him to go to sleep for a while. Aiden wanted him to tell Harriet he'd call her when he's had some time to process all this."

Harriet hung her head.

"Once again Michelle comes between us and I'm not the person he feels like he can talk to."

Aunt Beth put an arm around her shoulders.

"Let's not make this about you. If you had something like this happen, would you go to him? Or would you come to me?"

Harriet looked up. "Okay, point taken. I just feel so helpless."

"It's going to take him some time," Mavis said. "He'll come to you when he's ready."

"And he's going to have to get to the point where he can acknowledge that what you were telling him about his sister all along was right," Beth added.

"I just want this to be over," Harriet said.

Lauren, Jessica and Sharon joined them by Harriet's car.

"Hey, anyone want to go for one last coffee with our guests?" Lauren asked. "Sharon and Jessica are both leaving in the morning."

"Why not," Harriet said. "I don't seem to be able to do anything productive today."

They moved to their respective cars and headed to The Steaming Cup.

Chapter 32

Jessica sat down at the round table with her mocha and a cranberry orange scone.

"So, let me see if I have this right. Michelle collected saliva from Aiden over a month ago, saying it was for a DNA test at the genealogy website. She kept his saliva and substituted her own, knowing the report the company generated didn't reference gender identity. Fast forward to now. She somehow got Marine to leave her rehab program, probably with a promise to get her a lead part in the local production of *Blythe Spirit*, and got her back on drugs again."

"Sounds right so far," Lauren told her.

"I'm guessing they crossed paths in a counseling program in Seattle. Michelle had to go to a program a few months ago. On the other hand, Marine had been close to Michelle's mother, so she may have initiated the contact. If she's been on drugs until recently, she might not have known Michelle's mother died last spring," Harriet suggested. "Or she was finally able to express her condolences. Who knows?"

"So, Michelle took Marine to Aiden's, maybe telling her there were animal drugs there," Jessica continued. "She overdoses Marine, drops saliva and hairs from Aiden's brush or something, covers her with the electric blanket, drives by us saying Marine disappeared and she's looking for her."

Lauren sipped her cup of chai and set it back on the table.

"I think she bought a phone, used it first to call Aiden a few times, and then changed the registration to Marine and gave it to her. I also think she taped a phone to Aiden's bumper and used a 'find my phone' app to see

212

where he was when he was looking for the injured dog. She waited until he was fairly close, removed the blanket and left. Marine's body would still be warm, causing the medical examiner to misjudge the time of death."

"Wow, she really put some thought into this." Jessica said.

"You don't know the half of it," Harriet told her. "Michelle has been trying to get the money Aiden inherited from his mom since the day Avanell died." She shook her head. "She's been mentally ill to some degree her whole adult life. Aiden just couldn't see it."

Lauren's phone buzzed, and she stood up and walked away from the table before she answered it. The group sipped their drinks and watched her. She tapped on her phone then put it to her ear again briefly before she ended her call and came back to the table. She pulled a pad and mechanical pencil from her messenger bag and copied some information from the screen.

Harriet looked at her and raised her eyebrows.

Lauren folded the paper in half and held it out to Sharon.

"I have the information you wanted. I also have two pieces of advice for you. First, be sure you really want to go down this road. Once you start, there's no going back. Second, if it were me, I'd hire a private detective to scout the situation for you before you act on the information."

Sharon's eyes widened. She took the paper and held it to her heart.

"I never thought this would really happen," she said.

Harriet put her hand on Sharon's arm.

"I'm happy for you. I think Lauren's got a good idea, though. Have a PI check the family out. Have him or her get a sense for what sort of people the adoptive parents are and what sort of kid your child is. Of course, your child is your child, no matter what, but it's good to be prepared."

"I'm scared." Sharon said.

"Honey, we're all here for you, no matter what you decide to do," Mavis assured her.

Lauren wrote another note on her pad and tore it off.

"Here are the names of a couple of private investigators I've done computer work for in the past. They're both ethical and very discrete."

"Take a deep breath and then finish your drink," Aunt Beth told Sharon. "You don't have to make a decision or take action today. You can take some time."

"It seems like that's what everyone needs," Harriet said. "Time."

✂- - - ✂- - - ✂

Several days passed before Aiden called, and it was another two before he asked her to meet him for dinner. His Bronco was already in the parking lot of Hot Diggity Dog. Harriet was surprised he chose to return to the place he'd been arrested.

"I'm a bit surprised we're eating here," she said as she slid into the plastic booth seat.

"Jorge says I need to make new memories to replace the bad ones. I decided to start here. Besides, I really like their hot dogs." He smiled, a hint of the old Aiden showing through.

"How are you?" she asked.

"Let's enjoy our food before I drag us both down by talking about me."

"Okay," she said softly.

For his part, Aiden kept the conversation light with stories of his dog Randy and his friend Julio. Finally, after he'd eaten hot dogs, fries, a milkshake and an ice cream cone, there was nothing left to order.

"I get the feeling you're stalling," she told him.

He hung his head briefly then looked up and reached across the table, taking her hands in his.

"I need you to listen to what I'm going to say and not think it's about you. I've talked to Jorge and Julio, and I talked to Dr. Johnson at the clinic. I'm not ready to go back there yet. I have a lot to think about, and I don't think I can stay in the house where my sister lived, and my mom before her."

"What are you saying?" Harriet asked. She could feel tears forming and fought to hold them off. Her heart raced.

"I called my old research team." He paused. "Dan has to come home to be with his mother while she has knee replacement surgery. He'll only be stateside for three months, but they said they'd love to have me come take his place for that time. Dr. Johnson said he's willing to keep my place open until I get back."

Harriet took a deep breath.

"When will you leave?" she whispered.

"I'm going back to Seattle with Julio tonight."

Tears fell on the plastic table unchecked. Aiden slid out from his seat and moved in beside her, taking her in his arms and resting his chin on her head as she cried.

END

About The Author

ARLENE SACHITANO was born at Camp Pendleton while her father was serving in the US Navy. Her family lived in Newport, Rhode Island, before settling in Oregon, where she still resides.

Arlene worked in the electronics industry for almost thirty years, including stints in solid state research as well as production supervision. She is handy, being both a knitter and a quilter. She puts her quilting knowledge to work writing the Harriet Truman/Loose Threads mystery series, which features a long-arm quilter as the amateur sleuth.

Arlene divides her time between homes in Portland and Tillamook she shares with her husband and their dog Navarre.

About The Artist

APRIL MARTINEZ was born in the Philippines and raised in San Diego, California, daughter to a US Navy chef and a US postal worker, sibling to one younger sister. For years, she went from job to job, dissatisfied that she couldn't make use of her creative tendencies, until she started working as an imaging specialist for a big book and magazine publishing house in Irvine and began learning the trade of graphic design.

From that point on, she worked as a graphic designer and webmaster at subsequent day jobs while doing freelance art and illustration at night. April lives with her cat in Orange County, California, as a full-time freelance artist/illustrator and graphic designer.

Made in the USA
Middletown, DE
13 July 2015